THE HOLLYWOOD ILLUSION

The Hollywood Illusion

ALLEGRA POPE

This is a work of fiction
Names, characters, places, and incidents are products of the
author's imagination or are used fictitiously. Any resem-
blance to actual events, locales, or persons, living or dead, is
entirely coincidental.

Contents

Chapter 1

Paul Max lived high above it all—literally, in the clouds.

Sunlight bled through the wraparound windows of his Beverly Hills fortress, splashing across polished floors and cold minimalist furniture. Art from Paris. Imported. Expensive. Untouchable.

The place looked staged. Because it was. Page 48, *Architectural Dreams*.

Paul Max stood barefoot by the glass, shirtless, coffee in hand. Abs sculpted. Pecs like stone. He knew the camera would approve.

Sometimes he still couldn't believe it. One film—*Murder in the South*—and his life detonated. Every year after, another release. Another smash. Another headline.

Then came the ad deals. The endorsements. Magazine covers. And the money. Always the money.

The critics called him charming. Said the camera loved him. Oscars? Not a single one. Maybe that was the missing piece. He told himself it didn't matter. Not really. Not yet.

It didn't bother him. Not so much that anyone would notice.

Still, he was one of Hollywood's highest-paid. A name that guaranteed a million-dollar opening. A face that sold out theaters worldwide.

A breeze nudged the palms. Sky, impossibly blue. The kind of morning that whispered: you're untouchable. Paul knew better.

It was the kind of morning that made you believe life was safe. But Paul had stopped believing in safe and untouchable *the moment the first note slid under his door.*

Behind him, Lola laughed. Soft. Carefree. Dangerous.

The world knew her as *Lola Flemming*, Hollywood's Next Big Thing. In his kitchen, in his shirt, she was just Lola. His Lola.

Her face stopped conversations cold. Full lips. Cheekbones sharp as glass. Eyes like honey catching fire. They could warm you. Or scorch you alive.

Her hair was chaos perfected—dark waves that made you wonder: bedroom or runway? Didn't matter. Men would trade souls for that look.

"Eggs or just coffee?" she asked, pulling open one of three refrigerators. She didn't look back. Didn't need to.

Paul moved closer, smile in place. "Whatever you're having."

He pressed a kiss to her neck. She didn't flinch.

She laughed low. "Careful. I might forget breakfast."

"That's the plan," he whispered.

He remembered their first meeting—Peter Woodford's party. Peter, the producer, the kingmaker. Attendance wasn't optional. It never was.

The party stank of money and rot. Drugs on trays. Dancers in paint. Beautiful people with ugly secrets. Ten years ago, Paul thrived on it. Now it just made him tired.

That night, he planned to ghost early. The whispers about his divorce were everywhere. Everyone wanted dirt. He had none left to give.

Peppy La Font. His first wife. Older. Magnetic. Loaded with power. They adopted kids. Played house. It worked for a while. Until it didn't.

Peppy wanted quiet afternoons in Colorado. Paul wanted more scripts, more lights, more applause. They outgrew each other. The divorce was loud, messy, public. Of course.

And then—just when he'd had enough—he saw her. *Lola.*

What is it with some women? A glance? A smile? The way they bite their lip? Lola was all of it. And none of it. She was a spell. And Paul? Already caught.

She stood under the lights, curvy, amused, radiant like she owned the air. She looked at him. Smiled. And that was it.

They left together. Ended up at his place. In the backyard. And they talked. Really talked. All night long.

Now, months later, she was here. In his kitchen. In his shirt. Humming like she belonged.

They were that couple. Beautiful. Annoyingly perfect. Instagram come to life.

Paul Max. Box-office king. Face carved from stone, lit by million-dollar teams. And beside him—his goddess.

He had it all. The mansion. The cars. The girl. The illusion.

But deep down, in the quiet dark, the whisper never left: This won't last. Nothing this perfect ever does.

Because, in the end, his life was just an illusion.

Today felt safe. Normal. But that was the lie.

Texts from Otto, his assistant. A revenue call. A gala he skipped. Notes from his lawyer. Routine. Harmless. Nothing dark. Not yet.

He poured Lola's coffee.

That's when he heard it.

Not a knock. A whisper. Paper sliding across wood.

Paul turned. *Maybe another note*, he feared.

An envelope lay on the floor. Someone had slipped it under the front door.

"Delivery?" Lola called. He shook his head. "No knock."

He walked over, bent down, and picked it up.

Thick, cream-colored paper. No stamp. No logo. No return address.

Just one word, written in careful, black ink:

Paul.

He frowned. Not "Mr. Max." Not "To the Resident." Just Paul.

"Fan mail?" Lola asked, sipping her coffee.

"Maybe," he muttered, but his gut clenched.

He opened the door fast, scanning the front steps.

Whoever dropped it was gone.

Maybe they were still nearby, behind a bush or tree, watching.

The thought chilled his blood.

This was the first left at his house.

He shut the door.

"Babe? What was it?" Lola called from the kitchen.

"Nothing. Just some local ad." He lied without blinking.

He tore it open. One sheet. No name. No signature. Just a paragraph. Paul read it once. Again. A third time. The words cut deeper each pass.

"I know what you did ten years ago.

I know you're a murderer.

I have proof. Bring $2 million in cash. Wait for instructions.

Tell no one—*or Lola dies.*"

The rest blurred.

One line seared into him, louder than the others: *I know you're a murderer.*

And they weren't lying

Chapter 2

Paul gripped the steering wheel like it might disappear.

The road stretched empty. Moonlight slid across the asphalt like oil. Behind him, the city lights shrank to nothing.

Headlights flared in his mirror. A car. Getting closer. His pulse spiked. Was it them? He held steady. Kept the speed. They wouldn't hit him here. Not on an open road. The car closed in. Inches now. His throat dried. Then—whoosh—it swung past, leaving him rattled and alone again.

False alarm. He exhaled, shaky. Too jumpy. Too nervous. No use pretending—*he was scared.*

Hollywood shrank in the rearview. The dream. The illusion. Gone. His mansion. His toys. His perfect life. All of it fading into the dark.

And the past, like most illusions, wasn't real.

Maybe he'd always known it was fragile. That everything—the success, the glamor, the admiration—was built over something violent, dark, and unfinished.

His past hadn't disappeared. It had waited—patiently, quietly—ready to pounce at the first opportunity.

Out here, there was nothing but blacktop and desert breath.

A perfect mirror of his life.

The leather bag sat in the passenger seat. $2 million in cash. Packed tight. Heavy. Dead weight.

Otto hadn't asked questions at first. Just blinked. Then blinked again.

"You need what?" he'd said that morning, standing in Paul's kitchen, still holding a half-drunk green juice.

"Two million," Paul had repeated. "Cash."

Otto paled. "That's... a lot."

"I know."

"What for?"

Paul didn't answer. Just sipped his coffee. Stared out the window like the palm trees might explain it.

Otto had tried again. "Paul, man. What's going on?"

Still nothing. Paul made a huge effort to look calm and collected, but Otto knew him well. Otto knew that something was wrong, very wrong.

Later that day, Paul sat alone in his office, blinds closed, watching shadows shift across the floor. The silence was louder than any scream. His phone lay face down on the table. No missed calls. No texts.

Just waiting.

It felt like years.

Who the hell could it be?

A desperate nobody chasing a quick score?

Or a ghost from his past—someone who's been nursing a grudge, waiting for the right moment to strike?

He'd been careful. Obsessively careful. No loose ends, no witnesses, nothing left to chance.

What happened was buried. Cleaned so thoroughly it should've vanished from the world.

And yet... someone had found a way to drag it back into the light.

He hadn't told anyone about the note or the two million.

Not CC. Especially not CC.

She could smell fear the way a shark smells blood in the water.

Maybe that was his mistake—keeping it all to himself.

His phone buzzed. Finally.

"Old Sunoco Station. Hwy 14. 10:00 PM. Alone. Car clean. No phones. We're watching. Don't try anything stupid."

Otto came back around 8:00 PM. Pale, sweating, holding the bag.

"No suspicion?" Paul asked.

Otto shook his head. "Told the bank manager you were throwing one of your weirdo theme parties. Said you needed cash for realism. He laughed."

Paul nodded. Still didn't smile.

Otto's hands trembled. "You sure you don't want to tell CC?"

Paul looked him dead in the eyes.

"Otto, listen to me. You can't breathe a word of this to anyone—especially not CC."

Otto went quiet.

Other calls came in.

Lola. Twice. Wanting to confirm if he'd be at the gala. She sounded excited. Happy. Picking a dress.

He said yes.

Lied.

Again.

Peter's text popped up first: box office numbers, international sales lagging behind projections.

Then the phone rang.

Paul didn't answer.

None of it mattered.

Not the money. Not the press. Not the next three films lined up.

Just Lola. Just that letter. Just the voice in his head saying: *You're dead, Paul. You've been dead since you opened that envelope.*

Now, the old gas station rose like a ghost off the side of the road. He saw it from half a mile away.

A broken sign dangled like a severed limb. The cracked lot was littered with rusted cans, busted glass, and cigarette butts from some decade no one remembered.

No lights.

No pumps.

Just a rotting shell in the middle of nowhere.

He pulled in slowly—engine rumbling, then silence.

Nothing.

No other cars. No wind. Just the buzz of desert insects and a faint oil stink from the cracked concrete.

He got out, grabbing the bag. The weight almost pulled his arm from the socket. The air was bone-dry, hot. The moon hung overhead like a dead bulb.

Paul looked around.

"Okay..." he muttered. "I'm here."

Still nothing.

Minutes passed. Then a full hour. Was he in the right place?

Then a car. Far off. Headlights slicing through the dark.

It pulled in fast. Too fast. A silver sedan. Modern. Tinted windows. Long beams stayed on, blinding.

Paul shielded his eyes.

A door opened. A figure stepped out. Unclear. Shrouded in glare and dressed in black. Face hidden.

A voice came through a speaker or modulator—cold, flat, genderless.

"Open the bag."

Paul froze.

The voice repeated. Louder. "Open the bag."

He crouched and unzipped it. The stacks of cash looked ridiculous sitting in the dirt.

"Now drop it. All of it. On the ground."

Weird request.

"You want me to dump the money on the ground?"

"Do as I say. Move!"

Paul turned the bag over, bills spilling onto the dirt. Then he set the bag down.

He straightened; eyes locked on the figure in front of him.

"You've got the money. What else do you want?"

"You know what I want."

"What the f—"

"You know. Don't pretend. There's blood on your hands."

"I don't—"

"Don't lie, Paul. Not tonight."

Paul's hands trembled. "You want more money? Fine. I'll double it. Five million. Ten."

A pause.

"Forget the money. I only want you dead."

A gun rose. Not shaking. Not hesitating.

Paul backed up. "Who are you? What did I do to you?"

The figure stepped forward.

"Life's a bitch, Paul. You had it all. Now you have nothing."

Paul's voice cracked. "Please—wait—we can talk—"

But the figure wasn't talking anymore.

And Paul, for the first time in years, felt real fear.

Tears spilled hot, childish, unstoppable.

"I'll give you anything," Paul begged. His voice cracked, high and thin.

The figure stepped closer. "No. You already did."

The last thing Paul heard was the shot.

Then silence.

And darkness.

Chapter 3

Grace Fletcher hated mornings. Always had.

But crime scene mornings? Those were a whole new level of hell.

This one was worse—6:03 AM, Highway 14, middle of nowhere, with a corpse already trending on Twitter. Or X. Whatever they were calling it this week. Too many names. Too much noise.

She pulled the cruiser to the edge and killed the engine. Red-and-blue lights splashed against the desert like a rave no one wanted an invite to.

The reporters were already circling, vultures in designer sneakers. Cameras up. Eyes hungry. A couple even called her name, like she was the star of the show.

She kept walking. Rule one: ignore the circus. Always ignore the circus.

She carried a cardboard tray—Charlie's Americano, her skim latte. Ritual. Without it, the morning didn't start.

She stepped out into the chilly air, gravel crunching under her boots.

The scene stank—oil, piss, rot. A dead Sunoco station, half-devoured by time. Roof gone. Pumps gutted. Rust everywhere.

Except that silence was gone.

The scene buzzed—uniforms, techs, cameras, and plastic evidence bags. And money. Way too much money.

Scattered everywhere like dirty confetti.

Hundreds fluttered across the concrete, leaves in a sick wind. Bills skittering toward the highway.

Two uniforms scrambled after them, chasing cash like kids after candy.

"Jesus," Grace muttered as a rookie tech belly-flopped to snag a bill. "Raining cash."

Charlie Bonelli shuffled over, snatched his coffee with a nod. Hoodie under a blazer, hair wild, eyes bagged. He looked like hell. She probably did too.

"I know the question," he said after a sip. "And no—the money hasn't been touched."

"Do we know how much money we're talking about?"

"Not yet. The uniforms are still collecting, still counting. What we know—it's over a million. Maybe two. Give or take."

Grace sipped, hard. "So, Paul Max—dead with over a million at his feet—and nobody takes it?"

"Not a single bill. Just his wallet and phone."

Grace let that settle. Maybe the killer ran out of time. Maybe someone spooked him—or them. But then why hadn't anyone else touched it?

She scanned the mess. Techs were shoving bills into a duffel—Italian leather, of course. Paul's taste lingered, even in death.

Still, the bag screamed last-minute. Grab-and-go, not style points.

A man like Paul didn't own bargain-bin luggage, which meant one of two things—he didn't have time to choose... or he didn't give a damn.

Grace asked the only question that mattered: "What the hell was Paul Max doing out here?"

Charlie blew out a breath. "That's the million-dollar question. Literally."

They walked past the perimeter and ducked under the tape.

Paul Max lay sprawled near the wall of the station. Face pale. Eyes half-open. Chest slick with blood.

The scene was clinical now—photographed, measured, boxed in with cones and chalk—but the mess still felt fresh.

"He was shot three times," Charlie said.

Grace crouched. "Where?"

"Twice in the chest. One in the throat. No struggle. No defense wounds."

"Execution-style?"

"Feels like it. Could've been personal. Or professional."

"Time of death?"

"Medical's saying between 10 PM and 3 AM. We'll get more later."

Grace stood. "Any cameras?"

Charlie snorted. "This place barely has walls."

She turned to look at the desert again. Emptiness. Nothing but sand, scrub, and distant hills.

"So, how'd we find him?"

"Girlfriend," Charlie said. "Lola Fleming. Actress. She called dispatch around 1 AM, losing her mind."

Grace frowned. "She was with him?"

"No. She was supposed to meet him at a gala at the *Dolby Theatre*. He never showed. She went home to an empty house. Thought maybe he'd bailed. Then she checked the GPS in his car. It had been sitting out here for over an hour."

"Smart."

"But terrified. She begged us to check. Patrol sent a unit. Found this."

Grace glanced at the duffel bag again. "Nothing else inside?"

"Nothing. Empty—except for a few loose bills."

She took another sip of coffee. "So, he leaves home, drives to a ghost-town gas station in the middle of the night, brings nearly two million dollars, and ends up dead—no wallet, no phone, and no killer."

Charlie nodded. "Hollywood, baby."

"Did you find any other footprints in the area?"

"The footprints suggest Paul drove here and parked exactly where his car is now. It hasn't moved since. You can see his tracks circling the area—looks like he waited for a while, pacing around. We found traces of only one other vehicle.

"This place has been abandoned for years, so the scene's easier to read. That second car pulled up there,"—he pointed to a spot in front of the body, near the highway—"and we found footprints from another person moving around.

"We think the killer shot him near where the bag and body are now, then left. The prints aren't clear enough to estimate weight, but there's nothing to suggest a third person was here. No signs of interruption. It's possible someone tried to erase tracks, but not likely."

"So," Grace recapped, "Paul shows up here with the money, waits around, another car pulls in and parks just off the highway. The killer steps out, kills him, leaves the cash to blow around, and drives off."

"Exactly."

"How busy is this highway at night? Any chance of witnesses?"

"Very unlikely. The killer knew this stretch is almost dead after dark—and moved fast. No risks. Possibly someone saw something, sure. But the odds? Slim to none."

She looked toward the press line. Reporters shouted questions. Cameras rolled. Microphones stretched like weapons.

"This is gonna be a nightmare," she muttered.

"It already is."

Grace turned back to Paul's body.

Charlie hesitated. "One more thing."

"What?"

"Something weird. You need to see it for yourself."

He led her closer.

At first, she didn't notice. The blood was everywhere. Thick pools on the pavement, smeared across his chest. But then she saw it.

A word.

Someone had written a word in Paul Max's own blood—crude, but clear—across his chest.

MURDERER

Grace froze.

Whoever did this hadn't just wanted him dead.

They wanted to send a message.

She crouched again, staring at the letters. The blood had dried around the edges. It was done post-mortem. Probably with a glove or bare hand. Maybe even his own.

Charlie spoke softly. "You ever seen something like that?"

She shook her head. "Not in real life."

He rubbed his jaw. "So... someone kills a movie star. Walks away from nearly two million in cash, and decides to write this?"

Grace stood.

She didn't respond. Didn't need to.

She already knew.

This wasn't just a murder.

It was the final scene—Paul performing his last act for the world.

Whoever did it had staged it like a movie.

Paul's last role.

His final illusion.

Chapter 4

Mona's house smelled like cinnamon and dried lavender, like it always did.

Grace rang the bell once, then let herself in with the key she'd carried since she was eleven. The familiar chime echoed through the Spanish-style home in Whitley Heights.

Warm light spilled across walls crowded with art, crystals, and photographs that hadn't shifted in twenty years.

Mona appeared from the kitchen, wiping her hands on a floral apron. Her silver hair was tied up in a messy bun, cheeks flushed, eyes sharp as ever.

She was Grace and Becky's grandmother—the one who had raised them since they were little, after their parents were killed during a violent burglary. For both of them, Mona had been mother, father, and... grandmother.

"Smells like magic," she said, smiling.

Grace held up the dessert tray. "Fruit cake. Homemade. Glazed, not dry."

"Praise the spirits," Mona said, ushering her in. "Set it on the table. Becky said she might be late. Let's not wait."

They hugged, tight and briefly. Then Mona started scooping soup into mismatched porcelain bowls while Grace set down the cake and filled two glasses with water.

Dinner was light. Homemade lentil soup, rosemary crackers, and a chickpea salad with too many olives. It was Mona's idea of balance. Grace didn't complain. The food was good. Warm. Familiar.

"So," Mona said after a few bites, "you look tired."

Grace nodded. "I was up at five. Got a call. Big case."

"Anything I'd know?"

Grace gave her a look. Mona didn't miss anything.

"Paul Max," she said finally. "He was found dead. Three shots, two to the chest, one to the neck. Abandoned gas station in the middle of the desert."

Mona dropped her spoon. "*The* Paul Max?"

Grace nodded.

"Oh dear. Well, now I understand why my séance group is going insane."

Grace nearly choked. "Your séance group?"

"You laugh, Grace. Half of them are probably stoned. The other half? Scary intuitive."

Grace smirked. "Let me guess. One of them already predicted this murder?"

"Not exactly. But everyone's been talking about him. They're all convinced there's more to it. One of them even brought out the spirit board."

"Of course they did."

Mona leaned in, dropping her voice like she was telling a ghost story. "One spirit told us about how reality becomes elusive. And that people die sometimes because they are too fixated on living. Maybe a clue..." Mona said.

Grace just listened, allowing Mona to be Mona.

"In any case," Mona continued, "one spirit wrote *Hollywood Illusion* on the spirit board. My group was agitated after that. Do you think it means something?"

Grace raised a brow. "Maybe Mona. You know what I think about it. But please tell me that's not trending."

"Not yet," Mona said. "But give it time. What really shook them was the word the group started chanting."

Grace nodded, her tone steady now. "Yeah. Let me guess, *'murderer'* right?"

Mona's eyes flew open. "Yes! That was it."

Grace leaned closer. She suspected one of those *'scary intuitive'* mediums had probably seen it on TV, but she continued. "We found it written across his chest. In his own blood."

Mona went quiet for a second. "That's not random."

"No," Grace said. "It's either a lie meant to draw attention—or the truth. Something from Paul's past finally catching up."

"What do you think, dear?"

Grace exhaled. "Too early to say. Today was all forensics and paperwork. Working theory? Straight murder. He was lured out, carrying two million in cash—and never made it back."

Mona whistled softly. "Two million?"

"Yeah, close to it. Makes you wonder—what was he hiding that was worth that kind of hush money?"

They ate in silence for a moment.

Grace picked at a piece of lettuce. "It's not easy to kill a guy like Paul Max. He was always surrounded by people. Bodyguards. Assistants. Staff."

"Then the killer knew him. Or knew how to get close."

"Exactly. And it wasn't about money. It was personal."

"Or they wanted it to look personal," Mona said. "Maybe the real goal was the message."

"Could be. Right now, we need to find the person who pulled the trigger. Whatever dirt Paul had in his closet, it can wait."

Mona reached for the cake and carefully slid it to her, as if it were made of gold.

"Alright," she said. "Enough death talk. Let's do something dangerous—sugar!"

Grace sliced the cake. Moist, tart, sweet. She poured a little whipped cream on top for both of them.

Still no Becky.

Grace checked her phone. Nothing.

She set the fork down.

"Mona."

"Yes, dear?"

"Tell me the truth. Where's Becky?"

Mona froze, then softened. "I don't know."

"You shouldn't try to protect her. When was the last time you spoke to her?"

"She called me last week—just to set up this dinner. Said she'd be here, maybe late. That's it."

"No texts since then?"

"I tried. Called a couple of times. No answer. But you know her."

Grace stared at her. "That's exactly why I'm worried."

Mona sighed. "I didn't want to trouble you. She disappears sometimes, Grace. You know that."

Silence.

Grace leaned back in her chair. "Not a single message. Not a single call. And now you're telling me she went dark on you too?"

Mona looked guilty. "She always comes back."

Grace looked at the cake. The glaze sparkled in the soft light. It had tasted like summer. But now it tasted like dread.

"She might be on one of her deep dives again," Mona offered, gently. "One of those stories she gets consumed with."

Grace didn't answer.

Becky was a brilliant investigative journalist—one of the best.

But she had an obsessive streak. In the past, she'd gone too far, dug too deep, and nearly lost herself.

The problem with Becky was that, to her, the world was a playground. She loved to play in it, blind to the risks. Deep down, she seemed convinced everything would turn out fine—even if someone were pointing a gun in her face.

Grace knew that feeling.

She knew that silence.

And now, she could feel it in her bones:

Becky was chasing a big story again.

Chapter 5

Grace shut the door with a soft click, the kind that made loneliness seem final.

Her apartment carried the faint ghost of Mona's kitchen—fruit cake, rosemary—like she'd smuggled the whole dinner home in her clothes.

She was full, more than full. Dinner had been warm, familiar, and a little heavy on the chickpeas. Rusty padded over, orange tail flicking like royalty summoning a servant. Two meows. Translation: *Feed me, human.*

"Yeah, yeah," she muttered. "Your Highness hasn't been forgotten."

She filled his bowl, scratching behind his ears as he buried his head in the food like he hadn't eaten in a week. He purred instantly. At least someone was predictable.

She made a mental note to pick up more cat food next time she passed a pet store—though ordering online was becoming a familiar routine.

Grace slipped off her coat, grabbed a glass from the counter, and filled it with a Merlot, then sank into the worn corner of her couch.

She reached for the remote and flicked on the TV.

And there he was. Paul Max. Hollywood's golden boy. Now trending corpse.

Every network had its package. Grainy red-carpet B-roll, fans sobbing on cue, shaky helicopter footage circling his gas-station grave.

His name crawled endlessly across the ticker, like tragedy had a brand manager.

PAUL MAX, 42, FOUND SHOT DEAD IN ABANDONED GAS STATION

One anchor, stiff as cardboard, read a statement from someone "close to the star." Another segment was already dissecting the final hours of his life.

In high-profile cases like this, it was always the same—the press not only speculated but somehow got hold of details that should've been confidential at this stage.

They knew about the money, which was no surprise; it had been scattered for anyone to see. But they also knew about the word 'murderer' painted onto Paul's chest, and every channel had its own "expert" trying to interpret it.

A *distraction*, one said.

A *message*, said another.

The *sick joke* of a disturbed mind. And so on.

A still from his last film filled the screen—Paul in a tight suit, jaw clenched, sprinting away from an explosion.

It was the seventh installment—yes, seventh—of the long-running action franchise *The Professionals*, about a team of spies battling not only villains, but governments and their own secret services.

The first three? Box-office gold. The latest one? *The Hidden Power*. Hidden, maybe, but not powerful.

It bombed. Critics called it tired, predictable. Even Paul's charm couldn't save it.

"Is that a reason to kill?" Grace muttered, directing the question to the cat.

Rusty tilted his head. Or maybe not. Grace caught herself—was she really reading expressions on a cat now? Yeah. That's how small her circle had gotten: work, family, and a furball with tuna breath.

That's why she was talking to him—because she didn't have anyone else.

But she didn't want to dwell on that. Not tonight.

The anchor speculated whether the sudden tragedy would drive more viewers to theaters—a death bump. The idea made Grace's stomach turn.

Money was always a powerful motive for murder. But if that's what this was, it was beyond cruel. Who kills someone just to boost ticket sales?

She reached for her phone and typed a note to herself: *Peter Woodford. Producer. Ask about money, pressures, recent contacts.*

Then the screen shifted.

A glossy shot of *The Hollywood Star*.

Grace froze.

Becky.

Becky works for *The Hollywood Star*.

Her sister's face rushed to her mind like a wave hitting concrete.

Becky was obsessive. Brilliant. But careless. She chased truth like a dog chased cars—fast, loud, and utterly blind to the danger.

Grace grabbed her phone and hit Becky's contact. Fourth time in the past three days.

No answer.

She hung up, chest tight, the silence worse than any busy signal.

This time, she sent a message.

"Becky, hi. Please call me."

Simple. Calm. Pleading, but not too obvious.

Of course, no reply.

She stared at the phone for another full minute, then set it down with a sigh. The wine wasn't helping.

The news kept blaring in the background, now looping old interview clips and celebrity tributes.

She turned it off.

The silence felt heavier.

Grace grabbed her laptop. Opened it. Searched Paul Max.

Page after page of glamour shots, film reviews, puff interviews, and tabloid garbage. It was hard to tell the truth from PR. But she kept scrolling. Kept digging.

She found articles about Paul's first wife, Peppy La Font, now living in Denver, Colorado. In the photos, she looked happy—smiling with her two adopted children, wrapped in snow and sunlight. Maybe she was.

Surprisingly, she didn't seem bitter. In an interview from three months ago, Peppy spoke warmly of Paul.

She told the reporter, "I have great memories of him. Life has different seasons for different people, and that's okay. You shouldn't fight it. If you love someone—and that someone wants something different—you let them go. That's love. And I loved Paul."

She even mentioned plans for a cameo in one of Paul's upcoming films.

She sounded honest. Too honest, maybe.

Grace made a mental note to follow up, but for now, Peppy didn't strike her as a suspect—although wives, former or not, always made the list.

Then she found an article about Peter Woodford, Paul's longtime producer. It had been published just before Paul's last movie hit theaters.

Woodford had known Paul since his breakout role nearly a decade ago—a film adaptation of the best-selling novel *Murder in the South*.

The story followed a lawyer who uncovered a massive corruption scheme inside a Savannah law firm. Sharp script. Skilled director. Paul's raw, ridiculous charisma.

Boom—instant blockbuster.

After that, Paul never slowed down. He went on to star in twenty-two major box-office hits, becoming a Hollywood legend by the time he turned 40.

And Peter? He rode that wave all the way to mogul status. An empire-builder. An insane millionaire, if the articles were to be believed.

But the word on the street was that he had a gift for burning through money—lavish parties, ridiculous mansions, super yachts, even a struggling football club in England that bled cash.

Ten more minutes in, she found something that made her pause.

A headline from three years ago.

And there it was, in bold capital letters from the archives of a fringe tabloid:

PAUL MAX IS A MURDERER

Chapter 6

Becky Fletcher stared at the headline glowing on her tablet screen, barely believing it.

FAMOUS ACTOR PAUL MAX FOUND DEAD AT ABANDONED GAS STATION. LAPD CALLS IT HOMICIDE.

Her coffee sat untouched. Outside her apartment, the city buzzed with early morning life—but inside, everything felt still.

Becky had been up since dawn, working through her notes for the day. She'd just switched on her tablet, and now she couldn't believe what she was reading.

No. Impossible. She'd spoken to Paul. Two days ago. His voice still echoed in her head. They'd been working together for a month. Interview sessions. Notes. Off-the-record conversations that danced around secrets.

Paul wasn't just her next profile—he was the biggest piece she'd written in years. This piece had consumed her life. Becky had been working around the clock, twenty-four-seven, sacrificing friends, family, everything. Her phone was full of unread messages, unanswered texts—some from people she loved, all pushed aside in the name of the story.

She'd even forgotten Mona's dinner the night be-fore. She'd have to apologize.

Eventually.

Once the piece was done. Once the world read it and understood why it mattered.

But Paul was dead.

And that would make finishing the story much, much harder.

Becky re-evaluated the situation. Her first reaction had been pure panic and shock, but now her mind was shifting—considering other angles.

A murder.

An opportunity.

A wave of shame washed over her. Paul had been murdered—a man she'd known, someone close—and here she was already thinking about how to use his death. How to use that and what she had and spin it into a great story.

But she was an investigative reporter. This was her job. And, if she was being honest, maybe it was her duty to Paul. A way to serve him even now that he was gone.

Maybe she could help bring his killer to justice.

Yes—that's what she needed to do. No hesitation. No doubt. She had to work this.

Besides, she'd already gathered a mountain of in-formation on Paul: private conversations, confidential notes, and... yes, plenty of details from the trial.

Maybe this brutal murder was tied to the trial, Becky thought—the one from last year. The case that brought the world to a standstill for weeks.

The case that turned Paul Max from Hollywood's golden boy into a courtroom defendant.

Becky remembered it all too well.

Paul had been filming *Silent Sun*, a period thriller. The director, Thomas Preminger was a celebrated name in the industry—known for helming films that had won Oscars for actors, crew, and technicians alike.

Preminger called himself an artist. Everyone else called him temperamental, demanding, impossible.

In one of their conversations, Paul confided to Becky that *Silent Sun* was his first real attempt at aiming for an Oscar. He claimed he hadn't told anyone else.

But Becky had already guessed it, knowing Paul's history and ambitions, but hearing it straight from him carried more weight.

Silent Sun was one of those gritty, high-art projects designed for awards season. The set was a mix of high-caliber talent and bad blood. Serious actors, the kind who didn't like sharing scenes with someone they saw as a pretty face, reluctantly standing under the same lights as Paul Max.

In a pivotal scene, he was supposed to fire a gun loaded with a stun round. But someone had swapped it for a live bullet.

The actress opposite him—Rebecca Fontaine—was hit in the chest. She'd collapsed mid-take.

Chaos erupted on set. An assistant director immediately called the police while crew members scrambled to help, pressing against the wound to stop the bleeding.

Paul, according to witnesses, was in shock—trembling, pale. Moments later, the ambulance arrived.

It was no use.

She died on the way to the hospital.

Becky had been glued to the news the second it broke. Paul Max had shot and killed a woman. By accident, they said. But people whispered otherwise.

As soon as the story hit, she marched into the office of *The Hollywood Star* and asked her boss, Jim Bamford, to let her cover it.

Jim didn't hesitate. It was the story of the moment, and Becky was, by far, his best reporter. And when Becky was determined, there was no force in the world that could stop her.

So, just like that, Becky was in court, notebook in hand, recorder in her purse, sitting close enough to see Paul's face every day.

He looked awful. Haunted. Thin. Tired. Shocked.

Maybe it was all performance—he was a good actor, after all. But if it was, it was the performance of a lifetime.

He didn't look guilty. He didn't even look nervous. He looked devastated—like a man drowning in grief, processing something too heavy to name.

She remembered the trial in vivid flashes.

Sad photos of Rebecca Fontaine lying on the set floor, blood soaking her blouse. Footage of EMTs rushing in. Stories from friends who said she was finally getting a break.

She'd scraped for years—bit parts, commercials. *Silent Sun* was supposed to be her shot.

One security expert testified about how firearms were handled on set. Or rather—mishandled. Safety protocols skipped. Checks ignored. Prop-master overwhelmed.

The production was small but fast-moving. Corners had been cut.

And Paul? He wasn't just the lead actor. He was also one of the executive producers.

Responsibility landed heavy.

Some speculated that Paul might have swapped the bullets himself. After all, it was an unusual *accident*—too surreal to be just a mistake.

That led people to wonder: what if Paul had changed the bullet on purpose?

But why? The motive was the missing piece.

There was no apparent reason for Paul to want Rebecca dead. He'd hired her. He knew her from years ago, back in the indie scene. Old colleagues, maybe even friends.

But then came the witness.

A sound tech who testified, under oath, that he'd heard a loud argument from Paul's trailer the week before the shooting. Shouting. Rebecca's voice. Paul's too.

He couldn't hear the words.

Just anger.

Just volume.

Just heat.

That changed everything.

Could Paul Max have intentionally killed Rebecca Fontaine?

Chapter 7

Paul's legal team didn't let the case fall apart without a fight.

Just when it seemed like the tide had turned against him, they pulled out a letter—signed by thirty crew members—affirming that the on-set safety protocols had been followed to the letter.

No shortcuts. No negligence. The production had done everything right.

Becky remembered the moment it was introduced. A ripple ran through the courtroom. Suddenly, doubt crept back in.

What looked like recklessness a few days before now appeared organized, professional—even airtight.

The crew's signatures carried weight. If the people on the ground—lighting techs, camera ops, production managers—believed things were handled correctly, how could the jury disagree?

The prosecution fumbled to recover.

They brought up the argument again.

That heated exchange in Paul's trailer a week before the shooting.

But they had no second witness. Just the sound tech, who heard raised voices but couldn't say what was said.

It could have been just a disagreement, something relatively normal in sets with enlarged egos, artists' eccentricities, and a lot of money around, making people very susceptible.

Paul claimed it was a creative disagreement—that Rebecca had a different interpretation of how she wanted to build her character.

Tempers flared, but it wasn't serious.

Convenient. Clean.

Probably too clean.

Still, it wasn't enough to make the charge stick. The prosecution tried—they interviewed dozens of people, searching for any hint of bad blood between the two. But nothing surfaced.

Everyone described their relationship as good, and no one recalled ever seeing them argue.

The real turning point, Becky thought, was the gun.

The weapon had been locked in a safe. Two keys. One held by an assistant. The other? Paul.

The gun and the blanks—bucketed and labeled—were checked the day before filming. Everything accounted for. Witnesses confirmed it.

The assistant loaded them into the safe and locked it.

That assistant called in sick the next day, so Paul used his own key to open the safe.

It was around 10:00 AM. He arrived, unlocked it, grabbed the gun, and filmed the scene.

Dozens of people were present. No one noticed anything strange.

But here's the thing.

Paul had full access to the studio—all hours.

He had his own key to the lot and to the soundstage.

There were no cameras in the weapons room—only security guards making thirty-minute rounds.

That became the prosecution's final angle.

The theory was simple: Paul could've slipped in the night before, swapped the rounds, locked the safe, and vanished without a trace. No one would've seen him.

But it was still circumstantial—a maybe, a what-if.

No witness could place him at the studio. Security reported nothing unusual. The gate attendants never saw him.

There were, however, other ways in. He would've had to scale walls, dodge patrols, and make his way back the same way. The prosecution argued that it was not only possible but would have been almost easy for a man in good shape like Paul.

And with that, suspicion began to grow.

The prosecution insisted it was possible—and that the only key to the safe was in Paul's control.

Since switching the round during the filming day would've been impossible, they argued the only logical option was that he'd snuck in during the night.

No concrete proof supported it, but in their view, it was the only way it could have happened.

And it wasn't just the prosecution's view. The jury bought it.

But all that changed the day Peppy La Font took the stand.

Becky remembered that moment perfectly—because it shifted everything. She had been watching the jury every day, reading their faces, catching the smallest gestures.

It was remarkable how much you could tell about which way a trial was leaning just by studying them.

Before Peppy testified, Becky's read was clear: the jury was convinced Paul was guilty.

Not just because of the killing itself, but because he was a producer—the one who had opened the safe the night before, the only time someone could have swapped the bullet.

But everything shifted after Peppy.

Peppy was calm. Elegant. Still stunning under the courtroom lights. And she didn't flinch.

She told the court that she'd been with Paul that night.

The entire night.

They had dinner. Talked. Slept together.

The next morning—around 10 AM—she left him on set.

They'd even had breakfast together. Peppy mentioned that Paul had cooked, bringing the tray back to her while she was still in bed.

Scrambled eggs with feta cheese and cherry tomatoes—just the way she liked them.

Her statement was a bombshell.

Not just because it gave Paul an alibi—but because of what it implied.

Peppy had no reason to protect him. They were divorced. Hadn't worked together in years.

And yet there she was, under oath, saying he couldn't have committed the crime because he was in bed with her when it would've happened.

The prosecution tried to break her. They brought up the possibility of manipulation, guilt, and lingering affection. But Peppy held firm.

Becky remembered watching the jury's faces during her testimony.

They believed her. The smiles, the nods, the way the jury seemed to connect with Peppy—appreciating her as an honest woman, courageous enough to tell the truth.

She'd been in another relationship at the time, which made her testimony all the more difficult.

The moment Peppy stepped down, Becky knew what the verdict would be.

There were other details in the trial—technicalities, expert opinions, legal maneuvering—but none of it carried the same impact.

That alibi sealed it.

Paul Max was acquitted.

Some people cheered. Some called it justice.

Others, like Becky, sat in stunned silence.

Because even with the acquittal... the questions would never go away.

Could he have done it?

Would a man like Paul—charming, gifted, adored—really go that far to silence someone over an alleged creative dispute?

Or had he simply been in the wrong place at the wrong time?

Becky didn't know.

But someone thought they did.

Chapter 8

There it was.

Becky stared at the screen, reading the words again as if they might change.

The word *"murderer"* was written on Paul Max's chest. In his own blood.

No matter how many times she read it, the meaning didn't shift.

That wasn't just violence.

It was a message.

Someone hadn't accepted the verdict. Someone believed Paul Max was responsible for Rebecca Fontaine's death. Someone thought he was a murderer—and wanted the world to see it.

But why?

Becky remembered how Paul looked during the trial. Not the press conferences. Not the headlines. Not the close-up photos from the red carpet before everything fell apart.

She remembered the version of him that only the people in that courtroom saw.

Defeated. Hollow. Like he'd been carved out and left to dry.

And to make it worse, he was alone. No family. No friends. Not even Peppy. No one was there for him when it mattered most.

What was going through Paul's mind?

Maybe he finally understood that being adored by millions didn't erase the crushing solitude of his existence.

Because when he needed someone the most, no one was there.

Paul was surrounded by people—millions who admired him. But in the end, that too was an illusion.

None of it was real.

Behind the façade, there was no one.

Becky had watched him closely then—surrounded by professionals and technocrats, all focused on legal strategy and procedural details.

But no one was tending to him. Not his emotions. Not his disappointment in people. Not his broken heart. Not his fear.

He looked like a child. Like a little boy waiting outside a school long after the bell rang, hoping his mother would come—but knowing, deep down, she wasn't coming. And he would be alone.

For the rest of his life.

Their eyes had met that day, during the second week of the trial. It happened just as Becky saw him not as a celebrity, not as a defendant, but as something smaller.

A boy left behind.

And Paul had looked back at her and had held her gaze.

It wasn't flirtation. It wasn't curiosity.

It was something else.

Sadness. Recognition. Maybe even a silent plea.

Maybe he's seen, in her expression, a flicker of understanding.

Maybe, for the first time in days, he realized someone saw him—not the headlines, not the scandal, but the man underneath.

And maybe, in that moment, Paul Max had felt a little less alone.

She'd never forgotten the look. And from that day forward, she'd noticed him scanning the room each time he entered—until he spotted her.

Then he stopped looking. He never smiled. Never nodded. But he looked relieved.

Like her presence meant something.

Like she was a constant. The mother who finally showed up. The one who didn't leave him behind.

And somehow, a strange, invisible bond was formed. Not friendship. Not trust exactly. But something real.

Maybe that's why he chose her.

After the trial, Becky tried to land the interview. She contacted his team, emailed his publicist, reached out through Otto—his assistant—but got nowhere.

Paul Max wasn't giving interviews. He had vanished from the public eye.

But Becky didn't give up.

And then, one afternoon, everything changed.

She went to his house—on a whim, maybe, or a hunch. She stood outside the front gate, watching the sun set behind the hedges.

She wasn't sure what she was doing. It felt desperate. Stupid.

Then headlights appeared. A black car pulling into the driveway.

It was Paul.

He saw her. Slowed down.

He could've ignored her. Driven in. Let the gates close behind him.

Instead, he stopped the car, stepped out, and walked toward her.

"Hi," he said.

"Hi," she replied.

"You're the reporter from the trial."

"And you're the actor from the trial."

Paul's lips curved into a faint smile. For a long second, neither of them spoke.

"Thank you," he said softly.

"Thank you?" Becky asked, confused.

"For being there. I know you were just doing your job, but I felt... I don't know. I felt like you understood what I was feeling."

"I think I did," she said.

He nodded slowly. "What are you doing here?"

"I want to apologize in advance for showing up unannounced," she said, taking a breath.

"I've tried to go through the proper channels. Otto... wouldn't let me through. I just wanted a chance to ask you—face to face—for an interview."

Paul tilted his head.

"I'm not after headlines. No scripts. No agendas. I want to talk about the real you. The man behind the fame. Your life, your victories, your failures. Love. Hate. Regret. Hope."

Another pause.

He stared at her for a long moment. Thinking.

"If there's someone who could understand me," he said finally, "I believe it's you."

More silence.

Then: "Call Otto in the morning. I'll let him know today."

Becky smiled, caught off guard.

"Nice to finally meet you," he added, turning to go.

"Becky," she said. "Nice to meet you too."

He got back in his car, opened the gate, and disappeared into the house.

The next day, Otto treated her like a VIP.

From then on, they met regularly. Short, structured sessions at first—always in Paul's office, always with Otto nearby. But over time, the walls came down.

Paul never acted like someone hiding a crime.

If anything, he was trying to unpack one.

He told her about Rebecca Fontaine. How they'd known each other years ago—back when they were nobodies.

Just two hopefuls in a little acting group called Red Stage. Before his first breakout role. Before fame swallowed him whole.

They'd lost touch, but two years ago, they bumped into each other at a festival. He was filming *Silent Sun* and offered her a small part.

He thought it might help her get back on track.

He said she was good. Always had been.

One evening, during a quieter moment, Paul's eyes went glassy. He spoke slower. Softer.

"It was an accident, Becky," he whispered. "That's all it was."

His hands trembled.

"I didn't switch the bullets. I didn't touch that gun before the scene. Someone missed something. Maybe the day before, someone messed up a check, but I didn't do it."

His voice cracked.

And then, suddenly, he collapsed into sobs.

Becky froze.

He bent forward in the chair, elbows on his knees, face buried in his hands.

She reached out—hesitant—and placed her hand gently on his back.

He didn't flinch. Didn't move.

He simply grabbed her hand and held it.

He looked up through tears.

"I didn't do it," he said again. "I swear to you. I didn't."

Becky believed him.
She wasn't sure why.
But in that moment, she did.

Chapter 9

Jack Taylor sipped his coffee slowly, eyes on the muted television screen across the hotel room. Channel after channel flashed the same headline.

Paul Max Found Dead – LAPD Investigating Homicide.

He set the mug down on the glass-top table. Black coffee. One shot of espresso. No sugar—he hated sugar. Said it cluttered the taste.

He was staying at the Beverly Hilton, one of the quieter suites, high enough to avoid foot traffic but not so extravagant as to attract attention.

He'd checked in under a name that didn't belong to anyone alive anymore. No one knew he was there. Not even the concierge.

He arrived in L.A. last night, just after midnight, straight from O'Hare. The Chicago job had gone as smoothly as silk, but he still felt off. Not because of logistics. Not because of the target.

Because of what she was.

He hadn't wanted the job when it came in. An old woman? Weak. Alone. Minimal security. It offended his instincts. And... his morals?

Was he starting to care about the difference between what was simply wrong and what was truly unacceptable?

Could a paid killer have rules—draw a line in the sand and think, *Yes, I'm a bad man, but even bad people have limits*?

The reality was, it didn't matter whether morality clauses for murderers could pass Kant's standards. What mattered was how he felt. And that thought struck a nerve.

Maybe it was bad—all of it.

Maybe it was time to stop. To be the kind of man who worried about lawn care and nosy neighbors instead of how best to stop a woman's heart in the middle of the night.

But the pay was too generous. Ridiculously so.

And Jack was not the kind of man who asked why.

He was a professional.

He executed.

The intel had been precise. A key to the back door. The alarm code. A house layout complete with highlighted entry routes.

She'd been asleep when he entered. Second floor. First door on the right.

Jack figured whoever hired him was probably close to the old woman—maybe a grandson, a granddaughter.

That made the job revolting. Or worse, maybe a son or daughter. Someone eager to get their hands on her inheritance. So, they'd paid someone like him to "resolve" the problem.

Despicable.

But Jack was there to do what needed to be done. No hesitation, no questions, no doubts.

He preferred plans—precision. Backup plans for the backup plans. Improvisation was a last resort, a sign that something had gone wrong.

The fact that this job was so meticulously prepared, with so much intel, made him feel better. In control.

He could improvise. He had, in the past. But it was never clean. He hated that.

He verified the old woman's identity—same face from the photo, even with the wrinkles and white hair.

Then he placed the pillow over her head.

She didn't struggle much. It was over in seconds.

No cameras. No witnesses. No signs of forced entry.

If anyone asked, she died in her sleep.

That was last night. He'd received half the payment a week ago. This morning, when he checked his account, the rest was there.

Today, he got up early, feeling rested. He decided to watch the circus unfold on the morning news. Paul Max's name was plastered everywhere. Reporters speculated on motives—jealousy, blackmail, maybe a drug deal gone bad.

Others hinted at old grudges from within the industry.

One image stuck with him: Lola Fleming. *Gorgeous.* The reporter stood outside Paul's house, explaining that since the accident, Lola hadn't left.

Paul's longtime assistant, Otto Fisher, issued press releases and media updates. Aside from Otto and the delivery services bringing food and supplies, no one else had been seen going in or out.

And then the theories came back. One analyst—a retired LAPD detective—wondered aloud whether Paul might have "a few bodies buried in his backyard."

"Few bodies?" the reporter asked.

"Well," the detective said, "it's possible."

No one knew anything.

Not really.

And Jack?

Jack watched with the detached indifference of a man who had been orbiting death his entire adult life.

There was nothing sacred about fame. Or wealth. Or talent.

People died the same way—alone and afraid. Jack had seen it too many times to pretend otherwise.

He recognized the hypocrisy, the stunned disbelief in the eyes of those who thought they were untouchable, when suddenly faced with their own mortality.

That was the moment the illusion shattered. And it would never return. Because this was the end.

He knew. He'd seen it in the final flicker of *dozens* of eyes—when the end was near and there was no way out.

When God, or nothingness, stood right in front of them. That's when they pissed their pants. Every time.

And all the grandeur, the fame, the carefully constructed myth of their lives? Gone.

What was left was raw, panicked fear.

The moment of truth.

The moment when the illusion we call life collapses—leaving you staring straight into the void. Everything you thought mattered suddenly feels imagined, hollow, meaningless.

In the end, we are all mortal, and all the things we once held so dear take on a different, humbling perspective.

He took another sip of coffee. It had gone cold. He hated cold coffee. Reaching for the hotel phone, he called room service and ordered another—exactly the same as last time.

Paul Max. Hollywood's golden boy. Now headline meat. Blood on his chest. Word on his chest was *"murderer."*

He glanced back at the screen. Paul Max. Shot three times. Middle of the night. Desert gas station.

The reporters were already dredging up last year's trial—an on-set accident in which he'd allegedly killed actress Rebecca Fontaine. They speculated about a lone avenger, someone hungry for justice for Rebecca.

Then his burner phone rang.

The cheap, plastic one. The one he never used unless someone was ready to pay.

He stared at the number.
He recognized it. And it was important.
He picked up.

Chapter 10

Like most mornings, Grace stopped at the coffee shop down the block from the station. One black Americano. One skim latte.

It was how her workdays began—small rituals wrapped in caffeine.

She liked routine. Craved it.

In homicide, chaos was constant. Victims. Theories. Crime scenes. Lies. Noise. Maybe that was why Grace clung so tightly to structure.

It gave her something to hold onto when everything else spiraled.

She smiled to herself.

She'd spent the last few days worrying about Becky's obsessive tendencies—how she threw herself headfirst into her work like a bullet in a steel room.

But wasn't she doing the same? Filling her mind with theories and evidence, trying to make the noise fit into some kind of shape?

The difference was that Grace clung to structure.

Becky... ricocheted.

She walked into the station, greeted by the usual controlled chaos: people arguing at the front desk, officers heading out for calls, others filing reports, typing, drinking bad coffee.

Grace made her way to the second floor, where her desk sat across from her partner's.

"Hey you," Charlie Bonelli called out. "Just in time. Lola Fleming's waiting in Interview Room 2."

"Morning," Grace replied, handing him the black coffee and taking her seat. She opened a binder containing notes on Lola.

Then she turned to the evidence board, eyes scanning the names and photos, the half-connected dots.

Fifteen minutes later, they entered the interrogation room.

Lola sat at the table, red-eyed and pale, her hair undone, makeup smeared. She wore a hoodie far too casual for someone used to gowns and cameras.

Her posture was slumped. Exhausted.

Grace sat across from her while Charlie remained standing, arms crossed behind her.

"We appreciate you coming in," Grace began gently. "Before we start, I want to remind you that you're here voluntarily. You have the right to an attorney—"

"I know my rights," Lola said quickly, voice scratchy. "I'm here to tell you everything. I want you to find the son of a bitch."

Her tone cracked on the last word. Her face trembled. She was making an effort just to be there.

Grace leaned in. "Did you notice anything unusual in Paul's behavior in the last days or weeks?"

Lola closed her eyes for a long beat.

"No," she whispered. "Life was perfect."

A tear slipped from one eye.

"We were in love," she continued. "I moved in three months ago. We were happy. Laughing. Even the work stuff didn't get to him. The movies, the pressure—it didn't matter. We were just... good. Very good."

"Tell us about that last day," Grace said.

Lola recounted it in soft fragments: breakfast together, Otto's arrival, then her morning run.

"What time was that?" Grace asked.

"Maybe around ten?"

"And then?"

"When I got back, Paul and Otto had left for the office. I texted him—just a smiley face—saying I'd see him at the gala. He said he had meetings all day and would go straight from the office."

"Did he say what the meetings were about?"

"Just usual stuff," she said. "The last movie wasn't doing great. He mentioned meeting a producer, maybe Peter... something about marketing. But nothing strange."

She continued with her activities: a meeting with her publicist, a quick stop at her stylist. She got home late afternoon, sent another message to Paul about wearing the silver dress they'd picked together.

"We talked briefly. Then he stopped responding to my texts," she said quietly. "Not even a smiley. I didn't think much of it then—I was running late. I figured we'd talk at the gala."

Grace nodded. "So, you arrived at the gala..."

"About 8:30. He wasn't there. I bumped into a friend, chatted, but by 9:00 I started to get worried. I called. No answer. I called Otto. He said Paul had left the office at 8:00. That he should be on his way."

Her voice cracked again.

"I texted him again. No reply. I started to get mad. I'd dressed up for him. I thought he was being rude."

"You went home?"

"Around eleven. He wasn't there. I made something small to eat and turned on the TV. By midnight, I called Otto again. He hadn't heard anything. I called Paul. No answer. That's when I started to really worry. I called his security."

Grace leaned forward. "What did they say?"

"They said he dismissed them for the rest of the day. At 7:00 PM. That made no sense."

She swallowed.

"I called Otto again. He was panicking. Then I remembered the GPS in Paul's car. I had access through the app."

She paused, steadying her breath.

"I saw he'd left the office after nine, took a weird route, and stopped... out in the middle of nowhere. Off Highway 14. Parked at 9:44 PM. And still there."

Grace nodded slowly.

"I called the police. I begged them to check. I also called the security team and made them send someone. I waited."

Another breath.

"Then the call came. Around 3:00 AM. They told me..." Her voice broke. "They told me Paul was dead."

She went quiet.

Grace and Charlie exchanged a glance.

"I think I passed out," Lola added, voice barely a whisper. "I remember EMTs... flashing lights. Otto crying. The police. A doctor gave me something. I was just... gone."

"I'm sorry for your loss, Miss Fleming," Grace said softly. "Do you remember anything else? A call he received? A meeting he didn't mention?"

"No. Everything felt normal. He had no enemies. Everyone liked him. Maybe a few jealous people, sure, but nothing dangerous."

Grace kept her tone steady. "Anyone unusual around him recently?"

Lola thought.

"Just one thing. He was doing an interview. With a reporter. She came to the house a lot. I thought it was strange—Paul hated interviews. But he said he trusted her."

Grace's heart skipped.

"Do you remember her name?"

Lola dug through her purse, pulled out a business card, and handed it over.

Grace read it.
Of course.
Becky.

Chapter 11

G race Fletcher leaned against the passenger door of the unmarked car, coffee cooling in her hand, mind spinning faster than the traffic around them.

Grace was worried about Becky.

Paul Max had been murdered while she was in the middle of conducting an in-depth interview with him, and now Becky had gone dark. That could only mean she was in over her head.

And Becky had a knack for finding trouble.

When they were kids, she'd once tried to investigate a drug ring for the school newspaper. She got so involved that she started receiving threatening notes—at school and at home.

Mona had gone crazy with worry, but Becky managed to uncover one of the main distributors, who eventually ended up in jail.

If others were involved, no one ever found out.

Becky was ecstatic, even winning a school award for her investigative piece. Mona, however, was furious. She'd had a long, closed-door conversation with Becky afterward.

Mona never spoke about it much, but Grace suspected Mona'd struck a deal with someone high up—a top guy who decided to sacrifice one of his mid-level players and pull the operation from that school.

Mona must have had serious leverage to make that happen.

Luckily, the story died there. But that was Becky—naïve, smart, and dangerously irresponsible.

The city rolled by in streaks of concrete and sunlight as Charlie drove them across town to their next interview. The silence between them wasn't tense—just full.

Charlie knew Grace was processing. That's how their partnership worked. When she needed to talk, she would.

Charlie had been working with Grace for about six months. At first, it hadn't been easy. Grace was still accustomed to the style of her previous partner, Henry Woods, who had transferred to New York when his mother fell ill.

But now, they understood each other. Grace was a consummate professional—one of the best in the force—and Charlie was glad to work alongside her.

He'd started his career in Phoenix, but when the opportunity in L.A. came up, he didn't hesitate. It was a chance to work in a larger district.

His first cases there hadn't been glamorous, but they were challenging and engaging. Now, this case felt like his real shot at the big leagues.

And now, she spoke.

"You remember when I told you Becky mentioned working on something big?" Grace said, eyes still on the road ahead.

Charlie glanced over. "Couple weeks ago, yeah?"

"She said it was an interview with a Hollywood star. That's all she said. Nothing more."

"You didn't ask who?"

Grace shook her head. "No. I didn't think it mattered. She's always doing profiles, always chasing some new angle."

But now?

Now it mattered.

Becky had been interviewing Paul Max—the Paul Max—and then he turned up dead. And she went silent at the same time?

That wasn't just a story.

That was a lead.

"It was Paul Max. I don't remember her saying his name," Grace added. "And I think I would've remembered it. But honestly? I'm not sure."

Grace had always been honest with herself about one thing: she wasn't into the current Hollywood scene. Never cared for celebrity drama, red carpet fights, or social media meltdowns.

That wasn't her Hollywood.

Her Hollywood lived in black and white reels, smoky close-ups, and orchestral swells. She could tell you about Glenn Ford slapping Rita Hayworth in *Gilda*, or the raw desperation in Frank Sinatra's eyes in *The Man with the Golden Arm.*

But the stars of today? The Paul Max types?

They existed in a different orbit.

Of course, she'd heard something about his trial. Everyone had.

But it was background noise.

She had been knee-deep in a triple homicide last year, and there were only so many tragedies a mind could hold at once.

But now, it was impossible to ignore.

Paul Max was murdered.

A year after the trial.

Someone had written 'murderer' across his chest.

And Becky—her sister—had been interviewing him.

And now Becky wasn't answering her phone.

Again.

Charlie pulled up to a stoplight, glanced at her. "You thinking what I'm thinking?"

"That Becky's involved in something dangerous?" Grace muttered. "Yeah."

"Think she's hiding something?"

"I don't know. But I do know that she hasn't responded to a single one of my messages in almost a week."

"That's normal?"

Grace let out a breath. "Define normal. Becky gets obsessive. Tunnel vision. She shuts the world out when she's chasing a story. But this time... something's off."

She scrolled through her phone. A dozen unan-swered texts. Five missed calls. All delivered. None read.

"It's too much of a coincidence," she said softly. "She's working with a famous actor—he ends up dead in the middle of nowhere—and at the same time, she goes dark."

Charlie pulled onto the freeway ramp. "You think she's in danger?"

"I think it's time to activate Plan B."

Charlie raised an eyebrow. "Plan B?"

"Becky's always been unpredictable. But she knows I worry. So, we made a deal years ago. If she ever van-ished for more than a week without a trace, I'd use her emergency key."

"You're going to her place?"

Grace nodded. "Tonight."

"And if she's not there?"

"Then I start digging."

Silence settled between them again. The freeway stretched ahead like a long breath. Grace looked out the window, her thoughts ticking like a metronome.

Someone had killed Paul Max.

And whoever it was had a message to send.

Maybe justice.

Maybe revenge.

Either way, Becky was too close to the story.

And Grace could feel it—deep in her gut, beneath the layers of discipline and instinct she'd built over years in homicide—

Something wasn't right.

And this time, the case wasn't just about solving a murder.

This time, it was personal.

Chapter 12

Otto Fisher gripped the steering wheel until his knuckles went white.

He hadn't slept. Not really. Not since the call. Not since the news began flooding every screen, every headline, every whispered conversation in the city.

The media had gone wild over Paul's death—he was everywhere. Every channel. Every newspaper. Every tabloid.

The world was ravenous for details about him, about his death, about his past. Even if you tried, you couldn't escape the avalanche of coverage pounding away all day and all night.

Paul Max was dead. His boss. His mentor. His friend.

And Otto had done nothing to protect him.

It still felt like fiction—a tabloid rumor that would unravel by noon. But it wasn't.

He was driving to Paul's office—his office now, technically—but his mind kept short-circuiting, refusing to accept what that meant.

Paul wouldn't be there. Not today. Not ever again.

His stomach churned.

The plan for the day had been simple. Morning meetings. Lunch. Wardrobe fitting. A studio call. Paul had even joked about skipping the last one if the food at the new restaurant was good.

Otto wiped at his face, angry at himself for crying again.

He'd done it all night—on the floor of his apartment, in the shower, curled up in bed like a child.

It wasn't supposed to end like this.

He'd worked for Paul for five years—five perfect, chaotic, beautiful years. Before Otto, Paul had burned through assistants like tissue paper. No one lasted. No one could keep up.

Then Otto came along. He understood Paul. Finished his sentences. Read his moods.

Knew when to disappear and when to step in.

He still remembered his first day—messing up a private airline booking. Paul had been furious, but Otto had pulled off the impossible and fixed it.

Paul had been impressed. Pleased. He appreciated efficiency and quick thinking.

And Otto had been there through everything: the bitter divorce from Peppy, the trial that nearly destroyed Paul, the whirlwind romance with Lola that spiraled into a sickly-sweet soap opera.

Otto never liked Lola.

There was something manufactured about her—too polished, too controlled. Volatile beneath the surface. The kind of woman who inserted herself into every detail of Paul's life—his wardrobe, his press, his dinner parties.

And Paul let her. He was blind to what she was.

A gold digger with a grip on him so tight, he couldn't see the trap he was in.

According to Otto's own digging, Lola Fleming was born Mary Ann Krushensky in Vincennes, Indiana—a nowhere town she spent her life trying to erase.

Her father walked out when she was five.

Her mother remarried a priest with a hand like a ruler and a heart like stone. The house was a place of sermons and silence, where affection was rationed and mistakes were met with scripture.

Lola learned young to keep her distance. At sixteen, a back-alley abortion went wrong. It left scars the doctors could see and others they couldn't. She'd never have children.

Maybe she never wanted them after that.

She left home before she was eighteen. First stop—Chicago. Waitressing by day, hostessing by night.

Her beauty bought her a seat at tables she had no business sitting at.

One of those seats belonged to a man with mob ties. For a while, she played the girlfriend. When that turned sour—and it always turns—she skipped town.

L.A. was a clean slate, or as clean as she could get. She picked up a few modeling jobs, enough to meet a film director who promised her the movies.

She took the promise and the name change—Mary Ann Krushensky became *Lola Fleming*. Her first real role was in *Maribel Dreams*.

She was raw, natural, magnetic. People noticed.

A brief, high-profile fling with a second-tier actor made her a fixture in gossip rags and teen magazines. Behind the photos were bruises and screaming matches.

She walked away before it killed her.

Time passed without a serious relationship. She drank too much sometimes, but she was smart—smart enough to keep the cameras pointed where she wanted them.

Then came the role that changed everything: *Sex and Lolitas*. She played a venomous, ambitious young woman who could charm and destroy in the same breath. Audiences couldn't get enough.

The show made her famous.

Now, with the fourth season about to start filming and movie offers stacked on her desk, Lola Fleming was at the top of her game.

On paper, she was a survivor.

In the right light, she was a star.

But Otto knew better.

Under the gloss and the smiles, there was steel, and maybe something colder.

Paul lavished her with gifts. Took her to Venice, to Iceland, to some private island that probably doesn't exist on Google Maps.

Otto remembered Lola's birthday in Paris—Eiffel Tower views, custom lighting, rose petals, and a string quartet flown in from Vienna.

Excessive. Exhausting.

But Otto made it happen.

Because if Paul was happy, he could deal with anything.

He'd have done anything for him.

And now Paul was gone. And Otto was carrying a secret that tied him to it.

He pulled into the private garage beneath the building. His pass still worked. Of course it did. He parked, sat there for a moment, the engine ticking. His mind flashed back to the night Paul died.

He'd lied to Lola—told her Paul left the office like normal. That nothing was out of the ordinary.

But that wasn't true.

He knew exactly what happened.

Paul had asked him to withdraw two million dollars in cash.

No explanation. No questions. No one could know—not Lola, not security, and especially not CC.

Otto obeyed.

And never saw him alive again.

Now he was left holding the guilt like a bag of bricks. Should he have followed? Called the police? Brought CC into it?

He didn't know. But he felt responsible.

He'd lied before—about his age, his past, even his sexuality. But this was different. This lie could bury him.

And worse, it betrayed the trust of the one person who had truly understood him.

Paul had helped him when he was still wrestling with his identity. Never judged. Just listened. Supported.

That made this worse.

Otto took a deep breath, got out of the car, and headed for the elevator. The building felt colder, quieter—like even the walls were in mourning.

Inside, Denise, Paul's longtime receptionist, gave him a tight-lipped look.

"Morning, Otto. You... you don't look too good. Can I get you something?"

"Don't worry, Denise. I'll be fine. But grab me a Tylenol, will you? My head's killing me. Are they here?"

"They're here," she said softly. "Detectives. Conference room."

Of course they were. They'd called the day before, requesting an urgent meeting first thing in the morning.

They wanted answers—what had happened, what he knew.

And he needed to decide exactly what to tell them.

Otto walked past the framed movie posters lining the hall, the air still carrying Paul's cologne, as if he'd just stepped out.

He paused outside the door.

His hand trembled.

Inside, two detectives were waiting. Questions would come—about the money, about Paul's movements, about that night.

He had a choice.

Keep the lie alive.

Or finally come clean.

Either way, nothing would ever be the same.

Chapter 13

O tto Fisher stepped into the conference room and froze.

A female detective sat at the center of the table, sipping from a paper coffee cup.

Calm. Watchful. In control.

In the corner, the male detective stood, arms crossed, studying a framed movie poster on the wall—Paul Max in mid-stride, drenched in Venetian rain, face stoic, shirt unbuttoned just enough to look dangerous.

"Mr. Fisher?" the woman said, rising and extending her hand.

"Yes," Otto said, swallowing. "I'm Otto Fisher. Personal assistant to Paul Max."

The male detective turned.

"Detective Charlie Bonelli," he said, stepping forward. "Always admired Paul. This one's from that film he shot in Venice, right? Heard he didn't use a stunt double. Did he really jump from that plane?"

Otto let out a quiet sigh. "He jumped. Not exactly from the plane, but yeah. He jumped."

He didn't want to explain the nuance of camera tricks and wire rigs.

Some people never understood that Hollywood doesn't sell movies—it sells illusion.

A projection of common, mortal desires dressed up as something bigger.

Hollywood was an illusion in every sense. Not just because viewers sat in front of a screen watching someone else's fantasy unfold in two dimensions. But because the entire system was designed to deceive—to simulate a version of reality that didn't exist.

These days, much of it was AI-generated. Scenes enhanced, faces smoothed, emotions digitally stitched.

What audiences saw were lab-grown images, curated to manipulate.

An illusion from start to finish.

Even the lives of the actors were false—massaged, polished, and rebranded to create parasocial bonds.

Carefully tailored to feed the need.

To keep the illusion alive.

It didn't matter now. None of it did. He gestured toward a chair.

Bonelli sat down.

Otto remained standing for a second too long before easing into the chair across from them. His skin felt wrong—too tight, too hot.

"I'm Detective Grace Fletcher," the woman said. "We're investigating Mr. Max's murder."

Murder.

That word hit harder than "case." It was the right word. The one Otto had been avoiding. His chest tightened.

"Could you walk us through what happened that day?" Grace asked, her voice steady.

Otto hesitated.

Then he began.

"I went to Paul's house in the morning. Like always. We usually did a quick debrief—mapped out the day, coordinated calls, promo schedules. That kind of thing."

"Was Lola there?" Grace asked.

"For a moment. Then she went for a run."

"What happened next?"

Otto looked down. His fingers tightened on his knees.

"Paul asked me to get him two million dollars. In cash."

Charlie raised his eyebrows. "That the same two million found at the crime scene?"

Otto nodded. "I assume so, yes."

"What did he say it was for?"

"He didn't. I asked. He refused to explain. Just told me to get it and keep it quiet. No one could know."

Grace's pen moved slowly across her notepad. "So, what did you do?"

"I went to the bank where Paul keeps most of his funds. He's treated like royalty there. I met with the branch manager—told him Paul was planning a themed party and needed the cash for props, atmosphere, whatever."

"And he believed you?"

Otto gave a faint shrug. "People knew Paul had... eccentricities. The manager laughed and said, 'Paul will always be Paul.' Then he got me the money."

"You asked for it in hundreds?"

"Yes. I brought a bag with me. We packed it and I left. He asked if I had security with me—I lied and said yes. But I was alone."

Otto paused, deciding what to say next. He knew the bank manager would talk—maybe already had. That was part of why he'd decided to come clean.

"Denise can give you the manager's contact," he added, glancing toward the hallway.

The detectives didn't react. They'd probably already spoken to her.

"Then you returned to the office?"

Otto nodded. "It was close to eight. Paul was there. Waiting. He looked... off. Nervous. He wasn't taking calls, but he kept checking his phone—like he was waiting for something."

Grace leaned in. "Did he message Lola?"

"I think so. I didn't see the message, but I saw him typing. He talked to her briefly, then he turned to me and said I could go. *That everything would be okay.*"

Otto's voice cracked.

"That was the last thing he said to me."

He paused, swallowing hard.

"Did you call anyone?" Charlie asked.

"No. Paul told me not to. I waited. I thought maybe he'd call and tell me everything was fine. But then Lola called—past midnight. She was hysterical. So, I told her I'd try to reach Paul. I thought he wouldn't mind if it came from her."

"And?"

"He didn't answer. I called her back. She checked his GPS and said he'd gone out to some remote place. She called the police."

"Why didn't you tell her the truth then?" Grace asked.

Otto's eyes welled up. "Because I promised Paul I wouldn't. And because I was scared. And because... I hoped it was just a misunderstanding."

Silence followed. Grace let him sit in it.

"Did Paul seem afraid?" she asked.

Otto nodded slowly. "Yes. More than I'd ever seen him."

"Did he have enemies?"

"Not that I knew of. He was loved—adored, even. Especially lately. He was happy with Lola. Between films. Resting. Traveling."

"What about the trial?" Charlie asked.

Otto hesitated. "It was hard. But it was an accident. Everyone knew that."

"You're aware someone wrote *murderer* on his chest?" Grace asked.

Otto looked away. "Yes."

"You think someone didn't believe it was an acci-dent?"

He didn't respond right away. His chest felt like it might cave in. He knew he needed to say yes—and keep them focused on the trial.

Otto didn't want to steer these detectives toward other enemies—ones long buried in the past, where they belonged.

Some things were better left untouched. Safer. Cleaner.

It was better to keep their attention on the trial. On the enemies everyone already knew about.

"Maybe. Yes. Maybe someone never accepted it. But who? It could've been anyone. A relative. A fan. Some-one who watched the trial on TV and saw something we didn't."

That was a lot of people for them to consider.

"What about Rebecca Fontaine's family?"

"She didn't really have any. Her mother's in a care facility. No spouse. No kids."

Grace scribbled something. "Anything else you re-member? Anything strange in the last few weeks?"

Otto hesitated again.

"Nothing I can recall," he said. But he wasn't sure if that was true.

"Thank you, Mr. Fisher. We'll follow up soon. Can we arrange it through Denise?"

"Yes," Otto said, the weight returning like an avalanche.

The detectives stood and left.

Otto remained where he was, breathing in the silence, trying to order the noise in his mind.

Then he reached for his phone.

And made the call.

Chapter 14

"This is too much! The police were here! I... I don't know what to do!"

Otto Fisher's voice shrieked through the phone, raw and unfiltered.

His breathing came in quick bursts. He paced the narrow hallway of Paul's office, tugging at his collar like it was strangling him.

On the other end, Connie remained silent.

She was sitting in her sleek home office, surrounded by blackout curtains and thick silence. She didn't flinch.

She let Otto scream, let him burn through his panic like a candle on its last inch of wick. And yep, as always, Otto was loud.

Emotional. Unraveled.

Behind the noise, she was already calculating. She'd dealt with panic before.

As a former FBI special agent, Connie Carson had been trained to recognize hysteria for what it was: noise. But she hadn't been with the Bureau in years. Fired. Disgraced.

Not because of failure, but because her boss couldn't handle a certain important individual with a fragile ego and a taste for scapegoats.

She'd been the scapegoat.

Thrown to the wolves to protect a man's career. Dishonorably discharged.

A stain on her record that she never bothered to scrub out.

She didn't look back.

She went private, made millions cleaning up messes for powerful men who couldn't manage their own shadows.

And the biggest mess of them all?

Paul Max.

A man-child with the face of a god and the impulse control of a dog off leash.

This time, the mess was too big.

He was already dead.

There was nothing Connie could do to protect him anymore.

But loose ends had a way of strangling you if you didn't cut them fast—evidence, whispers, people with too much to say.

For years, Connie had been the one scrubbing Paul Max's world clean, burying the mess where no one would ever find it.

But some skeletons still had her fingerprints on them, and if they clawed their way out, they could drag her down with them.

There were skeletons tied to Paul, and she needed them to stay buried—far from the public eye, the detectives, or anyone who knew enough to be dangerous.

People like Otto.

Otto was a liability.

He was good at color-coding a calendar and picking out Paul's tailored jackets, but under pressure? He cracked like cheap glass.

"Okay, calm down," Connie said finally. Her voice was ice in a steel cup. "Tell me exactly what you told them."

"I told them everything! About the money! That Paul asked me for it, how I went to the bank, what happened after, even what I told Lola—everything!"

She closed her eyes. One slow breath in.

Idiot.

"Did you mention Red Stage?"

There was a pause. Then came Otto's confused voice.

"Red Stage? What the hell does that have to do with anything?"

Of course. Typical. People like Otto couldn't see two meters in front of themselves.

Couldn't tell when the ground was shifting beneath their feet. Couldn't understand how the past could explode into the present if you gave it just enough air.

"No," he continued. "They didn't ask about that. I didn't bring it up. Why would I?"

She bit back the words. Because you're too dumb to know when you're in danger.

Instead, she said, "So you kept the enemy conversation focused on the trial?"

"Yes," Otto said quickly. "They think the killer was someone angry about the verdict. I leaned into that. I didn't mention anything else."

Silence. The first real silence between them.

Then: "Okay. Good," Connie said. "That's what we need. Keep them looking in that direction. Far from Red Stage."

"I still don't get it," Otto muttered. "What does Red Stage have to do with any of this?"

She almost laughed. But not the funny kind.

If the police dug into Red Stage—the contracts, the betrayal, the prison time, the deaths—they'd uncover the rot.

They'd trace the chain reaction that began ten years ago. The one she had been part of. The one that had made Paul call her in the first place.

Otto hadn't been around back then, so his understanding was only fragments—shadows of what really happened.

But enough to be dangerous.

"You don't need to get it," she said flatly. "You just need to keep your mouth shut."

Otto hesitated.

"Okay. Okay. That makes sense. I guess."

Connie leaned back in her chair, fingers drumming on the armrest. Otto was unraveling. She could picture him: sweating, pale, blinking too fast.

The kind of guy who'd confess just to relieve the pressure in his chest.

He was dangerous.

But for now, he was contained.

"You did well," she said, her tone softening just enough. "Just stay quiet. Stay calm. Everything will be fine."

Otto went silent.

The last time he'd heard those words—*Everything will be fine*—they'd come from Paul.

Hours before he was murdered.

He didn't mention that to Connie.

"Who was blackmailing Paul?" Connie asked.

"I don't know. Paul didn't say. He never even used the word *blackmail*. He just asked for the money. But... we shouldn't talk about this over the phone."

"You're right," Connie replied smoothly. "I'll meet you at your place tonight. Ten o'clock. In the meantime, I'll start working to close some loose ends. Tie things up. Clean the house. I'll let you know if you need to do anything."

"Okay," Otto said, his voice small.

"Good."

"Thanks, CC," he added, with a tired breath. "I feel much better with you involved."

CC smiled, cold and controlled.

"Of course."

Then she hung up.

And Otto was left staring at the phone, hands shaking, wondering if he'd just saved himself—*or sealed his fate.*

Chapter 15

CC felt it in her gut—something was about to blow. And Otto was the weak link. Always had been. He was unraveling fast, and she couldn't afford that.

She hated Otto Fisher. Always had.

Long ago, she made a pact with Paul Max: she'd operate outside his "official" team. Out of sight. Out of reach. No brunches, no birthday parties, no team-building garbage.

That arrangement kept her away from Otto—thank God.

She couldn't stand his jittery energy.

He was soft, emotionally leaky, desperate to please. She didn't trust people like that.

People who break under pressure. People who talk.

She remembered something from years ago. A black site. Cold cement. Fluorescent lights that never flickered.

They had a suspect in custody—a Nazi scumbag with blood on his hands. She was tasked with getting intel. Crucial intel.

Her partner, though, was a square. Rigid. Weak. The kind of man who followed rules because he was afraid of what would happen if he didn't.

She hated his guts.

But she had to work with him. The guy reminded her of Otto—so wrapped up in himself and his own fears that he couldn't see the real world.

The world with all its miseries and unfairness.

The real world, where only the strongest survive.

Where rules don't matter—only results, and the power to control the story and the people making the decisions.

The law? That was for people without power.

The suspect looked tough. But she saw through it. He was paper-thin. Bravado masking rot.

She pushed hard. Pressure. Words. Then pain. The bastard started to crack—she could see it in his eyes.

And then her partner tried to stop her.

Told her it was enough.

Tried to pull her off.

She tried to talk him down. Keep him quiet.

Convince him she had it under control.

But he wouldn't listen.

She didn't remember the exact moment she hit him. Maybe it was instinct. Maybe it was rage. One moment he was barking orders, the next he was out cold on the floor.

She got what she needed.

The intel was critical—it led to documents linking the President's inner circle to the nazi gang.

But no one cared about that later. Internal review. Charges. Her boss, at the end, backed her partner. Said she'd gone too far. And when things got messy, he hung her out to dry.

That's when she learned.

You don't trust people.

Not even the ones on your side.

Especially not them.

And Otto was about to talk.

CC sat in her fortified bunker beneath an abandoned industrial building at the edge of the city. Some called the area lawless. She called it perfect.

Her lair was built beneath the bones of a collapsed factory—entry only through a narrow stairwell, shielded by fake brick, steel, facial scans, and enough alarms to make Fort Knox blush.

Inside: self-sustaining generators, three satellite uplinks, a freshwater filtration system, and non-perishables to feed her for over a year. Guns. Ammunition. Enough to arm a squad. Maybe two.

She had three exit routes, all hidden, all secure. Some days, she didn't surface at all.

Lately, she hadn't left in weeks.

Paranoia? Maybe. But paranoia had kept her alive.

She moved like a ghost—changing her routines, wearing different disguises if she went out, switching vehicles.

Even inside, she kept the lights dim and the bunker had no windows. She didn't trust anything. Not people. Not cameras. Not silence.

And definitely not Otto.

CC was tall and powerfully built—a woman shaped by years of martial arts and intelligence training.

From an early age, she understood the importance of control and power. Raised in a middle-class family, she grew up in the shadow of her older brother, her parents' clear favorite.

Their attention barely brushed her; she was invisible.

Living in the shadows wasn't easy, but over time it became her second nature.

When she was fifteen, everything changed. Her brother died in a motorcycle accident while practicing for a motocross competition.

The tragedy shattered her parents.

They continued living together, but their souls seemed hollow, existing in a haze of grief they could never shake. From that moment, CC knew she was on her own.

She took charge of her life because there was no one left to do it for her.

The army became her proving ground.

There, she grew tough—very tough. She served in Afghanistan and came face-to-face with the chaos and moral ambiguity of war.

On one mission, she was captured and tortured. It was the worst experience of her life, leaving scars that still marked her body. She had been close to breaking when a Marine rescue team found her.

Soon after, she hunted down two of the men who had tortured her.

She gave them exactly what they'd given her—and more.

Both died at her hands.

The most chilling part wasn't their deaths—it was her own reaction. She felt nothing. No remorse. No guilt.

Only the cold, clinical satisfaction of exercising power and delivering revenge.

From then on, CC became colder still. Meticulous. Professional. Emotionless.

A machine.

Her skill and discipline drew attention, and she was eventually trained in intelligence work before being recruited by the FBI.

She excelled in the field, but her psychological evaluations flagged concerns about her mental stability.

When accusations were later brought against her, those reports became ammunition.

Maybe they were right—maybe she didn't belong in the FBI.

But CC didn't care. She knew the truth: the world offered plenty of other ways to succeed.

She walked barefoot to the VR command center built into the far wall of her living area. Powered on the curved screens, slipped on her haptic gloves, and started digging.

Red Stage.

The name flickered in front of her in a series of archived news clippings, old contracts, buried legal threats, and barely-documented production credits.

She leaned in, narrowing the search. Dug through litigation archives.

Pulled up estate transfers.

She worked through the afternoon, eyes darting between columns of data. Cross-referencing aliases. Sifting through airport logs.

Pulling down encrypted files from half-dead forums where paranoid weirdos exchanged conspiracy theories.

Some of them weren't so crazy.

Paul had secrets. Secrets where she was involved.

And there was a missing link. She could feel it. Like a breath held in the dark.

She stopped only when her alert chimed.

A reminder.

She leaned back in her chair, pinched the bridge of her nose, and sighed.

She had a meeting with Otto at his place, and she needed to get ready.

So, she made the call.

Chapter 16

Another text from Grace.

Becky Fletcher rolled her eyes and tossed her phone face down on the bed.

My God, how intense can one woman be? Grace had sent three texts and a voicemail in the last six hours.

Becky didn't need that right now.

She was in the middle of the biggest disaster—or possibly the biggest scoop—of her career.

No middle ground. No gray areas. Just chaos.

Paul Max was dead. So, he could not save her.

Her interview—months in the making, delicate as glass—was now nearly useless.

She didn't have enough. Not enough to publish. Not enough to make it sing.

Too many gaps.

Too many threads left dangling.

And the man who could tie them together? Gone.

She felt like she was stranded in the middle of the ocean—sitting on a tiny island, no food, surrounded by sharks.

She couldn't stay where she was.

There was no story here.

But to swim meant diving into dangerous waters.

Still, she was Becky Fletcher.

Becky Fletcher didn't do waiting. She didn't do starving.

She was a survivor—the sharpest investigative reporter the West Coast had ever seen. Sitting still meant dying, and Becky had no intention of dying.

Not here. Not now.

She got her harpoon, strapped on her fins, and jumped headfirst into the bloody tide.

"Let's go shark hunting."

And she smiled—a sharp, dangerous curve of the lips.

This was the Becky Fletcher she trusted most.

The one with her back against the wall.

The one who'd burn through every obstacle to reach the truth.

In that moment, she stopped being just a journalist.

She became a weapon.

Her hunch—no, not even a hunch, more like a flicker of a thought—kept coming back.

Something about Rebecca Fontaine.

Not just the trial. Not just the accident on set.

It was the past. The *before*.

Back when Rebecca and Paul helped build something called Red Stage.

More than ten years ago. A little acting company with big dreams.

Paul had mentioned it, vaguely, but never followed up. Becky had written it down. Twice.

And now it echoed.

What happened between them? Why didn't they stay in touch?

Why did Rebecca end up bouncing from one miserable job to another for years while Paul climbed Hollywood's Mount Olympus?

Why hadn't he helped her... until she conveniently "*bumped into him*" a year ago?

Sure, it could've just been life.

Careers diverge. People forget.

Maybe seeing her again stirred something in Paul—guilt, friendship, pity.

Maybe that's why he gave her the role in *Silent Sun*.

Maybe.

It was a story. A soft one, maybe—not Pulitzer material—but with the right color, the right angle, it could still land.

Deep down, she knew Paul's death was connected to Rebecca's.

To find the link, she'd have to travel back—ten, maybe twelve years—to the beginning of Red Stage, to when they first met.

She didn't know what she'd uncover. Maybe nothing tied directly to Paul's death.

But something was there. She could feel it.

Paul had always been slippery when talking about Red Stage—offering only vague references, skirting around specifics.

When she pressed, he waved it off, claiming it was too long ago, that he didn't remember clearly.

Her heart seized at the thought: *What if I pour time and money into this and find nothing?* She could almost taste the sting of failure.

But then she straightened, pushing the doubt aside.

Her instincts—the ones that had never failed her—told her something didn't sit right. And when that happened, she knew she was on the trail of a real story.

The deeper she dug into Red Stage, the more questions emerged.

Especially after she found Mark Zambrano, detective, Boise PD.

Marcus O'Brien, one of the co-founders, was dead now. Died a couple of years ago.

Becky had been trying to track him down, and instead found Mark. It was Mark who dropped the bait no reporter could resist.

"Come to Boise," Mark had said. *"I'll tell you everything I know. And I promise—you won't be disappointed."*

That got Becky's full attention.

A local detective involved in a story tied to a long-dead acting company and the death of an actor?

No-brainer.

She picked up her phone and made the call.

"Hello?"

"Hi, Mark. How are you?"

"Fine," he said. His voice was calm, clipped. Detective-like.

"Are you still good for tomorrow?"

"Actually," Becky said, already slipping into her sneakers, "I'm flying in tonight. Late. I figured I'd rather be fresh and ready for the morning."

"Great," Mark said. "I've been waiting to talk to you. I've got files ready. A lot of background you'll want to see."

"Perfect. I'll see you at ten tomorrow morning."

She hung up and took a deep breath. Then sat back down and did what she always did: double-check the source.

She researched Mark Zambrano.

Young. Sharp. Six years with the Boise Police Department.

A solid performance record, with a commendation for his role in a high-profile corruption case two years ago.

By the book. Smart. Ambitious. Son of a cop.

Everything checked out.

For now.

She still didn't know what Mark's connection to Paul Max was—or why a local cop was neck-deep in a story about a long-forgotten acting company.

Was he investigating Paul's murder?

Had he uncovered something linking it to Red Stage?

She would find out.

Because she wasn't turning back now.

She packed her laptop, charger, and recorder. Checked her notes—then checked them again. She pulled a suitcase onto the bed, but it felt too big.

So, she reached for the smaller one. More logical for a short trip.

She had three days of clothes, four days of caffeine pills, and one unfinished story that could become her career-defining piece—or her downfall.

She glanced at her phone. Another text from Grace. Ignored.

She opened her Uber app and called for a car. The airport was 30 minutes away.

And Becky Fletcher was already swimming.

Swimming with sharks.

Chapter 17

Jack Taylor waited. Still as stone. The alley was narrow, boxed in by brick walls that sweated moisture in the night air.

Somewhere far off, a bottle shattered, followed by laughter. The sound didn't reach him—it was background noise, like the faint hiss of a streetlamp behind him.

He stood in the shadows, leaning just enough to see the mouth of the alley. His hand rested casually in his coat pocket.

Not on the gun. Not yet. He had time.

A mouse skittered by, pausing to stare at him with glassy eyes before disappearing into a drain. Jack didn't move. He barely blinked.

The damp air smelled of garbage and wet cardboard.

He'd been here an hour, shifting only once when his leg cramped. He could feel the familiar ache in his lower back, the kind you ignore because the job comes first.

A car rolled past, its headlights sweeping the alley for a second.

Jack eased deeper into the shadow.

Then—footsteps. Slow. Unhurried.

His pulse stayed steady. He breathed evenly, shifting his stance to get the angle right.

The figure emerged at the far end. Head down. Hands in pockets.

An old man.

Perfect.

The type who wouldn't notice him, wouldn't remember him.

Jack waited as the man reached the building's entrance and pushed inside.

The door began to swing shut—slowly, too slowly.

Jack moved at the last moment, catching it before the latch clicked.

Inside, the old man was already stepping into the elevator. Jack slipped past, letting the doors close.

He took the stairs. Two flights up. Quiet steps.

At the landing, he stopped in front of the door he'd come for.

A glance down the hall. Empty.

From his pocket, he pulled the tools. Quick, precise work on the lock.

The door gave.

He slipped inside, eyes scanning every corner.

Time to arrange everything.

Jack laid out his tools, then searched for the perfect place to wait.

He killed the lights, making sure they wouldn't flick on. When the room was set, he poured himself a bourbon—careful not to leave prints—and drank it slow.

Then he waited in the dark.

Motionless. Focused. Patient.

This part—the stillness before the act—was his favorite. A personal ritual.

In the silence, his mind sharpened.

He imagined each step, each breath, each twitch of panic from his target.

He ran the scene again and again in his head, recalibrating timing, refining response, analyzing the moment the illusion of control shattered in his victim's eyes.

That flicker of realization. That silent scream buried under futility.

It was about power.

Not rage. Not hate. Just pure, cold control.

Being the hand that decided who lived. And when that life ended.

Normally, Jack preferred to let it unravel slowly. Painfully. A process. A performance.

But not tonight. Tonight wasn't about indulgence.

Tonight was work.

The client wanted the death to look like suicide. Not suspicion. Not noise.

Just another quiet tragedy buried in a coroner's file.

So, Jack adjusted.

The plan was straightforward: inject a potent paralytic, something fast and rare. Something the average coroner wouldn't test for unless they had reason to.

Then place a gun in the victim's own hand, fire a single shot into the skull, and leave the scene tidy.

No struggle. No fingerprints. Just the illusion of despair.

It wasn't perfect. Nothing ever was.

If the forensic team became suspicious, they might order a more thorough toxicology report and discover the compound.

But that wasn't the point. The point was delay. Confusion.

A dead person couldn't explain anything. And the people who mattered would move on before the truth caught up.

Jack didn't ask why. He never did.

But he was told, "Make it convincing. That's all."

That was the hard part.

Normally, Jack liked to tailor the scene. Learn something about the target—a vice, a fear, a buried failure—and weave it into the narrative.

People believed a story when it had layers. The right background. Some texture.

But this time, there wasn't enough time.

So, Jack improvised.

He planted incriminating evidence on the victim's computer.

Downloaded files no one could defend. Obscure websites.

A browser trail soaked in perversion. And just to tighten the noose, he linked it to an open investigation—a murdered child.

A case that still had the LAPD spinning in circles.

Enough to justify why someone like that might take a bullet to the head.

Not elegant. But functional.

Jack checked the time. The victim was almost there.

The house was dark. No pets. No cameras. The security system had been disabled fifteen minutes earlier. The victim's schedule was provided to him.

Then—the click of a key in the lock.

Jack stood perfectly still in the shadow of the hall closet.

The door opened. A soft creak. Footsteps on the hardwood floor.

Jack stepped out silently, already moving.

The victim turned. Confused. Then terrified.

Jack grabbed the victim from behind, pressing the injector into the neck before the victim could scream. A swift hiss of air. One second. Two.

Then dead weight.

The victim collapsed to the floor, breathing but frozen. Conscious. Paralyzed.

Jack crouched beside the victim.

"No fuss," he whispered. "Nothing personal."

The victim blinked slowly. Eyes wide. Terrified.

Jack dragged the body to the bedroom and laid it on the bed.

He lifted the gun—clean, untraceable—and curled the victim's fingers around it, just so.

Then, steadying the wrist, he angled the barrel up toward the temple.

Checked the alignment. Close-range. Classic suicide angle.

And pulled the trigger.

The sound was muffled, but final.

Blood pooled fast. The body sagged.

Jack moved quickly, wiping down everything he'd touched.

He returned the injector to his bag. Reset the victim's hand on the grip.

Tilted the monitor on the desk toward the open browser window.

Obscene. Disturbing. Enough to cloud everything.

He exhaled. Looked around the room one last time.

Clean. Cold. Convincing enough.

He stepped out the back door, slipped into the night, and disappeared.

Chapter 18

G race Fletcher was exhausted.

The last twenty-four hours had been a blur of subpoenas, phone calls, interviews, and cross-checked timelines.

Her desk looked like a war zone—folders half-open, notes scribbled in haste, a cold coffee that had lost its soul hours ago.

Everything was in motion.

Acting quickly on subpoenas, they'd secured Paul Max's cell phone records. And there it was—confirmation that he'd received several calls from an unidentified burner phone during the critical hours leading up to his murder.

The timing matched what they had heard from multiple sources.

That part of the puzzle was real.

They were still waiting on a secondary warrant to dig deeper—location data, call metadata, any crumb the burner might have left behind.

But it was a start. A hard, concrete lead.

They'd also confirmed details surrounding the infamous two million dollars. The bank corroborated Otto's story: he had withdrawn the money on Paul's behalf.

Even the part about the manager joking that "Paul will always be Paul."

The financial trail—and Otto's story—checked out. Charlie was still digging into the financials of Paul's inner circle to see if anyone stood to benefit from his death.

So far, nothing.

Then there was the security team.

Grace and Charlie had spoken with the firm Paul hired for personal protection. No one wanted to talk at first—NDAs, privacy concerns, standard crap.

But under the shadow of a homicide, walls began to crack.

Quiet confirmations emerged. Timelines were compared. Patterns noted.

They confirmed key pieces of Otto's version: Paul dismissed his security at 7:00 PM that night. Unusual, but not unprecedented.

The security team confirmed they hadn't seen anything suspicious in the weeks leading up to Paul's death.

They had been monitoring for stalkers, obsessive fans, or anyone getting too close—but nothing unusual ever came up.

Their work had been routine. Standard protection. No red flags.

The dismissal on the day of the murder was the first and only time Paul had ever asked them to stand down.

Even during romantic getaways, the security detail had always been nearby.

Which meant one thing: Paul was instructed to dismiss them.

Whoever blackmailed him may have known about the security team—and made it clear they had to go.

Maybe they threatened him directly. Viciously. In a way that truly scared him.

Scared him enough to go it alone.

They were finally getting a clearer picture of Paul's last day.

Still, something didn't sit right.

The deeper they looked, the more the evidence seemed to rule out the people closest to Paul. Lola. Otto. Even the staff.

Everyone had some version of grief, yes—but not murder. Not motive.

And yet Paul Max had ended up dead in a gas station with murderer scrawled in his own blood.

So, Grace started thinking in another direction.

What if this wasn't calculated?

What if it was emotional?

A lone operator. Someone acting not for money or revenge, but justice.

Maybe for Rebecca Fontaine.

If that were true, it could take weeks—months—to crack. No clear suspect. No money trail. Just raw emotion and time.

So, they expanded the scope of the investigation.

Experience—and data—suggested that most homicides were committed by someone close to the victim.

But Paul Max was a public figure, which opened the door to a more complicated possibility: the killer could have been a complete stranger.

A random person. A fan. Or a fanatic.

Still, the most logical starting point was the trial.

The people in Rebecca Fontaine's orbit—friends, colleagues, anyone who might have carried resentment like a disease that never went away.

And some of what they'd already uncovered supported that theory.

Rebecca's mother was alive, yes—but far from a suspect. She was deep into dementia, living in a long-term care center. Insurance covered part of it, but the rest? Rebecca paid out of pocket.

And that wasn't easy. Her financial records painted a grim picture.

Years of low-paying gigs, gaps in employment, occasional side jobs just to keep up. The role in *Silent Sun* had been a lifeline.

A major part. A serious paycheck. It bought her some breathing room—and, Grace thought, some hope.

But then she died.

An *accident*, the court said.

But not everyone had to agree.

They were still mapping Rebecca's social circle. Theater colleagues. Friends. Former lovers.

No red flags yet. But Grace knew better than to trust the surface.

And Otto?

Something about him still felt off.

Too rehearsed. Too anxious.

Like he was constantly walking a tightrope strung over secrets.

Some of those secrets might have been about protecting Paul's image and reputation—but others felt like they were hiding something darker.

Grace couldn't say how innocent that "protection" really was.

All she knew was that her instincts didn't like it.

Otto appeared to be an extremely loyal employee—though it seemed he saw himself as more than that. Almost like family.

How far would someone go with that kind of attachment?

How much would he do to please Paul? To protect him?

Grace wondered if Otto had been drawn to Paul in ways he hadn't fully acknowledged—even to himself.

Maybe there were feelings there. Romantic feelings? Unspoken. Subconscious.

The kind that forged a quiet, sacred bond.

Their initial background check showed Otto had been single for a long time. No serious relationships. Not even anything casual.

Maybe no one ever measured up to Paul.

Grace jotted a note to herself: *dig deeper into Otto's movements in the days leading up to Paul's death. Credit cards, devices, emails. Relationships. Family. Motivations.*

Maybe he hadn't lied—but maybe he hadn't told them everything either.

She leaned back in her chair and checked her phone.

A new notification.

Message read.

Becky had finally read one of her texts!

Grace sighed, half a curse and half a relief.

That little shit. At least she was alive. Active.

But if it wasn't Becky checking her phone—a grim, unsettling possibility—why would someone else leave such a clear trace?

Unless they wanted it to look like everything was fine.

Or maybe it was just a mistake. The kind a non-professional would make.

Or maybe Grace was too far in her own head, chasing shadows, seeing ghosts where there were none.

Maybe it was just Becky being Becky—irresponsible, immature, selfish, and completely obsessed with whatever story had her spinning this time.

And she was still out there. Still chasing something. Still driving Grace crazy.

Grace took a breath.

Tonight, she'd swing by Becky's apartment. She'd been putting it off, convincing herself Becky would call when she was ready.

But enough is enough.

If her sister was actively investigating a murder case behind the scenes—and hadn't told anyone—Grace needed to know.

Because this case was growing colder by the hour.

And if Becky was sitting on fire, Grace needed to find out before it burned them all.

Chapter 19

Night had settled over the city.

It had been an intense day for Grace, but it wasn't over yet. She parked in front of Becky's condo, just off Melrose—a pastel building with clean hedges and a calm, tucked-away charm.

It looked quiet. Too quiet.

Grace knocked once. Waited. No answer.

She tried again—two sharp raps—giving Becky every chance to hear it, to come to the door. Silence.

Becky wasn't home.

Plan B. She hated even thinking it.

With Becky's erratic behavior—and the pact they'd made—this felt like crossing a line.

A violation.

Something she'd sworn she'd never do... unless there was no other choice.

The spare key was cold in her hand. Becky had never changed the lock—classic Becky, living like danger was something that happened to other people.

Grace slid the key in. Turned it. The latch gave with a soft click.

She pushed the door open and stepped into the mess, the air still carrying the faint trace of her sister's perfume.

And a mess it was.

Papers scattered across the table. Empty mugs. Dishes stacked in the sink.

A coat draped over the back of a chair.

The smell of coffee and unwashed laundry lingered in the air.

Becky's signature chaos—full creative hurricane mode.

Becky's disorganized life had been an issue between the sisters for as long as Grace could remember.

When they were younger and shared a room at Mona's house, it was a constant source of conflict—Grace's organized, orderly approach clashing with Becky's habit of leaving clothes, papers, books, and everything else scattered everywhere.

Now, looking at the familiar chaos, Grace remembered those fights with a trace of nostalgia.

"Becky?" she called.

Silence.

She stepped farther inside, scanning the living room.

A legal pad covered in scribbles lay beside an open laptop, its screen displaying a slow, aerial sweep of Hong Kong.

She moved to the bedroom. Same story.

The closet was half-open. Drawers halfway out. Clothes missing. On the floor next to the dresser there were always two suitcases. One was open on top of the bed. The other was gone.

Grace crouched beside it and spotted an empty toiletry bag tossed aside. In the bathroom, the toothbrush was missing.

Some makeup. Travel-sized shampoo.

Becky had packed in a rush.

In the kitchen, the fridge buzzed quietly. Grace opened it—half a carton of almond milk, wilted spinach, and three bottles of white wine.

Becky hadn't expected to be gone long.

Then she saw it.

A piece of paper on the counter, half-tucked beneath a jar of peanut butter.

Handwritten. Slanted, all caps.

MARK – BOISE, IDAHO

Grace stared at it. Read it again. Boise?

Was it possible Becky wasn't in the city—that she'd gone to Boise?

What the hell was Becky doing in Idaho?

And who was Mark? A potential source? A reporter?

She picked up the note and turned it over. Blank on the back.

A line from her childhood floated to the surface—something their grandmother used to say: *Follow the thread, even if it takes you through the dark. Because after the night, the sun will always rise.*

She scanned the apartment again, slower this time. Becky was definitely chasing something. And if it involved Paul Max—and now Idaho—it meant trouble.

No call. No text.

But this wasn't Becky hiding.

This was Becky in investigative mode. Which meant she was out there, exposed, and chasing a story that might kill her.

Grace's pulse ticked faster. She leaned on the counter, thinking.

Mark. Idaho. A scribbled note. A missing suitcase.

She walked back to the coffee table and sat on the couch. News clippings about Paul. Scribbled names. *Rebecca Fontaine* circled in red ink. A line drawn from her name to Paul's. Then another, to *Marcus O'Brien*.

O'Brien? Who was Marcus O'Brien?

Grace narrowed her eyes.

She grabbed Becky's laptop and tapped in her sister's usual password: *IloveMona*.

The screen flickered to life. Becky hadn't changed it.

Grace checked the recent activity—mostly emails. One stood out.

Subject: Meeting confirmed. See you tomorrow morning. – Mark Z.

Timestamp: today!

Now she had more—a first name, a last initial, a city, and a meeting date. And a full name connected to one of the deaths.

Grace closed the laptop.

Then she grabbed her phone and called Charlie.

"She's not in L.A.," Grace said the moment he picked up. "Becky's in Idaho."

"Idaho?" Charlie asked. "What the hell's in Idaho?"

"I don't know yet. But she left in a rush. Didn't tell anyone. And I think she's chasing a lead connected to Paul Max."

"She always dives too deep," he muttered.

"I'm worried," Grace said. "Listen, she's meeting someone named Mark—last name starts with Z. She wrote down Boise, Idaho. Can you pull anything up on that? I'll send you the email address he used. And please find out everything about a certain Marcus O'Brien."

"Got it."

"And one more thing. See if you can find Becky's travel records. When she flew. What airline. Everything. And Charlie—call me if you find anything strange."

"Will do."

She hung up.

The silence in the apartment returned, thick as dust.

Grace stood in the middle of the living room, the note still in her hand. She looked around again, eyes scanning the remnants of her sister's sudden departure.

Becky had been interviewing Paul... and then he was killed. Now Becky was in Idaho.

Becky was chasing something.

And Grace had the sinking feeling that whatever it was... it was going to chase back.

She took a breath and spoke to the empty room.

"Becky, what the hell have you gotten yourself into now?"

Chapter 20

Peter Woodford sat in his garden with a double espresso and a knot in his chest.

The morning was perfect—sunlight filtering through the bougainvillea. One of his dogs, a sleek black Cane Corso named Galileo, tore across the lawn chasing something that didn't exist.

Inside the mansion, his wife and daughter were still asleep.

They'd had friends over the night before and gone to bed late.

But Peter couldn't sleep. He'd tried for several minutes before giving up and heading downstairs. He poured himself a bourbon and tried to distract himself with a bit of late-night cinema.

He found *Shadow of a Doubt* and watched Teresa Wright and Joseph Cotten in a masterful story of suspicion and deception. Teresa had been a great actress—one who fought against the studios, choosing smaller films and stage work over the big paychecks.

The rules of the industry, he thought. Maybe the rules of life.

People with great power could shut you down. It didn't matter how good you were.

In the end, he drifted off on the sofa, the TV still murmuring in the background.

When he woke the next morning, a dull headache throbbed behind his eyes—a hangover's gentle punishment.

He swallowed an aspirin and leaned back, waiting for it to take hold.

"Rosa," he called, his voice still rough from sleep, "bring my breakfast outside, will you?"

He needed fresh air. The kind that might cut through the fog in his head, clear his thoughts, and keep the memories of the night before at bay—at least for a little while.

Rosa had just brought him a latte, a French omelet, and a croissant on fine china. "Thank you, Rosa," he'd said automatically, barely looking up.

He stared out past the pool and manicured hedges toward the rows of olive trees beyond the tennis court. Gorgeous property. Maybe too gorgeous. But he'd counted on keeping it.

It wasn't the end of the world, not yet. But it was close

He needed twenty million. Immediately.

Twenty just to survive the month. Forty if ticket sales didn't improve by next month.

And they weren't improving.

His last film—the one Paul starred in—was tanking. Box office returns had come in at less than twenty percent of projections. A disaster.

His investors were circling like vultures. Studio partners were getting cold feet.

And worst of all, the banks had stopped answering politely.

Banks didn't want to extend funds anymore. They knew the numbers and expected Peter to start paying down debt instead of increasing his lines of credit—because they were already maxed out.

He had about five million in liquid assets.

Enough to live like a mortal for a year, maybe. But Peter Woodford didn't do mortal.

His life had gravity. A mansion in Bel-Air. A summer estate in the south of France. A yacht moored in Nice that hadn't moved in months but still cost more than most people's homes.

His credit lines were tapped. One bank had already sent a warning letter. They wanted repayment on overdue interest. If he defaulted, the dominos would fall fast—and ugly.

And Otto, that weasel-faced little bastard, was ghosting him.

Three voicemails yesterday. Not a single callback.

Peter could barely contain his fury. Otto was managing part of Paul's finances.

Nothing major. Just a limited power of attorney Paul had granted during the shoot to handle expenses, clear payments, handle production emergencies.

But there was enough flexibility in the document—enough ambiguity—that Peter could use it. Access just enough to breathe.

Otto knew that. And Otto wasn't picking up.

Coward.

The media circus wasn't helping. The press had resurrected every dusty headline from the trial. *Paul Max: Tragedy or Villain?* Talk shows dissected courtroom footage like it was a season finale.

Legal pundits rehashed closing arguments.

Rebecca Fontaine's name trended again.

Think pieces popped up about accidental shootings on sets. Some people speculated that Paul's death was vigilante justice.

That someone had decided to do what the court hadn't.

Lola and Peppy had gone quiet. No statements. No appearances. Peter followed their lead. The last thing he needed was to stir more attention.

But silence wouldn't pay the bills.

He sipped his latte, staring at nothing. Somewhere in his gut, he knew the financial collapse was coming. And fast.

There was only one option left.

A long time ago, Paul had gotten into serious trouble. Peter never knew the details—only that it was bad. Very bad. Paul had done something. Something he never confessed to anyone.

But just like that, the problem disappeared.

Peter had always remembered that.

Sometimes in life, if you want to keep what's yours—protect the ones you love—you have to slip into the dark for a while. Just long enough to fix what's broken.

Just long enough to survive.

He thought of his wife and daughter, both still asleep inside the mansion. Peaceful. Unaware. It was his duty to protect them.

If something ever happened to them—because of him—he wouldn't be able to live with himself.

Or... was that an excuse?

Was he really worried about them? Or was he hiding behind them, using them as a shield to justify his own desperation?

The truth made him wince.

His father had been a loser.

Plain and simple.

A man who started a dozen businesses and failed at every single one. A man who dragged his family from one financial sinkhole to the next.

Peter still remembered the stupid grin he wore—smiling through it all, as if blind optimism could feed a family.

His mother had done everything to keep them afloat. Worked odd jobs. Took night shifts. Sewed clothes for neighbors.

All while his father played at being a dreamer.

She died young. Worn out. Exhausted. Probably from trying too hard to hold together a life her husband had no business building.

Peter hated that.

Hated watching her struggle while his father grinned through failure.

When the old man died, Peter didn't cry.

He looked down at the casket and saw only that same damn smile.

The smile of a man who lost everything and still didn't understand why.

He was determined not to become that man.

Peter Woodford was a success. A millionaire. A name people knew. A man who could drop a million dollars on dinner if he wanted to—and had, more than once.

"Tell me, Dad," Peter muttered into the air, "could you have done that?"

Of course not. His father hadn't earned a million in his entire lifetime.

But success didn't come from being soft. It came from being cold, ruthless, and calculated. The great titans of American industry were never kind.

They were sharks.

That's why they survived.

Why were their names remembered?

Peter had to be the same. Maybe it was for his family. Maybe it was to prove something to himself. Maybe it was to bury his father's memory once and for all.

Maybe it was all of that.

Or none of it.

But whatever the reason, it had to be done.

He leaned forward and picked up his phone.

Scrolled past Otto's name. Past the lawyers. Past the agents.

Until he found it.

Peter exhaled and dialed.

Chapter 21

"What the hell is going on?"

Peter snapped the moment CC answered the phone.

Probably not the smartest way to approach a woman like CC—but Peter didn't care.

He had bigger problems, more urgent fires to put out, and whatever reaction she might have was a distant second to the storm closing in on him.

"Good morning to you too, Peter," she said, cool and unfazed. "What exactly are you referring to?"

"Paul's murder," Peter said, pacing across the flagstone patio behind his mansion. "What do you think I'm referring to? Who killed him? Why didn't you do anything to protect him? Tell me everything you know," he demanded

There was a pause—tight, loaded. In the silence, Peter could almost hear her reaction forming. A flicker of doubt crept in. Maybe he'd come in too hard.

"Peter," CC said, her voice like ice, "let's get one thing straight—*I don't answer to you.* And I'm not here to babysit whatever's keeping you up at night."

Silence. Heavy, immediate. The kind that slapped him across the face.

Peter stopped walking. He was used to commanding attention, to getting his way. But CC was different. She had the kind of calm danger that made most men fold without realizing it.

And, worst of all, he needed her.

So, he folded.

And before she hung up, he quickly said, "My apologies, CC. I'm on edge. I'm devastated, and words are just... jumping out of my mouth."

She let the silence stretch a beat longer, her exasperation seeping into the single word. "Fine."

Peter exhaled.

He knew he was playing with fire—and in a territory he didn't understand.

CC came from another world entirely.

He'd heard the stories: war, killing, torture. A far cry from negotiating a new film deal or wrangling a temperamental director.

No, if he wanted anything from her, he'd have to tread carefully.

"I don't know who killed him," she continued. "Paul never brought me into whatever reckless mess he got himself into. He didn't want protection. Otto didn't say a word either. I'm working on figuring out what happened. But as of this morning? Nothing."

"You think it was someone connected to the trial?"

"Unlikely," she said. "No one cared enough about Rebecca to kill Paul over it."

"Then... Red Stage?"

That landed. He could feel it in her silence—dense, deliberate, almost like she was choosing her next breath.

Paul was the third Red Stage cofounder to die. Out of the original four, only one remained.

Peter leaned in slightly, his tone low but precise, as if measuring each syllable.

"Three of them," he said. "Dead. You really think that's just a coincidence?"

He didn't wait for her answer. He wanted her to sit with it, to hear the accusation under the question, to wonder how much she already knew.

Another pause.

"Yes," CC said. "I think it may be connected to Red Stage. I just don't know how."

"Well, we'd better find out. We're all implicated."

"I will," she said. "But until then—don't breathe a word about Red Stage. Not to your lawyer. Not to your wife. Not even to your damn dog. I don't want anyone connecting dots... or digging up bodies."

"I wasn't planning to."

"Good. Red Stage is buried. Let's keep it that way."

Peter walked back toward the table and sat down, pressing the heel of his hand into his forehead. The sunlight hit the French omelette Rosa had made for him. He hadn't taken a bite.

He braced himself. The next part of the conversation was a minefield, and one wrong step could blow everything apart.

"CC."

"Yes?" CC said, her tone edged with both irritation and anticipation—as if she already knew what was about to drop.

"I need a favor."

CC's immediate response was an exasperated sigh.

"I don't do favors," she said, firm and dry as stone.

"I can pay you... And I can be generous. I need something important, and I think you're the only one who can help me."

She went quiet again.

Peter had never come to her for anything—that had always been Paul's territory. Which meant only one thing: he was desperate. And desperate people paid better.

Peter waited, watching his dog run in circles by the pool. The ridiculous beast never got tired. Just spun and spun, chasing nothing.

Finally, CC spoke. "What do you need?"

A spark of confidence lit in Peter's chest. This was the moment—the pivot point. Time to be brutally direct.

"I need Otto to transfer twenty-two million dollars to one of my accounts."

She didn't respond.

"I know he can do it," Peter continued. "He has limited authority on Paul's accounts. Not full access—but enough."

"That's a lot of money, Peter," CC said. "Enough to raise eyebrows."

"Exactly why I need someone like you to handle it. Quietly. Smoothly. We'll say Paul authorized it before his death. A retroactive transfer. For a project, or a foundation, or whatever you come up with. You're creative."

"That's not just creative," she said. "It's criminal—and dangerously reckless."

"I'll pay you two million if you succeed."

Silence again. Not hesitation—calculation.

"Otto doesn't have that money," she said. "But you're right. He can move it."

"Then help me *make him* move it."

Another pause. Then: "Let me think about it."

Peter smiled. A cold, tired smile.

"Thank you, CC."

He ended the call before she could say anything else.

He stared out at the lawn, the trimmed hedges, the still surface of the pool. The croissant on his plate had gone dry. The coffee was cold.

He lit a cigarette, even though he hadn't smoked in years.

Twenty-two million.

He needed that money. Without it, he'd have to liquidate assets. Fire staff. Maybe even sell the estate in France—and quickly, which meant a heavy discount. That was not an option.

But Peter knew he'd made a pact with the devil.

Chapter 22

CC dropped the phone onto the concrete slab she called a desk.

Peter was no Otto. He didn't whimper. Didn't panic. Sure, he begged—but with a better attitude. And cash. That made all the difference.

She leaned back in her leather chair, exhaling slowly. The steel-paneled walls of her underground bunker vibrated with silence. Above her, the world spun like a drunken top.

Down here, everything was stable.

Backup generators. Solar panels. Food for a year. A wall of firearms. Six digital monitors blinking quietly. Even the air tasted cleaner.

People liked to say paranoia was irrational. But those people never had a gun jammed in their face, never smelled their own blood in the dirt.

CC had lived a different life. She'd been hunted. Tortured.

She'd made enemies in places where enemies didn't forgive, didn't forget.

Most of them were dead now—because she made sure of it. But a few were still out there. Breathing. Waiting.

Paranoia wasn't some nervous tick for her. It was muscle memory. A reflex burned into her from years of war and shadows. It kept her alive when training and luck couldn't.

CC didn't believe in being surprised. She believed in getting there first—making sure the other bastard was the one who never saw it coming.

Years ago, when she first crossed paths with Paul Max, he was nothing special—just another flashy, arrogant Hollywood brat with more ego than brains.

Desperate. Reckless.

The kind of kid who thought charm and a little fame could bend the world in his favor. And for a while it did.

They'd been introduced through a mutual acquaintance—a man who owed her a favor and knew better than to waste it lightly.

That alone made her curious enough to take the meeting.

Paul was young then. Green. Inexperienced. But ambition burned in him like a fever. A volatile mix—too eager to grab at the world, too naïve to understand how sharp its teeth were.

He came to her with a request. Something off the books. Illegal.

Not the smartest move, considering what he was trying to accomplish.

But at the time, Paul still shied away from truly drastic solutions.

He wanted it handled clean. Quiet.

Within what he thought were the "safest" boundaries.

Or at least, that's what he told himself.

She delivered. Flawlessly. No noise. No trace. No blowback.

Whatever storm he'd been facing evaporated, and Paul walked away thinking he'd outsmarted the game.

He never understood—he hadn't outsmarted it.

Everything in life has consequences.

And favors weren't free. She charged him well.

She also slipped in a gift—a spy virus. Subtle, recursive, and buried deep in Paul's system.

Every device he touched, every backup, every cloud folder.

Not just his. Otto. Peter. Peppy. Anyone orbiting Paul got swept in.

She didn't care about their texts or their petty scandals.

Tabloid crumbs meant nothing to her.

She wanted the real things—the conversations behind closed doors, the decisions that never made it to print.

She wanted leverage. She wanted control.

And if she ever needed to burn the whole thing down? She could do it in four keystrokes.

Paul never asked how she knew things. He wasn't that stupid. He understood the rule—know only what you need, and nothing more.

He just paid. And paid generously.

Over the years, she became the shadow behind the curtain.

The fixer. The ghost.

She didn't appear in any organizational chart, but when a problem surfaced, she solved it. Quietly. Permanently.

Otto and Peter knew better than to cross her.

Fear kept them cautious; self-preservation kept them distant. When it came to CC, the smartest move was staying out of her shadow.

Good.

Fear was leverage.

Now she had a choice—and she made it. Peter would get the money.

She already had one loose cannon in Otto; she didn't need another.

She stood, stretched, and crossed to her workstation. Four custom towers. Six screens. Fans whispering in the dark.

She pulled on her headset.

Eyes scanning the lines of code.

First step: the transfer.

She accessed Otto's laptop remotely using her backdoor virus. Navigated to the financial suite. Spoofed a local session.

Drafted a transfer request: $22 million wired to Peter Woodford, dated five days before Paul's death.

She synced it to Paul's digital calendar under a fabricated meeting: "Review distribution contract – P.W." Just enough friction to feel real.

Then came the email trail. Paul to Peter. Short, professional. Discussion of project financing. A rough contract. Time stamps, headers, metadata—all forged to perfection.

Next: the bank.

She logged into their system using admin-level credentials she'd secured years ago, courtesy of a deeply indebted IT manager with a gambling problem.

She forged the wire. Backdated it. Buried it in logs.

Adjusted the confirmation record.

She wasn't just planting evidence. She was building a reality.

Four hours later, it was done. Clean. Convincing. Untouchable.

She sipped cold coffee. It tasted like rust and victory.

Now Peter had his money. And she had Peter.

As the system backed up and encrypted the logs, she returned to the investigation.

Still no trace of the blackmailer.

No emails. No docs. No photos. Just a handful of burner texts—cold, clipped, anonymous. All traces scrubbed.

Whoever this was, they were good.

She'd scoured metadata, deep packets, and mirror images of Paul's cloud backups. Nothing. No slip. No misstep.

A professional.

A ghost.

She lit a cigarette and stared at the photo board tacked to the wall—faces from the past, the Red Stage crew.

Four co-founders.

The answer had to be there.

Either with the one she still hadn't managed to track down: Tom Harper, the elusive accountant, or with the only other co-founder still alive, Bob Malone.

She knew what had to happen next.

Find Harper. Locate Malone.

Before someone else did.

Chapter 23

G race Fletcher kicked the door closed with her foot and dropped her keys into the ceramic bowl near the entry.

Her apartment was in a quiet building in Hollywood Heights—safe, well-lit, with neighbors who nodded politely but minded their business.

Inside, it was clean. Organized. Like her mind wanted to be.

Hardwood floors stretched underfoot, the room wrapped in muted blues and soft grays. Books stood in precise rows along the shelves.

Near the fireplace, an Art Deco *Metropolis* poster shared wall space with another classic—*Vertigo*, its bold spiral frozen mid-swirl.

Routine. She needed it tonight. Too many hours working on this case.

Grace checked her phone. No messages from Becky—of course. Not even a stray text or voicemail.

The only texts were from Charlie, and she'd already seen them.

She sighed, thumb hovering over the empty inbox. When was the last time she'd had a real relationship?

Too long ago to remember without digging through dust-covered memories she had no interest in reopening.

Still, three weeks back, Matt McGregor—the sharp-tongued criminal lawyer she occasionally crossed paths with—had asked her out.

She hadn't answered. He'd followed up with a text two days ago, and she'd let it sit unread, convincing herself she was too busy, too tired, too focused on work.

The truth? She wasn't interested. Or at least that's what she told herself.

But now, staring at the silent screen, she caught herself reconsidering.

Maybe it wasn't about interest. Maybe it was about possibility.

She couldn't live on work and family alone forever. Not without cracking somewhere.

One night, she thought. Just one night. A decent dinner. An interesting conversation.

No expectations. No promises.

Her hesitation wasn't rejection—it was discomfort. She wasn't used to it anymore.

The vulnerability of stepping outside the safety of her routines, of her badge, of the walls she'd built around herself.

Her thumb hovered for another beat. And then she typed back, simple and direct:

Saturday works. Dinner it is.

She hit send before she could change her mind, then set the phone down.

It felt small. But in her chest, it also felt like something was shifting.

It was right then that Rusty meowed, weaving between her legs.

"Hey, you."

She crouched to scratch behind his ears, then opened a can of tuna and set it in his bowl. He dug in like he hadn't eaten in weeks.

Drama queen.

Grace poured herself a glass of Pinot, grabbed a couple of crackers with cheese, and flopped onto the couch.

She kicked off her shoes and stared at her tablet on the coffee table.

Tomorrow, she and Charlie would talk to Peppy La Font and Peter Woodford. The list of interviews was growing. The list of answers? Not so much.

And now Becky had thrown a wrench into everything.

She searched Marcus O'Brien. A few scattered mentions. Background roles. Local plays. No interviews. No social media. And then—nothing. He'd vanished. Off the grid.

She added Boise and Idaho to the search.

Still nothing.

Marcus O'Brien and Paul?

Just a sliver of information about an acting company called *Red Stage*. Nothing substantial—only a mention of one minor play featuring four actors: Marcus, Paul, Rebecca, and someone named Bob Malone.

Okay, this was interesting. Paul and Rebecca had worked together in a small acting company more than ten years ago.

But more importantly, Becky might have uncovered a connection between Paul's murder and a forgotten actor from his past—Marcus O'Brien.

And what happened with Bob Malone? Who was he?

She searched for Bob and found a story similar to Marcus's—some minor roles, then nothing. He'd disappeared.

And Rebecca?

She scraped through commercials, walk-ons, bit parts. A guest spot on a network procedural. Then a few more minor roles in B movies.

Until she reconnected with Paul.

And died on his set.

The only one who made it out was Paul. Big, bright, famous Paul Max.

Grace leaned back on the couch, wine in hand.

The pattern was clear. Paul soared. The rest? Faded. Disappeared. Or died.

But that wasn't a crime.

Maybe Rebecca's death was—but Paul had been acquitted in court. This was just Hollywood. A thousand versions of the same story: one rises, the others vanish. The city was littered with them.

She tapped her nails against the tablet, staring at the mess of browser tabs.

Something gnawed at her.

What was she missing? Her gut told her there was something to do with Marcus O'Brien or Red Stage—or both.

That familiar tightness formed in her chest. The one that always came when facts floated loose—close but not yet connected. Too many dots. Not enough lines.

She needed to focus.

She needed to bake.

Grace stood and moved into the kitchen. She pulled out butter, flour, brown sugar, eggs, and the last of the crushed pretzels from the pantry.

Brown Butter Toffee Pretzel Cookies.

Her specialty. The ritual grounded her.

Creaming. Measuring. Folding. It pulled her out of the anxiety spiral and into something solid.

She flipped on the soft jazz station—Miles Davis, smooth and slow.

Then queued *Murder on the Orient Express* on the living room TV. Volume off, subtitles on. She knew it by heart.

Twelve suspects. One corpse.

And in the end—more than one killer.

She stirred. Dropped dough onto parchment-lined cookie sheets. Rolled. Flattened.

Rusty jumped onto the stool and gave her a look.

"Don't judge me," she muttered.

The oven warmed the kitchen. The scent of brown sugar and vanilla filled the air. Her shoulders softened. Her breath slowed.

She glanced again at the tablet. Paul. Marcus. Rebecca. Bob.

The names felt heavier now.

But something was there.

Was it really a coincidence that Becky had managed to connect three of the four co-founders?

The links weren't entirely clear. Bob and Marcus had faded from sight. Rebecca had been killed—shot by Paul.

And now Paul himself was dead, murdered by an unknown killer.

The question was: what tied Marcus to all of this?

And then her phone buzzed on the counter.

Chapter 24

"Well, I've got interesting news," Charlie said.

Grace Fletcher straightened in the kitchen nook; phone pressed to her ear. The cookies were already in the oven, ticking away on the timer.

Good—she had just enough time to take the call.

She'd been waiting for this call. She needed to know if she was jumping on a plane to Idaho—or if Becky had just chased a dead lead.

"Talk to me," she said. "What did you find?"

"Let's go step by step," Charlie said, voice steady. "Marcus O'Brien. From Boise. Used to be an actor. A long time ago."

"Red Stage," Grace cut in.

Charlie paused. "How'd you know?"

"I found a few things online."

"Alright, then you know the basics. Four co-founders: Paul Max, Rebecca Fontaine, Bob Malone, and Marcus O'Brien. Small acting company. One obscure play, a micro-budget film, some contracts. That's all."

"Yeah, I saw pieces of that," Grace said.

Rusty padded over, brushing against Grace's legs—a rare request for attention. She crouched, letting her hand glide over his back.

He arched beneath her touch, tail stretching high in quiet satisfaction.

"Well, the initial data showed Red Stage operating for a couple of years before two co-founders, Paul and Marcus, left—leaving the other two, Rebecca and Bob, to keep it going for another year before shutting it down. They just couldn't make it work. But, turns out Marcus didn't just leave—he got kicked out. Embezzlement. And guess who uncovered it?"

"Paul..." Grace guessed.

"Correct! How'd you know?" Charlie asked. Without waiting for an answer, he went on, "Paul found out, reported Marcus to the group, and the accountant confirmed the theft. Marcus was arrested."

Interesting. If Marcus was tied to Paul in Becky's notes, maybe it all traced back to this case.

Could Marcus have been responsible for Paul's death? Revenge?

Had Becky already uncovered the killer?

Grace blinked. "That... definitely wasn't in any of the articles I read."

"Not surprising. Paul wasn't famous yet. No media attention. Quiet case. Guilty plea. Barely a ripple."

"Jesus. This might be our first real lead in Paul's murder."

"Wait. That's not all," Charlie continued. "After a short imprisonment, Marcus moved back to Boise and unraveled. Battery charges. Public intoxication. Multiple DUIs. Lost his license. Medical records show severe cirrhosis. He was in and out of the hospital."

"And?"

"Five years ago, he was found dead at home. Alcohol poisoning. He drank himself to death."

Grace exhaled. "So that's three of the four Red Stage co-founders gone. Marcus, Rebecca, and Paul."

Dead end. Marcus wasn't Paul's killer.

"Correct. But not under the same circumstances. Marcus's death was self-inflicted. Rebecca's? Still possibly an accident. And Paul... well, Paul was executed."

"With '*murderer*' smeared across his chest."

"Yeah. That's not exactly subtle."

Grace's thoughts spun.

"But what's the connection? Rebecca's death might be related—if someone believed Paul was responsible. But Marcus?"

"Could be nothing," Charlie said. "The guy spiraled. Doesn't scream conspiracy."

Grace rubbed her forehead. "The logical explanation is Becky just stumbled into Marcus's name while researching Paul. Followed the thread. Not foul play—just reporting."

"Maybe. But you know Becky."

A beat of silence. Grace rewound the story in her mind, retracing every step, trying to see how the pieces might finally fit.

Her phone buzzed. A text—Matt McGregor.

Great! See you at Mario's Cantina at eight on Saturday. Can't wait.

Grace caught herself smiling.

She didn't want to acknowledge it, but there it was. Excitement.

A spark she hadn't felt in too long. She'd told herself work and family were enough, that the routine kept her steady.

But the truth was, she wasn't dead inside—and Matt was proof.

Attractive, smart, charming. If she had to choose someone, he would've been her pick.

She hesitated, then tapped out a single smiley face in reply. Small. Safe. But it said enough.

And then she pushed it aside.

Back to the case.

Becky had been conducting in-depth interviews with Paul—and then he was killed.

If I were Becky, what would I do? Grace thought.

First, finish the article. But what if it wasn't anywhere near finished? Then Becky would need more information—maybe to fill in some gaps.

That made sense.

A possible approach.

She'd just been wrapping up the final interviews before the article could be complete.

That was fine. And somewhat soothing.

"Well... at least Becky doesn't seem to be in immediate danger," Grace said.

"No. Not imminently."

Grace stood and began pacing the kitchen, her glass of water forgotten on the counter. She was never able to stay quiet when something was sparking in her mind.

"So, Marcus is dead. Rebecca's death still has unanswered questions. Paul was murdered. And the only one left from Red Stage is Bob Malone," Grace continued.

"It could all be coincidence," Charlie offered.

Coincidence? Or was Becky quietly shifting the article toward the murder?

If you thought like Becky, you knew she'd chase the biggest prize—she wouldn't settle for simply finishing the piece.

Grace felt her own perspective shifting, unease creeping in.

Everything was starting to look too suspicious.

Too many coincidences.

"Maybe," Grace said, though her voice was tight. "But Red Stage wasn't just some failed creative experiment. There's something else buried in it. I can feel it."

"And Becky may be standing right in the middle of it," Charlie said. "Oh—and I checked her travel records. She's flying back tomorrow night. Quick trip."

Grace tried to come to terms with the facts. Becky had found something in Boise—maybe just colorful background for her article, nothing tied to murder.

She was interviewing someone there, likely someone who had known Marcus and could shed light on the past.

But the pattern nagged at her. Only one person from Red Stage was still alive. That was hard to ignore.

Could that last co-founder be in danger too?

Was someone trying to eliminate the rest of them?

"Have you started looking into Bob Malone?"

"Not yet."

"Start. We need to find him. Fast."

"Why?"

"He could be the next victim."

Chapter 25

Grace Fletcher arrived at the Hollywood Community police station balancing a cardboard tray of coffee and a Tupperware brimming with cookies.

Morning light stretched across the bullpen's floor tiles, too bright for the hour, but that was Los Angeles.

She set the cookies by the coffee machine—for everyone in the office to enjoy—then grabbed two and crossed the room.

The low hum of ringing phones and clacking keyboards mixed with the faint smell of burnt coffee, worn leather, and the ozone tang from the old copier in the corner.

A wall-mounted TV played the morning news at low volume, the anchors' muted expressions flickering in the background as detectives hunched over case files, already deep into their day.

"Morning," Charlie Bonelli called as she approached her desk. "So, we had a baking night, huh?"

Charlie had that plain, easy smile—the kind that made him look harmless.

Big guy. Tall, broad. Built like a bear, but without the claws.

Always on the sunny side of things. Sometimes a little too simple for this line of work, but he was solid—reliable, tireless, honest.

Grace was still getting used to him, but she knew she'd lucked out. Most detectives she'd worked with were pricks.

"My mind was racing," Grace said, handing him a cookie.

"Well, your anxiety tastes incredible," he said through a mouthful.

Grace cracked a smile. "Glad my mental instability is keeping morale up."

Charlie jerked a thumb over his shoulder. "Woodford's in Interrogation Three. Been here ten minutes."

"Good."

Grace grabbed her notebook and headed toward the room, Charlie in tow.

She glanced through the window before stepping in.

Peter Woodford sat comfortably, sipping police station coffee like it was aged scotch.

He was in his fifties, soft in the middle, clearly trying not to look it. No tie. Navy suit. Expensive shoes. A pale blue handkerchief peeking from his pocket like a calculated afterthought.

His skin was taut in a way that screamed discreet procedures. The kind of man who paid for good lighting—and better lawyers.

"Mr. Woodford," Grace said as she entered. "Thanks for coming in. I'm Detective Fletcher. This is my partner, Detective Bonelli."

Peter stood, offered a smile. "Of course. I was told you had some questions for me."

They all sat.

Grace didn't bother easing into it.

"You're the producer on Paul Max's last film," she said. "That production's in financial trouble, correct?"

Peter blinked, just once. "I thought we'd be discussing Paul's murder."

"And we are."

Silence.

Grace already knew Peter had an alibi for the night of the murder. He wasn't the shooter.

But she wanted to see what he would do under pressure. People said he and Paul were close. But two million in ransom had gone untouched.

And Peter, according to the police financial analyst, needed much more than that to survive. Two million was pocket change within the Hollywood elite.

"We're still okay," Peter said carefully. "Ask me again next month. Depends on how the numbers progress."

"Paul transferred twenty-two million dollars to you shortly before he died."

That detail hadn't come in until late last night—courtesy of Charlie's dig into Otto's laptop and a quick call to the bank.

"Yes, he did," Peter said, a little slower. "Paul wanted to become more involved on the production side. We drafted a private agreement—he'd invest, I'd manage. He'd receive a share of the profits."

"Why so late in the process?"

"He only decided recently. We had a talk—I was disappointed with the early projections. He thought the numbers would improve with more publicity. I told him, 'Put your money where your mouth is.' So, he did."

Grace nodded slowly. "A gamble, then."

"Not exactly. We were friends. This wasn't just business."

The slip in tense didn't go unnoticed. His voice caught on the word "were." His throat bobbed. For a second, Peter looked genuinely shaken.

"We had a good relationship," he added. "He believed in the film. So do I."

Grace leaned forward.

"Some of Paul's investors told us the movie's numbers have skyrocketed since his death—over 700% increase."

Peter froze.

"Yes, but that's just one day's data. We only got it today. We'll need more to know if it's just a short-term spike or a real trend."

"Correct," Grace said slowly. "That bump reflects increased interest in Paul's movies after his death. It's not unusual for numbers to rise when a major actor dies."

Peter frowned. "What are you suggesting?"

"I'm suggesting your projected losses are now projected profits. That Paul's death could make you rich."

His chair creaked.

"Are you implying I killed Paul? That I—what—hired someone?"

"You had motive. You were weeks from collapse. You had everything to gain."

Peter stood abruptly. "This is insane! I loved Paul. That man made my career—he's the only reason I'm still in business. Don't you think I would've made more money keeping him alive? Why would I kill my golden goose? Why would I kill him?"

"To preserve what little you had left," Grace said. "To protect your name. Your lifestyle. Your standing in the industry."

His voice rose. "I would never do that. There are other ways to fix a business, Detective. Ways that don't involve murder. Are you really intending to continue this line of questioning?

Grace didn't blink. "We have serious reasons to believe you had motive."

"I am not talking anymore without my lawyer present."

Grace closed her notebook. "That was all for today, Mr. Woodford. Have a good..."

But he was already gone—storming out with the whiff of cologne and indignation in his wake.

Charlie looked over at Grace.

"Well," he said, "he didn't like that."

"No, he didn't," Grace agreed.

She paused, then added, "But he's nervous. Too nervous. I think he's hiding something—something that's eating at him.

Maybe it's the money... maybe it's something else."

Chapter 26

"Well, what's next? I'm energized now," Grace joked, dropping into her chair.

Charlie grinned. "Peppy La Font will be here in about thirty minutes."

"Okay. I'll make a call in the meantime."

Grace walked back to her desk and pulled her phone from the drawer. She scrolled through her contacts and tapped a name—Jim Bamford, Becky's boss.

Before she could make the call, chief Wilkins appeared beside her desk, hands in his pockets.

"Grace. How's life treating you?"

He didn't go straight to business—always a bad sign. When the chief was in a good mood, it meant he wanted something.

"I tried one of your cookies," he said with a half-smile. "You're getting better—if that's even possible."

"Thanks," she said, careful to keep her voice neutral.

His smile faded. "Paul Max. Where are we?"

And there it was.

"Not much to work with," Grace said. "Killer used a burner. Calls were off the grid, no way to triangulate. I'd bet the phone's already smashed to pieces. No weapon recovered, and the bullets... they're not telling us anything."

"So, nothing from the scene."

"Not a thing."

"Leads?"

She exhaled. "That's where it gets murky. Paul didn't have obvious enemies. We're running through his inner circle, but nothing solid. The trial last year—when that actress was shot—could be connected. Could be revenge. But it's still just smoke."

Wilkins studied her for a long moment. "You know the mayor's breathing down my neck. The press too. They want a name, fast."

Grace met his gaze. "Sorry, they'll have to be patient. Rushing this will only get us the wrong one."

He nodded once, the kind that ended a conversation. But his eyes—hard, warning—said *Don't make me regret this.* Then he walked away, back to his office.

High-profile cases are a double-edged blade.

They bring resources, sure—but they also bring heat.

The kind you can't shake.

Reporters breathing down your neck. Politicians sniffing for headlines.

And Wilkins... always Wilkins. Popping in with his "helpful suggestions," checking your progress like you're a rookie with training wheels.

She shoved the thought aside before it soured her mood further.

Time to make the call.

The line rang twice.

"Jim Bamford," came the voice on the other end.

"Hi Jim, it's Grace Fletcher," she said.

A pause.

"Grace? Hey... is everything okay?"

Grace had only spoken to Jim a couple of times, and always in social settings. They'd never had a real conversation, so it made sense that he sounded surprised when she called.

She needed to tread carefully—press too hard, and she might spook him.

"Yes, all good. Or mostly. I tried to reach my sister before she left for Boise yesterday, but it was late, so I waited until today. Now she's not answering—might be in her interview."

"Oh yes," Jim said. "She's meeting Detective Zambrano from the Boise police department. About Marcus O'Brien."

Detective Zambrano. Grace didn't know how to react to that. On one hand, it was a relief—better a detective than some mobster or low-life thug.

But it also meant Becky was digging into Paul's murder, which meant trouble was close behind.

And yet, clearly, Becky was one step ahead of her.

Grace couldn't help but smile, a quiet swell of pride rising in her chest. Her sister—reckless as she was—had always been sharp, determined, and fearless.

Grace leaned forward. "Yes, she mentioned it briefly before flying out," she lied. "Maybe you can help," Grace said, keeping her voice calm. "You might not know this, but I'm the lead detective on the Paul Max murder case."

Jim exhaled, slow and heavy. "I had no idea. Becky never mentioned it."

Becky didn't know either, Grace thought—but the knot in her stomach tightened anyway.

"That case..." Jim paused, eyes narrowing. "Paul Max. Murdered. That's a whole different game."

"Yeah," Grace said quietly. "And Becky was writing a piece on him."

He gave a short nod. "Started as a profile, she told me. Turned into something bigger. Much bigger."

Grace's pulse ticked up. "Right. And now she's in Idaho—chasing Marcus O'Brien."

"I guess it's part of the same thread," Jim said, leaning back, "but I can't say for sure. Becky's careful—too careful. I only get scraps when she decides I should. But she did tell me one thing. Detective Zambrano's got something on Marcus O'Brien. Said it was worth the trip."

Grace felt her pulse quicken.

"Did she say why Zambrano thinks that?" she asked.

"No. He did not want to provide details over the phone."

Grace drummed her fingers on the desk. "Jim, you've been very helpful. I'll talk to Becky tonight and go over everything. If you hear from her in the meantime, will you let me know?"

"Of course. Do you think this connects to Paul's murder?"

"No. We are just exhausting all lanes of investigation. These two cases are not connected."

Another lie.

"Okay. Thank you, Jim."

"Take care, Grace."

Grace hung up.

What kind of information could a detective have about Paul's murder?

And why the secrecy? Why insist on meeting in person?

If he really knew something, protocol said he should've called the LAPD.

So why reach out to a reporter instead?

She sat there for a moment, staring at her phone.

So, Becky was digging into Marcus O'Brien. At least now Grace knew she was meeting with a detective, Mark Zambrano. But that wasn't enough—she needed to be sure.

Becky might've stumbled onto something big.

And dangerous.

"Charlie, I need everything you can find on a detective from Boise—Mark Zambrano.

I need it fast."

Chapter 27

Jack Taylor stepped into Becky Fletcher's apartment like a surgeon entering an operating room—controlled, sterile, purposeful. Every movement calculated.

He'd stopped by her office first, thinking he might catch her off guard.

Not there.

That was already a bad sign.

He didn't like chasing people.

He liked them right where he wanted them.

The smell hit him before the details did—a stale mix of old coffee, grease from takeout containers, and the faint tang of dust.

His eyes swept the place in one slow pass, cataloguing everything.

The sink is piled with unwashed dishes. Crumpled paper bags and plastic utensils scattered across the counter.

A half-empty mug perched precariously on a stack of dog-eared books. Her jacket was draped over a chair like she'd shrugged it off mid-thought.

His lip curled.

Mess. He hated mess.

To him, disorder meant something deeper—weakness, distraction, cracks forming in the surface. People who lived like this were almost always a step away from losing control.

Maybe she already had.

She wasn't here either.

Jack moved deeper into the apartment, his steps silent, his gaze dissecting the space as if it were a crime scene.

A laptop sat on the desk, lid closed but still faintly warm to the touch. No sticky notes with passwords nearby—too bad.

He clocked a scarf hanging from a doorknob, its fringe swaying slightly from a recent disturbance.

Then his eyes found the wall.

Notes and Post-its layered over each other like the scattershot remains of a long obsession—names, arrows, dates, half-finished thoughts.

The kind of clutter that didn't belong to a casual project. It was the mess of someone digging into something dangerous.

A single note on the table caught his attention. All caps:

MARK – BOISE, IDAHO

So, she'd left town.

That was bad.

Jack's jaw tightened. He hated it when things slipped through his fingers.

People on the move made mistakes, sure, but they also became harder to track. And right now, he couldn't afford Becky Fletcher becoming harder to track.

Not when she might already know too much.

He moved into the bedroom. Bed unmade. Clothes were tossed over it. An open suitcase, half-packed. A toiletry bag still damp from the bathroom counter. He didn't need to guess—she'd left in a rush.

"Shit," Jack muttered aloud.

She'd left recently—he could feel it in the air. The faint warmth in the room.

The lingering trace of her scent.

She'd escaped him by hours, not days.

If he'd been here yesterday, just one day earlier, it would have been different. She wouldn't have had time to run.

But now... it was too late for that.

He stood in the middle of the living room, jaw tightening. The gap between them wasn't big yet, but it was growing by the minute. And every minute made his job harder.

He needed to close it. Fast.

Reaching into his jacket, he pulled out the burner phone. He flipped it open and stared at the keypad for a moment, letting the weight of the choice settle.

Then he tapped in the number.

"She's not in the city," he said when the call connected. "She's in Boise. Following the Marcus O'Brien angle. I found a note. It seems that she will meet some-one called Mark."

Pause.

"No. She left yesterday. Probably still there."

Another pause.

"Ok."

He ended the call without waiting for a response.

The burner dropped back in his coat pocket.

But he didn't leave. Not yet.

Jack drifted through Becky's space like smoke, deliberate and quiet, fingers brushing over the fabric of her sweater still draped on the back of a chair.

It carried her—faint perfume, a trace of coffee, the warm, human scent that told him she'd been here not long ago.

He let it linger in his lungs before moving on.

The toothbrush in the bathroom. The shower curtain pushed halfway aside.

A bottle of shampoo with the cap still wet. He took in the small, private details most people never notice in their own lives.

But Jack noticed. Always.

He loved this part.

The invasion.

The intimacy.

Most people thought murder was about rage, about an explosion of anger, about taking something from someone who wronged you.

Or maybe about power—dominating another human being.

Revenge was another favorite theory.

Not for him.

For Jack Taylor, it was about knowing someone too deeply—more deeply than they'd ever let anyone else.

Learning their patterns, their weaknesses, their fears.

Knowing how they breathed when they slept, which glass they reached for in the cupboard, the exact drawer where they kept the things they'd never show the world.

Once he got that close, something inside him shifted.

It had always been this way.

Once he crossed the invisible threshold into their space—mentally, physically—there was no going back.

The pressure built until there was only one way to release it.

He had to kill them.

Not quickly.

Slowly.

It wasn't compulsion in the way people liked to label it. Not in his mind. This was craft. Precision. Art.

Jack stood in the middle of her living room, closing his eyes.

He could almost see her here.

Perched on the edge of the couch, drinking expensive wine from a glass that hadn't been properly cleaned.

Tapping furiously on that ancient keyboard, chasing a thread only she could see.

Or lying awake at two in the morning, eyes fixed on the ceiling, thoughts racing, the unanswered questions like mosquitoes in the dark.

He could almost feel her.

Almost.

And it made him want her gone.

But not yet.

Timing mattered.

Jack turned toward the door, his steps as silent as when he entered. But just before he crossed the threshold, a glint caught his eye—the hallway mirror.

His own reflection stared back at him, pale and unblinking.

A ghost in a city of masks.

"She's next," he whispered to himself.

Then he was gone, swallowed by the stairwell.

Chapter 28

Peppy La Font sat in the interrogation room like she owned the place.

One leg delicately crossed over the other. Coffee cup in hand. Head high.

She wore a cream silk blouse, tailored navy slacks, and a subtle gold brooch that sparkled just enough to whisper money.

Fifty-something, but in Hollywood years, that made her ancient.

Not that it showed. She was polished.

And still stunning.

Grace Fletcher entered with Charlie Bonelli at her side.

She carried a manila folder and a neutral smile. Charlie remained quiet in the corner while Grace took the seat across the table.

"Good morning, Miss La Font. Apologies for the delay. Crazy morning."

"Detectives." Peppy nodded graciously. "It's fine. My sister has the kids. I'm just trying not to overstay in Hollywood."

"We'll keep it quick."

Peppy gave a tight smile and sipped her coffee. It smelled expensive.

Probably everything around Peppy seemed expensive—not necessarily because it was, but because of the way she carried herself.

Somehow, the objects in her orbit absorbed her essence: exclusive, refined, unmistakably unique.

"We're interested in your deposition during Paul Max's trial," Grace said, not wasting time. "The testimony you gave in court, confirming he was with you the night before Rebecca Fontaine died."

Peppy blinked slowly. "You believe the trial is... connected to Paul's death?"

"Yes."

Poppy's eyes clouded, and she lowered her cup. "That was... last year. I'm still trying to process it all."

Grace opened her folder but didn't look down. "Why wasn't your testimony presented earlier? Paul's lawyer had to convince the judge to allow it late in the trial."

Peppy hesitated. Composed, but thinking.

"It wasn't easy," she said. "Paul was innocent. He didn't load that bullet. And the set followed safety procedures. I knew that. But I was... with someone else then. And Paul was too.

I didn't want to destroy two relationships to protect a truth I thought the court would recognize anyway."

"But then?"

"The trial turned." Peppy's voice dropped. "The prosecution twisted everything. The jury started to believe it was intentional. I couldn't stay quiet anymore."

"And your relationship?"

"Over," Peppy said flatly. "As you'd expect. Paul's didn't last long either."

Grace took a moment. "We've reviewed the gossip columns. The rumors were there, but we'll need names."

"I understand. I can give you mine. I don't know who Paul was seeing. Maybe Otto would know. Or his lawyers."

"We'll ask."

Charlie scribbled a note in the corner. Grace kept her focus.

"And the day Paul was killed—where were you?"

"Denver," Peppy said. "With the kids. A regular day. Gym in the morning. Grocery shopping. Then movies and dinner with my sister's family. I can get you the details."

"We'll send an officer to follow up."

Peppy nodded. Her hands stayed perfectly still. She wasn't nervous. She looked confident and open.

"Your divorce," Grace said, flipping a page. "It looked smooth. The papers mentioned some minor disagreements, but nothing major."

Peppy didn't answer right away.

"I loved Paul," she said finally. "Still do. We had a great marriage. But Paul needed more. He was hungry—for applause, attention. I was ready for less."

"You wanted out?"

"No," Peppy said, voice suddenly sharp. "I wanted peace. He wanted chaos. That doesn't mean we didn't love each other."

Grace leaned back slightly.

"If he'd told me," Peppy said softly, "that he wanted to disappear into the mountains with our kids and live a quiet life away from the industry... I would've gone with him."

She paused. A single tear rolled down her cheek. It wasn't theatrical—it was elegant, understated, like something from a black-and-white film.

Silence filled the room.

Grace didn't move. She believed her—she really did. But part of her—the seasoned detective—also knew when someone was too good.

Peppy had two Oscars.

She wasn't just convincing. She was masterful.

Grace had the distinct sense that, as an actor, Peppy could take a sliver of truth, stretch it, polish it, and turn it into something golden.

Maybe even something that wasn't quite true anymore.

Grace glanced at Charlie. He looked stunned.

They were both watching an artist at work.

"Thank you, Miss La Font," Grace said, standing. "My colleague will escort you to an agent who will take a more detailed statement."

Peppy stood. She gave a gentle nod, her posture perfect, her expression unreadable.

"Of course."

Charlie held the door. Peppy glided out like royalty. Not a single hair out of place.

Grace watched her go. She couldn't help it.

What a woman.

She thought of Greta Garbo. Grace Kelly. Those timeless actresses who held the screen with nothing but presence. Peppy had that.

And then she was gone, leaving behind a trace of something subtle. Something Grace could only describe as *glamour.* An old term, almost forgotten, yet perfectly fitting.

Was Peppy lying? Grace wasn't sure—but something about her made the hairs on her neck rise.

She could track down the people they'd both been seeing at the time, verify the timeline, and poke holes in the story if there were any.

Unless, of course, Peppy had been somewhere she didn't want to be found. That would take digging. Real digging.

On the other hand, Grace had to admit—Peppy had sounded convincing.

Maybe *too* convincing.

Ten minutes later, Charlie returned.

"Let me tell you who Mark Zambrano is," he said, holding up his phone.

"He's a *decorated* detective from Boise PD."

Grace's eyes sharpened. "Go on."

Chapter 29

Mark Zambrano didn't like loose ends. His work was about turning chaos into order—finding the pattern buried beneath the mess.

They scratched at the back of his mind, made sleep a shallow tease. His breakfast sat untouched on the table—two eggs growing cold beside a half-burnt slice of toast—as he checked the window for the third time in five minutes.

Suburbia stretched outside like a well-pressed image of stability. Trimmed lawns. Maple trees too young to cast real shade.

Identical fences. Identical houses. Safe. Quiet.

Mark was anxious. It happened when things weren't exactly where they needed to be. Logic mattered to him—lines, cause and effect, truth. But lately, things weren't aligning.

A few days ago, a reporter from LA called Boise PD asking questions about Marcus O'Brien. Most of the department didn't care. It was an old case, written off and buried.

One of his colleagues, Nick Mottola, strolled in late—as always—slipping past most people's glances with that slippery, untouchable charm of his.

Coffee in one hand, a powdered Dunkin' Donut in the other.

"Boy, my head is exploding..." he muttered, dropping into his chair.

As usual on a Friday, Nick was hungover. He was young, irresponsible, and addicted to late nights and club lights.

"Coffee should help," Mark said. He never knew exactly how to talk to Nick. They weren't far apart in age, but their lifestyles were worlds apart.

Nick took a bite of his donut, then leaned back. "Hey, you hear about this? There's a reporter calling around, trying to dig into what happened with Marcus O'Brien."

"Who?"

"Some big shot from L.A... Becky Fletcher."

Mark's brow tightened. "What does she want?"

"She called me yesterday. Asking every question in the book—when he died, how he died, autopsy, crime scene, you name it."

Mark leaned forward slightly. "But that case is closed."

"Of course it's closed. I told her that. But she wouldn't let it go. Pestering me. So... I got tired of it and..."

"And what?"

Nick hesitated, suddenly looking more interested in his coffee than the conversation. "Well... look, you've been poking at this thing yourself. It's more your realm than mine. I gave her your number."

Mark sat back, weighing it. The last thing he needed was a reporter sniffing around—but it might also be a way to pick up information he couldn't get otherwise.

"Nick..."

"Sorry, man," Nick said, holding up a hand. "I'm just done with it. That guy was a drunk, died in his element—alcohol. Period. I wasn't gonna waste any more time. But I know you're still chasing it."

Mark stayed quiet for a beat. Cases like this didn't do wonders for your reputation in the department. People already made jokes behind his back.

He knew it.

"It's fine," he said finally. "You did the right thing. I'll handle her."

Nick grinned, relieved. "Thanks, dude." He took a long sip of coffee and drifted away, clearly not interested in prolonging the conversation.

That had been a couple of days ago.

Then, the call had come.

Becky Fletcher.

He'd spoken to her briefly, just enough to get a feel for her cadence, her rhythm, the speed of her thoughts. She asked sharp questions. Didn't fumble. But he needed more.

He needed to see her. Read her. Decide if she was someone who could handle the truth—because what he had wasn't easy. It wasn't normal. And it sure as hell wasn't safe.

He wasn't worried about sounding crazy.

He was worried about being right.

But earlier that day, someone else had called him. A detective from L.A. wanted to talk—Charlie Bonelli, Grace Fletcher's partner. Becky's sister. He checked.

The names alone made his stomach tighten. This wasn't some random inquiry. Becky had already been poking around, and now her sister's partner was calling him directly.

And Bonelli's questions? They weren't about Marcus O'Brien.

They were about *him*.

The circle was tightening.

But that could wait. First, Becky.

Mark didn't want to meet at the station. Too much chatter, too many wandering eyes and whispered questions.

People would talk regardless, but he preferred to keep the noise down.

So, he invited Becky to his home on the edge of the city—low traffic, quiet streets.

His house was a modest, single-story Craftsman with wide eaves and a big front porch. The neighborhood was filled with families and retirees. Kids on scooters. Sprinklers running in the afternoon.

Inside, it was clean and sparse. Dark hardwood floors, beige walls, sturdy furniture.

A few framed commendations hung over a bookshelf—twenty years of service, two departmental awards for bravery.

He was still under forty, but already marked as a future chief. Fit, tall, sharp-eyed. His father had been in the force too, but made detective late—just before retiring.

Mark had climbed faster. He had farther to go.

The knock came sharp and on time. Just one minute past ten.

He opened the door.

"Hi," the woman said. "I'm Becky Fletcher, from *The Hollywood Star*."

"Hi. Mark Zambrano, Boise PD," he replied, offering a firm handshake. "Good to finally meet you in person."

"Likewise," she said, stepping inside.

She looked around briefly, alert but not nervous.

"This way," he said, guiding her down the hallway toward a studio off the living room.

"Can I get you something? Coffee? Tea?"

"No thanks," she said with a smile. "Already had too much caffeine today. The hotel you recommended—very good, by the way—has excellent coffee."

"Glad you like it."

He opened the studio door, and Becky stopped short.

A woman in her late twenties—or exceedingly early thirties—sat in one of the two chairs across from the desk, her hands clasped tightly in her lap.

She looked up with clear, intelligent eyes, her posture rigid. Her thick, curly red hair framed a striking face dusted with freckles. Her vivid green eyes were vibrant—but tinged with sadness.

Becky blinked. "Oh. I didn't know someone else would be here."

She turned to Mark, eyebrows raised. He nodded, calm.

"My apologies for the surprise," he said.

"Ms. Fletcher, this is Lisa O'Brien.

She's Marcus O'Brien's daughter."

Chapter 30

Peppy La Font felt unsettled after the LAPD detectives' interrogation. Paul had made mistakes in life—no doubt about that. But she had loved him, and in many ways, still did.

His loss pressed on her like a stone she could never set down.

And the children... they would suffer too.

She was doing everything in her power to soften the blow, to shield them from the worst of it.

But Paul wasn't someone who could simply vanish from their lives. His absence was too large, too heavy—it would leave a mark no matter what she did.

It had taken every ounce of her composure, every trick she'd learned over her acting years, to survive that interrogation.

She hated being questioned, but she'd endured it before—during the trial—and she'd endured it again.

For Paul. Always for Paul.

Peppy wasn't sure she'd convinced the detectives. In fact, she doubted it.

They would keep digging, trying to connect the dots—she could feel it.

She'd sensed something from the female detective, a flicker of admiration perhaps, but beneath it, doubt.

Not clear if it was about her answers or the case itself, but Peppy couldn't take chances.

Her story had to hold—untouchable, airtight. One crack, and everything could collapse on her.

Now, she needed to make a call, quickly. To keep her alibi alive. To make sure the story held.

Peppy drove up the winding streets to her sister's house in Beverly Hills.

Her sister, Minka, wasn't home—out at the mall with the kids, buying them the Apple Vision Pro headsets they'd been begging for.

Normally Peppy was strict, firmly against spoiling the kids—a risk all too easy given the life they lived.

Her rule was always to curb overindulgence.

But this time was different. This time, Peppy thought, a little distraction was necessary. Something to shield them, however briefly, from the brutal truth clawing at the edges of their lives.

Juanita, Minka's longtime maid, opened the door.

She'd been with the family for years—a kind, soft-spoken woman from Mexico, warm and patient with the children. In her fifties and a little overweight, Juanita was still quick on her feet, attentive, and unfailingly professional.

"Señora La Font, please come in."

"Thank you, Juanita," Peppy replied softly as she stepped into the mansion, her voice carrying a tired grace.

The cool air inside wrapped around her, a sharp contrast to the weight she carried in with her.

"Is it all right if I use the studio?"

"Of course. Please follow me."

Peppy had been there many times and knew the layout well, but Juanita insisted on guiding her.

"Would you like something to eat?" Juanita asked.

Peppy wasn't really hungry, but she knew food might help steady her. "Yes. Could you please make me a ham and cheese sandwich? With a cup of coffee."

"Of course. Here's the studio. If you need me, there's a button on the desk—it rings in the kitchen."

"Thank you, Juanita."

The studio was cool and quiet, paneled in dark wood with a wall of bookshelves and heavy velvet drapes that kept out the afternoon glare.

A leather-topped desk sat in the center, polished to a muted sheen, the faint scent of tobacco still clinging from her brother-in-law's cigars. In the corner stood a well-stocked bar, gleaming with bottles.

It was the kind of room designed for confidences—for secrets.

Peppy sat down, pulled out her phone, and scrolled to the number. She hesitated, rehearsed the words in her mind, then pressed dial.

"Jim? Hi. Long time."

She listened, the faint crackle of his voice in her ear.

"Yes, I'm fine, thank you. How are you? How's Penny?"

A pause, then she nodded faintly.

"Good to hear. Yes, they're fine—just a bit shaken, as you can imagine. They're with my sister at the mall now."

Her tone shifted, softening. "Jim, I need something from you. Remember what we talked about during Paul's trial last year?"

Another pause.

"Exactly. Darling, I need you to keep that story. If anyone calls, please hold to it."

She sat still, lips pressed thin, then spoke again. "Yes, the police are looking into Paul's death. They're circling back, asking questions about the trial."

A beat of silence.

"No, everything will be fine. That situation is old news—they're just tying up loose ends. The main focus is Paul."

Her eyes flickered, but her voice stayed smooth. "Yes, awful. Tragic."

She leaned back, letting him finish.

"No, they don't know anything yet. They're questioning everyone, trying to piece it together. Apparently, someone was blackmailing him—but they didn't take the money. Can you believe that?"

Her voice dipped low. "Yes, horrendous. They think it might've been revenge for what happened with Rebecca Fontaine last year. But honestly—who would want Paul dead? It feels so unreal..."

A final pause.

"Thank you, darling. You know I love you."

Her smile didn't quite reach her eyes.

"Thank you. Talk soon."

She hung up and exhaled slowly, relief washing through her. The call had gone well.

Even though she and Jim were no longer together, they'd managed to keep a good relationship. Now he remained the one man who could corroborate her story—the story she'd told under oath at the trial, last year.

Back then, Jim had been the man she was dating—the man she had to leave behind to shield Paul.

Her alibi hinged on that night, the night she swore she was with Paul... the night he might have switched the bullet.

A lie.

She hadn't been with Paul at all.

She'd been with Jim.

And now the weight of that lie pressed harder than ever.

If Jim slipped, even once—if he hesitated, faltered, confessed—the whole façade would shatter.

And Peppy knew: once a lie cracks, it doesn't stop.

It explodes.

Chapter 31

Mark Zambrano stood by the window.

Calm exterior.

Mind spinning.

He liked control. Liked facts that lined up. But this case? It didn't just refuse to line up—it laughed in his face.

He glanced back at Becky and Lisa.

The two women sat in opposite chairs. Becky leaned forward. Focused. Lisa was tighter. Jaw clenched. Fingernails biting her palms.

"I appreciate you coming," Mark said, tone level. "Lisa's here because she can offer a first-person perspective. Details that haven't made it into any file."

Lisa gave Becky a polite nod. "I've read one of your articles," she said. "The one about the producer found dead in his locked office. Incredible work."

Becky offered a brief smile. "Thank you. That one kept me up for weeks."

Lisa didn't respond. She sat in silence, one hand resting on her knee, the other tightening around the armrest of her chair.

Her jaw was set, but her foot tapped—barely perceptible, a quiet giveaway of nerves.

Becky cleared her throat, flipped open her notepad, and leaned forward just enough to close the distance between them.

"First of all," she said evenly, "I want to thank you for taking the time to talk today. I know they've all told me this case is closed—but I believe what we discuss could help make sense of what happened in L.A. recently."

Mark's gaze flicked to Lisa before he spoke. "Are you referring to Paul Max's murder?"

"Yes… exactly. But let me explain how this started for me."

Becky took a measured breath, pen poised above the paper. "I was working on an in-depth profile of Paul Max—his childhood, his early career, the movies, the actors and directors he worked with, his ex-wife, Lola… everything. Then suddenly he was killed, and my story was cut short. My main source was gone. And I needed to finish it—but where to begin? How?

Then something occurred to me. Something I hadn't consciously noticed while talking to Paul, but it had been nagging at the back of my mind. He was oddly evasive about his beginnings. Don't get me wrong—he talked about them. But the story always felt… polished. Too perfect. Carefully edited to project an image that didn't feel entirely real."

Lisa's fingers curled tighter around the armrest.

"And there were gaps," Becky continued. "Whole chunks of his past that he skimmed over. I remember one interview in particular—when we were talking about Rebecca Fontaine. I asked him when they'd first met. He told me they'd both been part of an acting collective, a small group called Red Stage. When I pressed for details, he minimized it—said it was just a short-lived experiment, not worth talking about—and moved on."

Mark glanced at Lisa and caught it—the tightening of her jaw, the flicker in her eyes. Something was stirring inside her. Since Paul's death, her mood had lightened; she seemed more alive, more relieved. But now, this interview was pulling her back—dragging her into painful memories.

Reopening this chapter of her life clearly hurt; the memories cut deep, but beneath the pain, there was a stubborn glint.

She wasn't just enduring it.

She was bracing herself.

Determined to see it through.

"I didn't think much of it at the time," Becky went on. "Until recently. That's when I learned Marcus O'Brien was part of Red Stage too, along with Rebecca and Paul. That got my attention. I started making calls, trying to dig up more about Red Stage."

Lisa's eyes narrowed just a fraction. Her voice, when it came, was quieter, tighter. "How much do you know about Red Stage?"

Becky gave a small nod, like she'd been expecting the question.

"Not much. There's almost nothing online. But I dug through old archives, found bits and pieces. Red Stage was co-founded by Paul, Rebecca, Marcus O'Brien—your father—and a man named Bob Malone."

Lisa's tapping foot stopped, and her knuckles whitened around her cup.

"Then you've read the lie."

Becky looked up. "The embezzlement?"

"He didn't do it!" Lisa snapped. "Paul accused my father. But it could've been any of them. Or all of them."

"But Paul had proof," Becky said. "Signed financial records. Witness statements. Your father served time."

Lisa shook her head. "Faked! All of it. My father told me. The signatures, the bank records—planted."

"That's a strong accusation," Becky said softly, choosing her words with care, trying to confront her in the gentlest way possible.

"I know. But there was someone else," Lisa said. "Tom Harper. He was the group's accountant. He testified against my father. But I'm sure he lied. I think he was paid off."

Becky frowned. At that time, no one in Red Stage had money. They were a struggling acting group. Unknown. Barely surviving. Why would someone go to the trouble of framing Marcus O'Brien?

The story felt thin. Off.

Becky tapped her pen against her notebook. "That name—Harper—it came up in some of the Red Stage contracts I found in a university archive. No photo. No address. Nothing since."

"Because someone made sure he disappeared," Lisa said softly.

Silence settled over the room.

Outside, a lawnmower buzzed faintly in the distance. Inside, Mark felt it again—that shift in the air. A pressure. Like something was starting to rise from the dirt.

Too many ghosts in this story. And one of them was whispering in his ear.

Becky leaned forward. "What happened to your father after prison?"

Lisa looked down. Her voice lowered. "He came back to Idaho. Tried to work. But the stain never went away. People wouldn't hire him. He bounced between mechanic shops. Construction sites. Day labor. He drank. A lot. I tried to help, but—I'm not rich. I'm just a teacher."

She paused. Swallowed hard.

"Then—" She stopped. Her voice cracked.

Mark moved closer, his hand finding her shoulder. She covered it with hers. He stayed there beside her—quiet, solid, present.

Becky's eyes flicked toward them. Mark saw the unspoken questions circling in her mind.

But she stayed focused.

"We need to find Harper," Becky said. "If he's alive, maybe we can get him to tell the truth—and finally clear this whole thing up."

Lisa shook her head slowly. "We tried. For years. After the trial, he just vanished. No trace. No word."

Her voice was steady now, but her eyes stayed wet.

Mark looked from Lisa to Becky. "Then maybe it's time we start searching again. This time, with better tools."

Because if Harper was still out there... he might be the last thread left.

And someone might have been working to make sure that thread was never pulled.

But Becky wasn't fully convinced. Why would anyone go to so much trouble? Was Lisa pointing to a real lead, or was she simply emotional—still reeling from the loss of her father?

"But there's more to the story," Mark said, his eyes soft as he looked at Lisa. "Something we discovered last year.

Something disturbing—*and possibly the most important piece yet.*"

Chapter 32

Mark Zambrano watched Becky Fletcher's face shift—first surprise, then curiosity, then something sharper. Conviction. She leaned forward, pen poised, focus narrowing like a lens.

"The most important piece?" she asked. "What is it?"

Lisa O'Brien's voice was calm, but the pain beneath it was impossible to miss.

"You need to understand the whole story. Let me go back a bit."

She took a breath.

"One night I went to my father's place for dinner. I'd brought food with me—he never kept much at home.

But that night, surprisingly, he was sober. We talked, and as usual, he drifted into the past. Only this time... his thoughts were clearer. More precise."

Her eyes hardened slightly.

"When the four of them—Paul, Rebecca, Bob Malone, and my father—founded Red Stage, Rebecca was clearly the most talented. Paul? The least. All he really had were his looks, and he knew it.

He spent hours in the gym, used expensive creams, fussed over his hair—every detail of his appearance was calculated. None of them believed he'd make it as an actor. Modeling, maybe. But acting? No.

My father believed Paul had crafted a personality designed to project one image while keeping the truth buried. He mastered the art of hiding behind a carefully built façade—an illusion.

He was the perfect magician, cloaked in layers of fiction. Paul might not have been a great actor, but he was a brilliant illusionist.

Bob was the other one with real potential. He didn't have Paul's polished good looks—he was rugged, more ordinary—but he was grounded and disciplined. He knew exactly what he wanted. He and Rebecca would spend hours rehearsing, reading plays, honing their craft.

Paul didn't.

Paul spent his time cultivating industry connections... and chasing women. He was a master at manipulating them.

All except Rebecca."

Lisa's voice tightened.

"She became a fixation for him. Everyone saw it. Bob too. Maybe it was because he was used to women falling at his feet. No one had ever resisted him. He couldn't handle Rebecca's rejection.

That wasn't love. It was pure ego.

One night, the four of them were eating pizza and drinking beer at the warehouse they used for Red

Stage. Rebecca and Bob lived there. Paul started in again—flirting with Rebecca in front of everyone.

At first, they pretended not to notice, but his comments turned into innuendos. He moved closer. She pulled away. He kept going. Finally, he grabbed her, tried to kiss her."

Lisa's hands curled into fists.

"That's when Bob snapped. He went for Paul. They fought. Hard. My father had to drag them apart. By the end, Paul had a black eye, Bob's face was red and swollen, and Rebecca was in tears.

Bob threw him out on the spot and told him that if he touched Rebecca again, he'd kill him. Paul shouted back, insulted Rebecca, and nearly started another fight. My father walked Paul away, trying to calm him down.

Told him Rebecca loved Bob. But Paul called her a whore. Said they were both losers. Swore he'd have nothing to do with them again."

Lisa exhaled slowly.

"My father always said that night was the real death of Red Stage. After that, they barely spoke, and my dad had to mediate everything."

She paused.

"A few days later, he saw Paul having coffee with Tom Harper—the accountant. Odd, because my father handled all the finances. He was the treasurer. Paul never wanted that responsibility.

When my father approached, they stopped talking. He thought it might be personal business, so he didn't push. Later, though, he wondered if that was Paul maneuvering behind his back."

Lisa's voice dropped.

"Months later came the embezzlement accusations. Paul walked into a meeting with documents in hand, accusing my father. He said he'd spoken to Tom about suspicious transactions. The others saw the papers, believed him, and turned against my father.

Tom backed Paul's story. My father denied everything. But it didn't matter. The trial came. The conviction. Prison."

Her jaw clenched.

"He never recovered. Prison broke him. He came home thinner, older, bitter. And he drank. God, he drank like he wanted to vanish. He took whatever work he could—mechanic gigs, warehouse shifts—but nothing lasted. Not with that reputation. Not with that weight."

Becky started to speak. "But surely after a while—"

"There was no 'after a while,'" Lisa cut in, voice firm. "He never got better. Watching Paul Max become a star wasn't just painful—it was the final twist of the knife. Paul accused him. Paul testified. And then Paul walked red carpets while my dad swept parking lots."

She swallowed hard.

"He got stuck in that moment. Relived it on a loop. Tortured himself. He went to every one of Paul's movies, sometimes screaming in theaters—'Liar!' 'Thief!' Always drunk. People laughed. Thought he was crazy."

Her voice cracked.

"It was too hard to watch him fall apart. To see someone suffer that much and not be able to save them."

Mark stayed quiet. He'd heard all of this before.

But Becky hadn't.

Mark could see it—the empathy in Becky's expression. The understanding. And beneath it, a flicker of something else: recognition of the rage that still burned in Lisa, quiet but unextinguished.

"And then," Becky said softly, "he died intoxicated."

Mark spoke before Lisa could answer.

"No. He didn't."

Becky's eyes jumped between them.

Lisa drew a slow breath.

"My father didn't die intoxicated," she said. "That's another lie.

He was murdered!"

Chapter 33

Peter Woodford swirled the ice in his glass, though the drink was long gone. Bourbon fumes lingered faintly, the ghost of better days.

He stood by the floor-to-ceiling window in his office, staring down at the Pacific Coast Highway.

Cars streamed by in smooth, pointless rhythm. He didn't see them.

The police thought he had motive.

Motive to kill Paul!

That was insane.

He didn't kill him.

Sure, Paul had money. And sure, Peter needed money. But that didn't mean he'd kill the man who, for better or worse, made him who he was.

Still... people talked. The rumors had grown teeth. And those detectives? They weren't just circling—they were snapping at his heels.

His phone buzzed once, then again. He ignored it.

A moment later, there was a knock on the door. "Yes?" he said without turning.

Karen, his secretary, stepped in. "Mr. Woodford, I just called Otto's office. Denise said he hasn't shown up today."

Peter turned.

"He took the day off?" he asked.

"Apparently, sir. Denise tried calling him at home—no answer. He's not responding to texts or emails. The police stopped by his office this morning. She said he had a meeting scheduled with them... but he never showed."

Peter's jaw clenched.

"Do you want me to reach out to his family?" she asked.

"No," he said quickly. "It's fine."

But it wasn't fine.

Otto was a pain.

A jittery little man with a permanent sweat stain on his collar—but he was essential. He controlled Paul's estate. He knew the books. And he was one of the very few people who understood how delicate everything really was.

And now he's taken time off?

What the hell was he doing? Was he trying to cover something up? Was he involved in the money transfer he'd asked CC to handle? Why had he suddenly disappeared?

Maybe he was jumping the gun. He didn't have answers. But he needed them.

Peter ran a hand through his hair. His reflection stared back at him in the window—tired eyes, tight jaw, skin pulled too tight from one too many cosmetic tweaks.

He looked successful. That was the point. Appearances.

But inside, everything felt like it was slipping.

He walked back to his desk and sat down heavily. Otto being gone was a problem.

A big one.

Because CC was involved.

And CC was a wildcard.

She'd probably think only of covering her own ass—maybe Paul's, at best. Beyond that, she'd throw Otto and him straight to hell if it meant saving herself.

He remembered warning Paul about her years ago—back when Paul still listened.

"She's dangerous," Peter had said. "Unstable. Maybe even sociopathic."

But Paul had just shrugged. "She gets things done."

"She could ruin us all."

"She already saved me—and more than once," Paul replied. "I owe her."

That was the last serious conversation they had about CC. After that, it was as if Paul was covering for her.

Protecting her.

Peter didn't know what she'd done for Paul, but whatever it was, he knew it must have been big. Paul was grateful—deeply grateful—and that said everything.

Still, Peter didn't want the details. Some things were better left in the dark.

At least that way, he could cling to deniability.

Or maybe she was blackmailing him. Peter wouldn't be surprised.

But again, he didn't want to know.

He picked up his phone and scrolled to CC's number but didn't dial.

Not yet.

He didn't want to deal with her unless absolutely necessary. Was this the moment he had to call her—or just a moment he could? He needed time to think.

He leaned back in his chair and stared at the ceiling.

Paul had secrets. That much was obvious now.

And Peter—stupid, complicit Peter—had chosen not to dig. He hadn't wanted to know what happened after the Red Stage days.

That was Paul's business.

Peter's role had been simpler: do what needed to be done.

The problem with secrets was that they had a nasty habit of surfacing. Always at the worst moments, usually when someone was dead.

And especially when they died badly.

He stood up again and paced the room. Otto being gone—just when questions about Paul's estate were becoming critical—was too convenient. Or too suspicious.

He needed to know what CC had done.

Obviously, she accessed Paul's accounts to get him the $22 million. But what else had she done? Forged something? Moved money around? Created trails that pointed back to Peter?

He pulled out his phone again.

"Karen," he said into the intercom, "cancel my meetings for the rest of the day."

"Yes, sir."

He hung up.

He sat down again and opened his laptop, fingers moving quickly. He logged into one of Paul's production company databases. The numbers were surging.

Since Paul's death, the movie had gone viral.

Ticket sales were up more than 700%. There was talk of Oscar buzz. International markets were opening up.

If the numbers kept trending that way, the movie would turn into a gold mine.

And the timing was terrible.

People would start connecting dots.

The man who stood to benefit most from Paul's death?

Peter Woodford.

He closed the laptop and leaned forward, elbows on the desk, fingers steepled against his lips.

He had to find Otto.

He had to get ahead of this.

He needed to make sure that CC hadn't left him holding the bag.

Because if she had... well, Peter might not end up on the red carpet.

He might end up in court.

Or worse.

He knew where he had to go.

Time to pay that little weasel a visit—*at home*.

Chapter 34

Mark Zambrano had been around grief before. Seen it. Studied it. Sometimes caused it.

But this was different.

Lisa's face crumpled, silent tears slipping down her cheeks. Mark leaned in, gently placing an arm around her shoulders—not as a detective, but as something more.

He caught Becky watching.

She had noticed the tenderness in his gesture, the quiet affection behind it. And Lisa didn't pull away. Her body language mirrored his—soft, open, accepting.

Whatever they were, it was mutual.

And visible.

"Miss Fletcher," he said, his voice calm but firm, "this is very painful for Lisa."

Becky nodded, sitting straighter. She noticed. The closeness. The way Mark hovered, protective, affectionate. She didn't say it—but she clocked it. And Mark knew she would.

He needed to explain.

"After her father died, Lisa kept trying to get someone to pay attention. No one cared. Everyone assumed it was just... what happens. He was a drunk. Everybody knew. So, when they found him at home surrounded by empty bottles, well, it was a no-brainer. Case closed."

Lisa didn't look up.

"But Lisa didn't let it go. She kept pushing. Asking questions. Sending emails. I saw her once outside the station—alone, waiting in the cold. Fragile, trembling... but strong. Determined. Against all odds."

Mark paused, his gaze locked on her with quiet, intense warmth—and something sweet behind it. Sunlight flickered in his eyes, catching on the edge of a tear that never quite fell.

"You have to understand the context," he said slowly. "At best, she was ignored. At worst, mocked. Dismissed. Treated like she didn't matter. That's how we met.

We started talking. And that night, when she told me her story... I didn't just hear it—I felt it. It got under my skin. My heart clenched, and I saw Lisa as something enormous—powerful—but also breakable. Isolated.

I decided I'd help her, whatever it took. We spent the next days talking. Long hours. Late nights. And then... the talking shifted. Became something else. Something you can't walk back from."

Lisa finally met Becky's eyes. They were wet, but steady—almost defiant.

"We fell in love," Mark said, without hesitation. "And I started getting involved in her father's case. We gathered everything we could on Red Stage. We tried to locate the accountant, Tom Harper, but without a broader investigation—or support from out-of-state law enforcement, maybe even the FBI—it was nearly impossible."

Mark continued, one arm still wrapped around Lisa, while his other hand remained clenched—tense, controlled.

"What we do know is this," Mark said. "Tom was alone. He lost his wife and son in a car accident a few years before Marcus's trial. No siblings. Parents gone. Then, one day, he closed his business and vanished—just like that.

No warning.

No trace.

He didn't go to family because he didn't have any. We couldn't find close friends or anyone significant in his life. We even tried tracking financial records, but without a court order, there wasn't much we could do."

Becky's pen hovered above her notepad. Then she lowered it.

"And last year," Mark continued, "we did something crazy. We had Lisa's father's body exhumed."

Becky blinked.

"You *what*? Did you get a court order to do it?"

"No... it was... outside official channels," Mark muttered.

"Okay, I don't need the details," Becky said, her voice sharper now. "But you do understand that whatever you found is unauthorized—and potentially illegal."

"Yes, we know," Mark said. "But we had to be sure. When Marcus died, the coroner performed a routine, bare-bones autopsy. No evidence of foul play, so it was treated like a standard case.

Just another drunk who drank himself to death. Everything else was circumstantial—bottles, reputation, assumptions."

He paused, then added quietly, "But when we had a private coroner examine the remains... he found a small puncture mark on Marcus's arm."

"A mark?"

Lisa nodded. "A puncture wound. Consistent with a needle. But here's the thing—my father never used drugs. He didn't even like taking aspirin.

During the original autopsy, it was obviously overlooked. They'd already assumed it was the result of alcohol intoxication. The team was predisposed to blame alcohol, maybe drugs, from the start."

"And our coroner found something else," Mark added. "Traces of residue—something consistent with medical-grade ethanol. Injected directly into the bloodstream. Not conclusive, but very possible. The coroner did it as a personal favor. Off the record. He couldn't push further or have his name anywhere near this."

Becky's mouth tightened. "So... not a drug injection."

"No," Mark said. "A deliberate alcohol poisoning. Fast. Clean. Cold."

"But that's just theory," Becky said. "Right now, it's a scar and some speculation."

"Exactly," Mark admitted. "Without a proper toxicology report, it's just a theory."

"You'd need a full forensic autopsy to prove it."

"Correct."

"And you couldn't get one?"

Lisa shook her head. "We tried. But no one wanted to touch it. Officially, he was an old alcoholic. No foul play suspected. It would mean reopening a closed file, challenging the original investigators. No one cared. No one wanted that mess."

They sat in silence for a moment. The buzz of a neighbor's lawn mower filtered in through the windows.

Then Becky leaned in. "But even if it was murder... why would Paul kill him after so many years?"

That question hung in the air like smoke.

Mark looked at Lisa. She looked away.

"That's what we keep asking ourselves," he said finally.

"Why then? Why after all that time?"

Chapter 35

Mark stood behind Lisa, one hand resting gently on her shoulder—a quiet gesture of comfort, but also a statement: *I'm here.* No words needed.

The room was still, save for the low hum of the air conditioner. Outside, a breeze rattled the bare branches, but inside, the silence pressed heavily.

Lisa sat across from Becky, her posture straight, her expression calm. But Mark knew better. Behind her eyes, a storm churned.

"We don't know why Paul killed Marcus after so many years... if in fact he did," Mark said, his voice low, deliberate. "But something happened five years ago. We just don't know what, but Marcus became a liability.

Up until then, whatever he knew—or didn't—wasn't a problem for Paul. Then everything changed."

Becky leaned in, pen poised above the page. "How can you be sure? Did you notice anything different about Marcus's behavior?"

"At the time, no," Lisa said slowly. "We were just living day to day. Life was already hard enough. I wasn't searching for clues. But looking back—yes. There were signs."

She drew in a breath. "First—my father drank less. Normally, his binges eased off for a day or two, never longer. But this time, it lasted for weeks. The last two weeks before he was killed, he was drinking less than I'd seen in years. He still drank, yes—but not like before.

I asked if he was finally quitting. He just said *maybe* and went quiet. I thought it was about his health—his liver was failing, and I figured perhaps he finally cared. But now... now I believe something else happened."

Her gaze drifted to the floor, voice tightening. "Second. My father rarely left Boise after prison. Once or twice, he went back to L.A.—old contacts, a cameraman friend. Those trips lifted him. But three weeks before he died... he vanished."

Becky lifted her eyes to her. "He *vanished*?"

"That's what we believe. Let me explain. I was out of town for a teacher's conference. I called him constantly—no answer. I even asked a friend to check his house twice. Empty, both times. Later, when I pressed him, he claimed he'd just been out drinking, depressed.

At the time, I believed him. It wasn't unusual. But he didn't look depressed. He was different. Lighter. Stronger. Almost as if something had been lifted off him. At the time, I didn't think too much about it.

He'd said he'd been depressed the week before, drinking himself numb, but now he claimed he was better. Was that possible? Yes—especially to someone like me, who wanted so badly to believe he was finally improving. So, I let it go.

But after his death, we spoke to people. My father was loud, impossible to miss—especially in bars, drinking.

Subtlety was never his strength.

None of the regular places remembered seeing him that week.

Not once."

She looked at Becky.

"Okay, Lisa, what do you believe happened?" Becky asked, clearly trying to understand her point of view.

Lisa drew in a breath. "Based on everything I've told you, it doesn't add up that he drank himself to death. Not at that moment. Maybe months earlier, sure. But not then.

I think he went back to L.A. while I was away. And something happened there. Something that shifted him. Changed him. I don't know what it was. I can only guess.

But two weeks later, he was dead. Think about it, Becky—may I call you Becky?"

Becky gave a slight nod in agreement.

"He died at the exact moment when he wasn't drinking heavily," Lisa continued, "when he actually seemed better. And the police expect me to believe he suddenly drowned himself in alcohol?

Possible, yes. Logical? Not a chance."

Lisa's next breath shuddered. "He found something—or learned something—that made him dangerous. A liability. And at the same time, it probably gave him relief. The truth. But then Paul silenced him."

Becky frowned. "But Paul was murdered afterward."

Silence.

"So, let's assume for a moment it wasn't Paul… who would want Marcus dead after all these years?"

Mark answered, his tone grim. "We looked. Believe me. No debts. No enemies. No money. Lisa paid his rent, his groceries, and even his meds. His world was tiny. Quiet. He was invisible. Except to Lisa."

"A dead end," Becky murmured, scribbling notes. "If Marcus was murdered, everything circles back to Red Stage—and the deaths tied to it."

Lisa's voice cracked sharp as glass. "He was killed because of that, something he knew, very likely about Red Stage, yes.

Even if Paul didn't kill him with his own hands, he destroyed him. He accused him. He testified. And then he sent someone to finish the job. Don't tell me he just died. Someone did this."

Mark said nothing.

He only watched Becky, reading her face.

He saw the doubt in her eyes. Maybe pity.

She wasn't convinced. How could she be? All they had were scraps—behavioral changes, missing days, a partial autopsy. No hard proof.

Becky leaned back, exhaling slowly. "Let me recap. Your theory is Paul killed Marcus—maybe out of fear, maybe to protect Red Stage's secrets."

Mark nodded. "That's right. In our view, Marcus knew something—maybe tied to Red Stage—and he was killed for it."

"But now Paul is dead. Rebecca Fontaine is dead. Marcus O'Brien is dead. That's three out of four co-founders." Becky's voice dropped. "That pattern can't be ignored."

A silence fell, heavy as smoke.

This wasn't just about Paul.

"It could be a coincidence," Becky admitted at last. "Hollywood's full of tragedies. Maybe Paul killed Marcus, and the others... maybe they're just unrelated."

Mark leaned forward, his tone like iron. "Only one Red Stage founder is still alive."

"Bob Malone," Becky whispered.

Mark straightened. "We've considered him. Especially after Paul's death."

Becky's pen tapped against her notebook, her eyes narrowing. "If Paul killed Marcus, then who killed Paul?"

Retaliation?

Or maybe someone's tying up every loose end.

Maybe all of this is about Red Stage.

Someone wants it buried, *permanently*.

She turned to Lisa, her expression sharpening. "Maybe it's Bob. Maybe he knows what Paul did."

Her voice sank to a whisper.

"Or maybe Bob's next."

Chapter 36

"Okay, listen to this. It is good," Charlie said over the phone.

His voice sounded clearer than it had in days—energized, almost optimistic. Grace leaned in, eager.

She was desperate for good news.

The case was murky, circling without direction, and she needed something—anything—to push it forward.

Right now, they were stalled.

Grace was seated at her desk, a yellow legal pad covered in red ink in front of her, but she dropped her pen immediately. "Tell me."

"We went to the care facility where Rebecca Fontaine's mother lives," Charlie continued. "She's... not in great shape, Grace. Dementia. Paranoid. Barely able to string thoughts together. We tried talking to her, but it was impossible.

The caretaker said she has rare flashes of clarity, but they only last seconds now—and no one knows when they'll come. She's deteriorating day by day. It's... sad."

Grace nodded, unsurprised. "I figured as much. But still—you found something."

"Not from her. This is the interesting part. On the way out, one of the caretakers flagged us down. Told us something strange."

Grace stood, pressing the phone tighter to her ear.

"She said that a few years ago, the facility received a sealed envelope—hand-delivered—from Rebecca. It was addressed to her mother.

At the time it was delivered, her mom was still lucid enough to understand, but she refused to open it. Told the staff to lock it away. Said she didn't want anything from her daughter.

Apparently, Rebecca hadn't visited her in a long time. Their relationship was... strained."

Grace could picture it. Rebecca visiting a mother who was slowly slipping away, who might not even recognize her anymore.

Maybe Rebecca still came, though less often, only to be mistaken for a sister or a caretaker.

Who knew? Her mother was fading from reality, piece by piece.

"Where's the envelope now?"

"That's where it gets even better," Charlie said. "The envelope sat there, forgotten, until recently. The staff only noticed it when someone—claiming to be from Paul Max's legal team—requested to retrieve it."

Grace's stomach flipped. Paul's legal team? What team? That didn't sound possible.

"When did this so-called 'team' request the envelope?" she asked.

"Yesterday."

Okay. Highly unlikely, Paul's legal team would be after an envelope addressed to Rebecca's mother. A year ago, maybe—but not now. And how would they even know something like that existed? Still, she needed to be sure.

Grace slid her notebook closer, flipped to a clean page, and looked up.

"Who made the request?"

"That's the problem. The name was fake. Burner phone. No court documents to back it up. The institution reached out to the clerk's office early today—no record of any official subpoena.

So, they froze the request and handed it over to us instead. Because by chance, we were there today.

Just in time."

This felt like more than a coincidence, Grace thought. They'd come looking to talk to Rebecca's mother—and instead stumbled onto an envelope they hadn't even known existed.

But someone else did.

Someone had been looking for it.

By sheer chance—luck, fate, destiny, call it what you will—they'd been there at the exact moment to intercept it. One day later, and it might already be gone.

Grace exhaled through her nose. "Someone wanted it bad."

"Someone who didn't want us to see it."

"What's in it?" Grace asked.

Her curiosity sharpened into something else—full-blown intrigue.

Charlie paused.

"More secrets," he said.

"Believe it or not, every time we dig something up, it's just a clue pointing to something else."

He hesitated, then added, "We opened it. Inside was a small key. And a note with a bank name, a box number, and an access code. I already sent an agent to retrieve the contents. He's on his way back now."

Grace sank into her chair, letting it all swirl for a moment.

Rebecca, dead on set. Her mother, in a home. And a sealed box no one knew about until someone tried to steal it using a fake identity.

It wasn't a coincidence.

Whatever lay in that box mattered.

It might even be the key to understanding everything.

"Let me know the moment it arrives," she said. "No delays. I want eyes on whatever's in that box."

"You got it," Charlie said. Then he hesitated. "There's something else."

Grace frowned. "More news?"

"Yes. It's been a busy day. I went to see Otto this morning."

Her pulse quickened. "And?"

"He wasn't at the office," Charlie said. "The secretary, Denise, told me he didn't show up today. But

I called yesterday and he confirmed he'd be in this morning. She even had me on the schedule.

"Then—nothing. No call, no text, no explanation. Otto hadn't said a word to anyone. He just failed to show up. Denise even tried his home. Nothing."

Grace closed her eyes for a beat. "And his family?"

"Denise offered to reach out. I told her no. Didn't want to stir panic until we know more."

She opened her eyes again. "Do you think he's running?"

Charlie hesitated. "I don't know if he's running. But I do think he's scared."

"Do you think he killed Paul?"

Silence.

"Charlie..."

"I don't know," he said. "But something's wrong. He knew everything about Paul's affairs. He had access. And if he thought someone was closing in..."

Grace stood. Her hand clenched around the edge of the desk.

"Send people to look for him," she said. "I don't care if we have to knock on every apartment in LA.

Find Otto."

Chapter 37

The coffee was lukewarm. Bitter. Becky didn't care.

She sat rigid in the aisle seat of a half-empty plane, the engine's hum a low, dull drone in her ears. Her notebook was open on the tray table, pages covered in looping arrows, underlined names, question marks like bullet holes.

She kept rewriting the same words.

Red Stage.

It came back to that. Every path, every death. Like an old scar the world forgot—but someone hadn't.

Rebecca Fontaine. Paul Max. Marcus O'Brien.

All dead.

One fact was clear: Paul had been murdered. The other two deaths were clouded in mystery. Now she knew both carried shadows. Rebecca's death had been written off as a freak *accident*. Marcus's—possibly a murder. Neither was certain. But both were far from clean.

And all connected by that tiny, forgotten acting company from twelve years ago.

Only two names remained in her notebook, circled in ink.

Tom Harper.

Bob Malone.

One vanished.

One alive.

She tapped her pen against the edge of the tray. Lisa and Mark had been generous. Brave. But also emotionally tangled. Lisa saw her father as a victim of Hollywood's cruelty. Mark saw Lisa as... everything.

And love had a way of softening corners that needed to stay sharp.

Becky didn't have that luxury. She had to stay objective.

Lisa and Mark were too close to it, too emotionally clouded. The story they pieced together was enough to raise doubts, yes—but not enough to point to Paul as the one responsible for Marcus's death.

If Marcus O'Brien was murdered, it was part of something larger. A story still being written. One where Paul and Rebecca were taken out not because of who they were—but because of what they knew.

And maybe what they did.

That was the worst part—no one in this story was clean.

Not even the dead.

Becky suspected Paul had never been a saint.

If anything, he was a narcissistic manipulator, wrapped in layers of lies and pretenses, his soul already tainted.

His obsession with Rebecca revealed as much—something he'd never confessed to her, and something conveniently absent from his trial.

Maybe because the only people who truly knew—Marcus, dead at the moment of the trial, and Bob, who wasn't involved—couldn't speak to it.

But it showed who Paul really was.

So, had he orchestrated the embezzlement that destroyed Marcus? Possibly.

But why Marcus?

Paul's hatred had always burned brightest toward Rebecca and Bob. That part didn't click. Maybe it was only because Marcus was the treasurer—the easy target.

And why, if he despised Rebecca, had he given her a role in one of his films? Was it a twisted favor? A calculated trap? An obligation, dues being paid for some other reason?

One theory gnawed at Becky: maybe the role was never an opportunity at all—maybe it had been a setup from the start. A way to kill her. But if that was true, it was a strange, convoluted way to end Rebecca's life.

Becky didn't like Paul, but imagining him deliberately killing someone that way was hard. And if he had meant to kill her, he'd been lucky. One shot. Fatal. She could just as easily have survived.

She flipped to a fresh page.

Why kill them all?

Who benefits?

What was Red Stage hiding?

Marcus went to jail for embezzlement. Or so the records claimed. But Lisa swore it was a setup. The only witness? Tom Harper, the accountant. The same man who disappeared the moment the trial ended.

Becky had tried searching him. Online databases. Public records. Nothing. The man was dust.

Either he ran from something—or someone made him vanish.

Could Tom Harper be the one killing all the Red Stage founders? But why? To cover his tracks? It didn't make sense.

The more reasonable explanation was that he'd just been a pawn. Maybe he helped Paul fake the documents that sent Marcus to jail—though why was still unclear.

Perhaps he'd been paid off, generously, by someone. But who? None of them had money back then.

Or maybe Tom was already dead, his body never found.

Chasing Tom Harper felt like chasing a ghost—a difficult path with no clear end.

That left Bob Malone.

The last standing member of Red Stage.

No interviews. No headshots. Not even a LinkedIn. Just one black-and-white cast photo from a local theater site, barely visible, his name printed under a blurry face half-turned from the camera.

Becky stared at the name again.

The plane hit a patch of turbulence, rattling her tray. Her pen skidded across the page. A jagged line slashed through Bob's name.

She would start with him. As soon as the plane landed, she'd make a few calls—people who could help. People who owed her.

She took a sip of the coffee and grimaced.

Something was building. She could feel it. That pressure behind the ribs. That sense of standing one wrong step from something that could swallow you whole. There was no doubt now—someone was orchestrating this.

One by one, the cast of Red Stage was being erased.

And Becky was getting too close.

Becky closed the notebook and leaned back, staring at the ceiling of the cabin.

She felt the engine shift pitch as the plane began its descent. The city stretched below like a glowing circuit board, beautiful and ugly all at once.

Los Angeles.

The illusion machine.

And now it was covered in blood.

The seatbelt sign chimed.

She buckled in, notebook pressed against her chest.

The last show of Red Stage wasn't over.

Not yet.

Chapter 38

Grace Fletcher turned the wheel with one hand, the other resting on her thigh, fingers tapping to the beat of a jazz station barely audible over the traffic.

The afternoon sun flared off the windshield. She hated being trapped in L.A. traffic, time bleeding away mile by mile.

But at least it gave her time to think.

Her phone buzzed in the cupholder. She glanced down—hoping for Becky.

Not Becky. Still ghosting her. The silence scraped her nerves raw, leaving her restless, anxious, furious. No one could imagine how much it exasperated her—and how much it *terrified* her.

But then she saw the name.

Charlie.

For a moment her shoulders eased. Not the message she wanted, but maybe the one she needed.

She hit the Bluetooth.

"Yeah?"

"Hey," Charlie's voice came through, clear but tense.

Grace straightened a bit. "What is it?"

"More news Grace. We pulled something from Paul's financials. Big payments. Not a one-off—installments. Over months."

Grace frowned. "Go on."

"They were directed to Peppy La Font. Started during the trial, continued for almost a year after. Substantial amounts. Spread out, just enough not to raise any red flags."

Grace's fingers froze mid-tap. "Payments for what?"

"Divorce alimony—but not exactly." Charlie's tone dropped, carrying a weight that made Grace sit straighter. "Here's the strange part: we checked the divorce filings. Those payments don't show up in the *original* settlement. In fact, the official alimony agreement was minimal. Almost symbolic. Paul paid generous child support separately, but these transfers? They don't match any of that."

Grace frowned. "So... what the hell was he paying her for?"

Charlie exhaled slowly. "That's where it gets interesting. During the trial, the divorce agreement was quietly amended—adding an extraordinary short-term alimony payment, paid in structured installments.

On paper, it appeared to be part of the settlement. The court signed off, so technically, it was all perfectly legal."

Grace felt her pulse climb. "So, what's your theory?"

"Our working theory?" Charlie said, his voice dropping. "Amending a marital settlement after the fact is rare—lawyers we talked to say it rarely happens without a fight. And legally, no reason is required if both parties agree.

Which means... Paul didn't need a reason. What I think happened is simple: he paid for her silence. For her alibi. They buried it in the divorce paperwork so it looked legitimate. She was his star witness, remember? She swore she was with him the night of the shooting.

That testimony flipped the trial. Without it, Paul was finished. The whole thing hinged on her timeline."

Grace gripped the wheel tighter.

"She sold the story," she said.

"Looks that way."

There was a long pause. Grace's mind drifted back to the interrogation room, to Peppy's careful words, her polished composure.

She'd looked untouchable then, perfectly rehearsed.

Grace let that memory linger, cold and sour between them.

Finally, she broke the silence.

"Goddamn it," she whispered. "It was all fake. Peppy wasn't answering questions—she was performing."

"She's so good at that," Charlie muttered.

Grace pulled into a gas station lot and parked. The AC hummed softly around her. In the rearview mirror, a mail truck trundled past.

She stared out the window, mind replaying Peppy's performance during the interrogation—how convincing she had been.

Too convincing.

"How sure are we?"

"We don't have an email saying 'thanks for lying,' if that's what you mean. But the timing... It's all there. Paul wires her money after she testifies. Then again, three weeks later. Then every month after that."

"That bastard."

She remembered Peppy's tears in the interview room. The tremble in her voice. The poetic regrets. The tragic romance.

It had been a performance.

A performance for the Oscars.

Of course it had.

But now Grace realized it hadn't started in the courtroom—it had begun much earlier.

Back when Peppy spoke to journalists about her love for Paul, her teary words about letting him go during the divorce, all that polished, practiced sentiment.

How could someone who truly loved him accept money for it? She could have stood by him for free—out of loyalty, out of memory, out of love for the father of her children.

But she hadn't.

She'd turned it into a transaction.

That made it filthy.

It reduced everything—the trial, the testimony, the grief—into theater.

A script, performed on cue. And the worst part was how easy it was to believe.

We, the audience, sat there swallowing it whole, innocent in our faith.

But Peppy? She knew better. She'd played her part to perfection. At the end of it all, there was no truth—only a façade. An illusion, carefully constructed by people who knew exactly what they were doing.

Grace swallowed hard. "We bring her in."

"Not yet," Charlie said. "We need more. If we confront her too early, she'll clam up or lawyer up. But I wanted you to know first. I think this changes things."

"It changes everything," Grace said.

A new silence fell. She didn't fight it this time. She just let it breathe.

Paul Max hadn't been lucky at trial.

He'd been clever.

He'd paid his way out of prison.

Paid the one person who could fabricate his innocence and make the jury believe it. Because everyone believed Peppy.

Everyone wanted to believe Peppy.

The aggrieved ex-wife coming to his defense. It had been a script. A perfect third-act twist. Another illusion.

"Peppy lied," Grace whispered. "And Paul killed Rebecca."

"Maybe."

"But why did Paul kill Rebecca? And who killed Paul?"

Charlie didn't answer.

Grace stared out the windshield at a mother holding a toddler's hand as they crossed the parking lot. She wasn't thinking about them.

She was thinking about Peppy La Font.

About her tears.

Her flawless makeup.

The way she held the silence like a monologue cue.

"And Charlie?"

"Yeah?"

"Keep digging into the person who contacted the institution. The one asking for Rebecca's box. It's clearly connected."

"Already on it."

"I will be at home if you need me."

The call ended.

Grace leaned back, phone resting on the seat beside her.

Paul hadn't been a victim.

He'd been a manipulator. A strategist. And maybe a killer.

And Peppy?

She wasn't just an actress. She wasn't a grieving widow.

She was a cold-hearted *accomplice*.

Chapter 39

Peter Woodford parked across the street, engine idling, eyes fixed on Otto's apartment.

He would confront him. Once and for all. He had to be certain Otto wasn't colluding with CC, setting him up to take the fall.

The afternoon light was fading, surrendering to night. Amber streaks bled into pink and blue, painting the sky in colors too beautiful for what he was about to do. The whole scene felt unreal—like a frame from some arthouse film, ominous yet distant, intense yet strangely vivid.

The lights were out. Curtains drawn. Stillness pressed against the windows like a held breath.

He killed the ignition and stepped into the night breeze. Cool, a little damp, it carried the faint smell of watered lawns and car exhaust. The quiet was wrong—too still, too expectant, as if the street itself was holding its breath.

A young couple walked past, their dog straining at the leash, both dressed in matching workout gear. They laughed at something private, carefree. Peter rolled his eyes. *Let's see where you are in ten years*, he thought sourly.

Still, he forced a polite smile—the kind meant to blend in, to look ordinary. The last thing he needed was anyone noticing him, anyone wondering. He was too exposed out here. He needed to move.

Crossing over, he slipped inside the building, timing it with an old lady stepping out. He climbed to the apartment and pressed the doorbell once. Then again.

Nothing.

He knocked. Waited. Knocked harder.

Still nothing.

Peter reached under the doormat—Otto's terrible excuse for a hiding place—and fished out the spare key. He hesitated, just for a beat, then slid it into the lock.

The door gave way with a soft click.

Inside, he punched in the code and silenced the alarm. Same one Otto always used: Paul's birthday.

For a man so meticulous, Otto left parts of his life dangerously exposed.

"Otto?" he called.

Silence.

He flicked on the lights. The place looked un-touched—immaculate, almost staged. A dusty ficus slumped in the corner. A stack of unread scripts lay neatly on the coffee table. Not a thing out of place.

Every detail whispered *Otto*.

But something felt wrong.

Off.

It wasn't anything Peter could put his finger on. Just a subtle feeling, seeping from the walls, from the air itself.

Not something visible—more like a current gone crooked, an energy out of tune.

A disordered aura, if that meant anything.

Whatever it was, it unsettled him.

His nerves tightened, his senses sharpened.

Peter stepped farther inside, moving almost unconsciously on the balls of his feet, careful not to make a sound.

His rational mind told him the house was very likely empty—but some deeper instinct refused to believe it.

The air was stale, heavy, the kind that made his skin crawl.

He drifted into the kitchen. Spotless. No dishes in the sink. Counters bare.

Not a trace of life.

Then he saw it.

On the dining table.

A single glass sat on the counter. Half-full.

Peter stepped closer. The liquid caught the light, a dull amber glow. He didn't need to smell it to know.

Bourbon.

He froze.

In any other house on the block—or anywhere in America—that glass wouldn't mean a thing. Just a half-finished bourbon left on the counter. Ordinary. Forgettable.

But not here. Not Otto.

One glance at the rest of the house told the story—everything in its place, nothing left behind. Otto would never abandon a glass half-full. Not his style.

And besides, Otto didn't drink.

Not for any moral stance—he just hated losing control. Said alcohol dulled his instincts.

In all the years Peter had known him, he'd never seen him take a sip. Sure, he kept a bottle for guests. But Otto's glass was always soda with lime. Always.

And now—no soda. No second glass. Just that lone tumbler, like someone had poured it... and walked away.

Peter's stomach clenched. His eyes scanned the room again, slower this time. The dining chair was pulled out, just slightly.

Otto would've straightened it.

He always did.

Peter backed up a step. The silence had weight now. No hum of the fridge. No tick of a clock. Just his own breath, ragged in his ears.

His mind fired in two directions at once.

One: someone had been here—a visitor. Otto hadn't poured his usual soda with lime.

And it couldn't have been CC—she didn't touch bourbon. Unless Otto had his regular drink and washed the glass, leaving only the stranger's behind.

But why leave it half-full? Why leave it at all? Sloppy. Un-Otto.

The other: Otto himself. A man pushed to the edge. Shaken.

Desperate enough to stare down the bottle he hated, pour a glass, even choke some of it down.

Maybe one glass is finished. Perhaps this was abandoned halfway.

The thought of Otto losing his discipline, his order—it didn't sit right.

Either way, the picture was bad. A nervous Otto. A disorganized Otto. Or worse—an Otto who wasn't alone.

He continued through the house. Carefully. Guest room—clean. Study—undisturbed.

Then he reached the bedroom.

And everything *stopped*.

Otto was there, on the bed.

Flat on his back.

A pistol in his right hand.

Blood pooled beneath his head. Bits of brain matter stained the wall.

It wasn't just a death scene.

It was carnage.

Peter's knees buckled. He stumbled into the bathroom, fell to the floor, and vomited into the toilet.

He wiped his mouth with a trembling hand, then pulled out his phone. His fingers hovered over the screen, his brain still trying to process the horror.

First Paul.

Now Otto.

He tapped 9-1-1.

The dispatcher answered with a rehearsed calm. "911, what's your emergency?"

Peter's voice shook.

"Please... send someone. Urgent.

My friend—*my friend is dead!*"

Chapter 40

Grace was at her apartment. Afternoon light slanted through the blinds, shadows stretching long across the floor.

She had left the police station early—she needed quiet, time to think, time to steady herself, to be ready if word about Becky broke.

By her estimate, Becky's plane should be landing in L.A. any moment now.

Grace didn't want to be tied up at the station when it happened. She needed to be able to jump in the car at once, no hesitation.

And beneath it all was the worry she couldn't shake. Becky.

The station hadn't dulled it; if anything, it had sharpened it.

As usual, she put a movie on in the background—*Double Indemnity.* Billy Wilder's classic about insurance fraud, with a script by Raymond Chandler.

Grace had seen it countless times, but she still lingered on that famous shot: Barbara Stanwyck staring into the camera while her husband was murdered. Cold. Beautiful. Damned. Great acting.

It reminded her of Peppy's performance in the interrogation room.

She fed Rusty, who meowed impatiently, then moved to the living room. Laptop open, a bowl of fruit beside her, she was nibbling grapes when her phone rang.

Charlie.

"You're not going to believe what we got," he said, breathless.

Grace sat up. "Try me."

"The box Rebecca Fontaine left for her mother. We got it. Grace, this is it! This is the missing piece."

"Stop circling—what's inside?"

"Documents. A lot of them. Enough to prove Marcus was innocent."

Grace's pulse jumped. "What?"

"It's all here. Marcus didn't do a damn thing. Guess who did?"

She closed her eyes. "Paul."

"Paul Max. Tom Harper. And a third name—only initials: C.C."

"Jesus Christ..."

Grace had started doubting Paul back in Peppy's interrogation.

The way he'd bought his way out of Rebecca's onset death—cold, calculated. A mind that could twist the truth. Deceptive. Ruthless.

And this new revelation only fits the picture. Paul Max—the golden movie star—hiding a very big dark secret.

"They forged everything. According to the papers, Rebecca Fontaine received the documents proving Marcus's innocence directly from Marcus himself."

"Marcus O'Brien?"

"Yeah. Turns out Tom Harper cracked. Guilt got to him. He sent Marcus the whole package—confession, proof, the works. And not just Paul and Harper. As I said, there's someone else, CC."

Grace let out a slow breath. "This is huge. But why? Why would they go that far?"

Charlie didn't miss a beat. "Peter Woodford. He was close to an actress who pulled him into Paul's orbit. She and a group of investors planned to back Paul's first movie. Remember—Paul was a master at manipulating women. They needed more money, plus Peter's connections.

Paul had the looks, the charisma, and just enough talent. Woodford said yes—he had a sharp eye for spotting potential in young actors. But then came the problem."

"Red Stage," Grace murmured.

"Exactly. All four founders had signed a strict contract. They couldn't leave for five years. If they did, they owed the others half their income for that entire period. It was Paul's idea, ironically.

Back then, he barely had income—just modeling gigs. The deal protected him. But when real money showed up, that contract became a liability. We're talking millions."

"And Paul found a way out," Grace said.

"Not exactly. Paul was never good at this kind of thing. CC was the mastermind. Came up with an embezzlement scheme—blame Marcus, cut him out, collapse the deal.

Tom Harper, the accountant, cooked the books, pushed by Paul and CC. Marcus took the fall. And Paul? He walked free. No penalties. From there, the money poured in.

His first five years of films made him a fortune—one he should've split under the Red Stage statutes."

Grace whispered, "So Marcus knew. And Paul killed him for it."

"Maybe. It fits. And Rebecca knew too."

"And that's why she died."

"It's a real possibility. Paul must've known about the documents. Maybe he killed them both—and perhaps he went looking for the proof, too. He could've even searched Rebecca's mother's room.

But who would've guessed it was tucked away in a forgotten envelope, locked in storage? The secret sat there for years, hiding in plain sight."

Just like in the Purloined Letter, the short story from Edgar Allan Poe, Grace thought.

Charlie pressed on. "With this, we can reopen Marcus's case. Maybe Rebecca's too. This ties everything together."

Grace hesitated. "One more thing. Do you think Bob Malone knew? That Paul killed the others, and he went after him in revenge?"

"Maybe," Charlie said. "But the documents don't mention Bob at all. Harper sent them only to Marcus—pure guilt, remorse for wrecking his life. Not Rebecca. Not Bob.

Unless Marcus shared them separately with Bob, but that's unlikely."

"There's one more thing that bothers me," said Grace. "If Marcus and Rebecca knew, why didn't they do anything with it? Were they both trying to blackmail Paul? And if Paul hated Rebecca..., why would he offer her a role in one of his films?"

Charlie had no answer. Too much of it was still conjecture.

Grace let out a hard breath. "So, let's recap: we've got proof Marcus was innocent. Proof Paul, Harper, and a mysterious CC framed him. And maybe the reason Marcus and Rebecca ended up dead. But our starting point—the big one, Paul's murder?"

Her eyes were fixed on the screen in front of her.

"That mystery's still wide open."

Chapter 41

L ife was shit.

Bob Malone didn't say it out loud, but it throbbed inside him like a second heartbeat.

He sat at a faded red plastic table outside a hole-in-the-wall Mexican joint on Whittier Boulevard, carnitas tacos still steaming in their paper wrap.

They were good—better than good. Maybe the best he'd ever had. Cheap, too. The kind of perfect combination that kept places like this alive.

In L.A., it paid to know the right spots, and this one was the real thing—owned and run by Mexicans who knew exactly what they were doing.

However, even the best carnitas in the city couldn't sweeten the taste of his life.

That, he knew, was rotten to the core.

He wasn't so much a man walking the streets of L.A. as a shadow dragging itself along—proof that no matter where he went, the stink of failure followed.

Life was shit. He told himself that often.

But sometimes, rarely, you stumble into something else.

A moment of joy. Love. Passion. The cry of a new-born son. The kiss of a beloved wife. Fleeting, fragile things.

He hadn't touched anything like that in ten years.

And when one of those moments came, you held it close.

You savored it.

Because you never knew when the next one would show up—or if it ever would.

He'd seen the headline on his cracked phone earlier that morning:

PAUL MAX FOUND DEAD IN SUSPECTED EXECUTION

Bob laughed out loud. Drew a few looks from nearby tables, but he didn't care.

He had carnitas in his hand, an ice-cold Modelo Especial sweating on the table, and the best news he'd heard in years.

Paul Max. Golden boy. Box office king. Academy darling.

And a liar. A traitor. A killer.

That smug bastard finally got what was coming.

Paul had forgotten where he came from.

Forgotten who built the foundation under his feet before he ran off to the hills, rebranded himself, and started living like a god.

He didn't just forget Bob. He forgot Rebecca. Marcus. All of them.

But he hadn't only forgotten.

He had done worse.

Paul killed Rebecca Fontaine.

And Marcus O'Brien? Maybe Paul didn't put the bottle in his hand, but he pushed him hard enough that he drank himself into the grave.

And now—now Paul was executed.

A little justice. At last.

He finished the taco, wiped his fingers on a napkin, and crushed the paper into a tight ball before tossing it into a nearby trash bin.

Across the street, his Toyota Prius waited—his lifeline, his one steady source of income.

The acting gigs still came now and then, but the pay was a joke.

Sometimes he was hired for parties, playing a role no one remembered.

Uber rides didn't pay much, but they paid just enough to keep the lights on in his one-bedroom in Boyle Heights.

Barely.

He slid into the driver's seat and drove back home.

Work was done for the day.

Tomorrow would come soon enough, and he needed an early start.

His left turn signal blinked too fast—a bulb going out. He made a mental note to fix it.

Bob's home was a one-bedroom in a tired old building—stucco peeling, rust crawling over the mailboxes—apartment 5B. Top floor.

The hallway reeked of weed and lemon cleaner, a mix that clung to the walls.

His key stuck a little in the lock—like it always did—before finally turning.

He stepped inside and shut the door behind him.

Cooler in here. Thank God for window units.

Bob dropped the work bag onto the kitchen counter—the same beat-up thing he carried on his routes, stuffed with tools, spare batteries, and whatever else he might need.

He took off his shoes, left them where they fell, and headed for the bathroom.

A quick shower, then bed.

Then Bob stopped.

Something was wrong.

He didn't know what exactly—just that tingle along the back of his neck, that whisper in his bones that said: *you're not alone.*

He turned slowly.

The apartment looked the same.

Couch with a blanket draped over the side.

Coffee table with an old script half-highlighted.

A stack of headshots he hadn't updated in five years.

But something felt off.

He'd never had trouble in this apartment. Sure, sometimes a couple screaming through thin walls, a fistfight breaking out in the stairwell—but nothing that ever touched him.

Robbery? Pointless. No one around here had a damn thing worth taking.

Most of the neighbors barely scraped by on minimum wage.

The rest hustled—drugs, tricks, whatever kept the lights on.

Who in their right mind would rob Bob Malone? Ridiculous.

But the thought, the feeling, wouldn't let go.

What he'd been laughing about, just minutes ago—Paul, murdered. Executed.

And now Bob... Bob was the last one standing.

The last surviving Red Stage founder.

A chill slid down his spine.

Was it a coincidence? Or was someone working their way through the names, one after another, until they all disappeared?

His laughter dried up.

Suddenly, the silence in the apartment felt louder than the shouts in the hall ever had.

And even the shadows weren't right.

He reached for the hallway switch.

Click.

Nothing.

That's when it hit him. The wrongness. The sudden, hollow drop in his gut. Fear crawled up his spine, sharp and cold.

"Who's there?" he whispered. His voice cracked, too thin, too quiet.

Silence.

Then movement.

From the corner of the room, near the window.

A figure stepped forward. Slowly. Like he'd been watching for a while.

Bob didn't move.

Didn't breathe.

Chapter 42

Finding Bob Malone wasn't hard.

The man had tried to vanish, yes—but not well.

He wasn't a professional at disappearing.

He looked more like someone desperate to outrun his past, to put distance between himself and the weight of old wounds.

It wasn't the careful vanishing of someone trained. It was clumsy. Human.

He didn't want to erase himself.

Jack Taylor knew the type—men who just wanted to start over.

He went by James Malone now. Cute. Same middle name. Same birthday. Same credit trail—just buried under gig apps and a PO box still tied to his old talent agent.

That alone was telling.

He didn't want to forget or erase his past. He wanted pieces of it within reach.

Maybe he thought some part of it was still useful. Probably just to keep his pathetic acting career on life support.

But that made him easy.

Easier than Jack expected.

People who really vanish—they cut clean. No loose ends. No nostalgia.

They kill the old name, bury the trail, and pick something forgettable.

A common name. A bland history.

Then they move halfway across the country and live like ghosts.

Those are the hard ones.

Unless you find the helpers. Or the family. That's when you squeeze. You send a message. Brutal, clear. If they don't talk, you go after the kids.

That's the rule: no links. No exceptions.

Jack remembered a guy once—caught him just as he was watching his little girl walk into school. That was his mistake. That was what gave him away.

Jack smiled when he traced it. People like Bob thought the world had forgotten them.

But the internet never forgets. And somewhere, there's always someone who remembers.

And Jack? Jack knew how to find them.

The apartment was a crumbling one-bedroom unit in Boyle Heights—apartment 5B.

End of the hall. Paint peeling from the doorframe. The kind of place dreams came to die.

Perfect.

It was the place Bob came to die.

Funny thing about men like him—men who spent years wishing for an end to their misery. When death finally brushed close, they always chose the lousy life instead.

That's the rule. No matter how rotten, how empty, how sick and broken—people cling to it. Paycheck to paycheck. Alone. Defeated.

Because when it comes down to it, we're all scared shitless of dying.

Jack waited until late afternoon, when the building thinned out.

A broken buzzer at the side door let him in. He picked the lock in under ten seconds—one of his oldest talents—and slipped into the stale apartment like smoke.

Logically, these apartments had lousy security, if any.

Some tenants bolted on metal doors, barred their windows, and tried to make a fortress out of rot.

Not Bob.

He had a regular lock—a cheap one, easy to snap—and nothing else.

He lived like a man convinced no one cared, like he had nothing worth stealing, nothing worth fearing.

The apartment smelled like microwaved beans and despair. Probably some bourbon.

A cheap place filled with cheaper furniture—sad, depressing.

But Jack gave Bob this much: it was tidy. Relatively clean. Maybe he spent his empty hours scrubbing, folding, keeping order where he could.

In Jack's eyes, that meant Bob wasn't completely lost.

The couch was secondhand. So was the mattress. Even the shelves looked salvaged, but Bob had filled them with books.

Real books.

Not dime-store mysteries or crumpled pulp, but solid reads—most of them secondhand, all of them worn, pages bent from use.

Another surprise. Bob kept his mind fed.

Who was he, really? A loser? Or just a man crushed by bad luck?

Someone who made one mistake too big to crawl back from.

Jack didn't touch a thing. Not yet. His professional rule was simple—leave as little a trace as possible.

Be a ghost, if you could.

He found the spot he wanted—a dark corner by the window, half-shadowed by broken blinds—and unpacked his tools: chloroform, cloth, the blade, plastic sheeting, gloves.

He also killed the hall light—darkness gave him the edge, and with it, the element of surprise.

He was good at waiting. Had been since childhood.

He sat in the dark and listened. The hum of the fridge. The whirr of a distant AC unit. Sirens somewhere far off. Minutes turned into nearly an hour.

Then—tires on asphalt.

A door slam.

Footsteps on the stairwell. Keys jangling. A door unlocking.

Jack tensed, breath slowing.

Bob stepped inside. The door clicked shut. He dropped a bag on the kitchen counter, muttering under his breath. He looked rattled—like a man dragging something heavy in his head.

He stopped mid-step. Froze. Suspicious? Jack hadn't touched a thing. He shouldn't know.

Bob edged toward the hall switch. Click. Nothing. Dead.

He lingered there, caught between moving forward or backing out.

"Who's there?" His voice cracked, thin in the silence.

Shit. He couldn't see him, but he knew. Knew someone was there—waiting in the dark.

Jack didn't wait anymore.

He moved. Quick. Quiet.

Two steps, and the cloth was over Bob's mouth—strong arms yanking him back into the room before he could even gasp.

Jack moved fast, merciless.

Bob thrashed, but Jack was stronger.

Always had been. Always would be.

Thirty seconds.

Then stillness.

Jack laid him down gently, like tucking a child in.

He stood over Bob, heart calm, pulse steady.

Plastic crinkled as Jack began to wrap him.

And then—

Knock. Knock.

The sound cracked through the room like thunder.

Jack froze.

Another knock.

Louder. Sharper. Impatient.

Chapter 43

Becky Fletcher sat in her car, engine off, windows cracked open to let in the dry Los Angeles air.

The street was dim, quiet. Just east of Boyle Heights, where the city forgot to gentrify.

Rows of worn stucco buildings leaned into the evening breeze; their surfaces cracked like old skin.

The kind of place where hope faded behind drawn blinds and no one asked questions after dark.

She glanced at her phone. 7:38 PM. A string of unread messages blinked from Grace, Mona, and even Jim.

She thought about calling Grace now—just to check in, maybe talk it through.

But no. Not the right moment.

Grace would ask questions she wasn't ready to answer yet. Not until she saw him.

Not until she heard it from Bob Malone himself.

She would call her tomorrow. Maybe they could have breakfast together.

Yes—that was a good idea. She'd call later, invite her out, and then they would finally have time to talk about all of this.

The notebook on her passenger seat was filled with scribbled fragments. Arrows. Names.

Doodles from the plane ride that hinted at theories she wasn't yet brave enough to voice. All roads pointed back to Red Stage.

Marcus O'Brien. Rebecca Fontaine. Paul Max. Now Bob Malone.

The last one alive.

Finding Bob hadn't been as easy as she thought. He was living under a different name—James Malone—in a forgettable apartment complex.

But Jim Bamford had helped.

He'd put people to work, digging through legal databases, and finally sent her the confirmation. A blurry cell phone photo came attached.

This is him, the message read. *Pulled from his DMV renewal. Be careful.*

Becky stared at the image again.

Time had weathered Bob Malone. Wrinkles deepened around the eyes, jaw sagged slightly, but there was no mistaking the face.

The same one she'd seen in old Red Stage programs.

The same one behind Paul in that forgotten photo.

At 7:52, a Toyota Prius rolled up the block.

Becky straightened.

This could be the moment of truth—the one she'd been waiting for since landing in L.A. a couple of hours ago.

She needed to talk to Bob.

To find out what he knew. And maybe to warn him that a potential serial killer was on the loose, targeting the remaining Red Stage members.

The driver stepped out, a Dodgers cap pulled low over his face, a bag in one hand.

He gave the street a quick glance before heading inside.

That was him. Bob Malone. The last survivor of Red Stage.

He looked fine—leaner than she'd imagined. Not overweight, not run-down. Still keeping himself in shape.

Was he still chasing the movies? Still holding out hope that one day the phone might ring, his agent's voice on the other end with a sudden role?

A flicker of doubt cut through her resolve. What if Bob *was* the serial killer?

He'd had bad blood with Paul ever since Rebecca. Could Paul's murder have been a delayed revenge?

And if Paul really had killed Rebecca... maybe that was Bob's motive to kill him.

How would he react if a reporter showed up at his door, talking about serial killers?

Shit. She hadn't thought this through.

She could be walking straight into the wolf's mouth.

Becky forced herself to breathe. She was here. She couldn't back out now.

And the odds of Bob being the killer? Minimal.

She had to believe that. She had her pepper spray in her bag.

If things turned ugly, she'd use it. And she'd keep herself near the door—always.

Decision made. She was going through with this.

Becky waited a minute. Then another.

Finally, she pushed the door open and stepped out, her heart tapping against her ribs.

This was it. No turning back now.

She crossed the street, notebook clutched like a shield, and made her way up the steps to his apartment.

The hallway smelled like grease and old carpet. Some lime. Apartment 5B.

She knocked.

No answer.

She tried again. Harder this time.

Still nothing.

But she'd watched him go in—just moments ago. Could he already be in the shower? That fast? She hadn't given him the time.

Her brow furrowed. She glanced around. The hall was quiet. Too quiet.

She reached for the doorknob on instinct—and felt it turn.

Unlocked.

A knot formed in her stomach.

"Bob?" she tried, gently pushing the door.

The room was dim. The blinds half-drawn.

And then she saw it.

A man. Bob. On the floor. Face pale, barely conscious, limbs twisted awkwardly. Covered in some type of plastic.

And someone crouched over him.

Another man. Wearing black, a ski mask, and gloves. Broad shoulders. He looked up.

Their eyes locked.

Becky couldn't scream, couldn't run—the man in black was on her before she even had the chance to react.

She tried to spin, but he was too fast. Her bag slid from her shoulder, thudding to the floor. The pepper spray tumbled out, rolling toward the center of the room.

A hand clamped around her arm—iron-strong, unshakable. The other smothered her mouth, cutting off her scream before it could rise.

She fought—kicked, twisted—but he was stronger.

His weight crashed into her, knocking her against the doorframe.

She gasped as pain spiked down her ribs and extended to her arm, face, and back.

She clawed at his face, nails raking skin.

He jerked, and she was sure she'd caught one of his eyes badly.

Then everything tilted.

Darkness slammed into her like a wave.

And she was gone.

Chapter 44

Shit. Shit. Shit.

Jack Taylor's pulse hammered in his temples. His hands itched.

This—this right here—was why he hated unplanned situations.

He lived by routine. Clean prep. Timed exits. No variables. No mess.

And now he couldn't see out of one eye. Blood was leaking down his cheek, hot and sticky.

He grabbed gauze from his kit, pressed it hard against the wound, and fixed it in place with a strip of bandage and a couple of Band-Aids—an ugly, improvised patch.

Crude, but it would hold. For now.

His vision was limited, but the bigger problem lay at his feet: a variable he hadn't planned for. A young woman sprawled unconscious on the floor beside Bob Malone.

She wasn't supposed to be here.

And worst of all—he had no idea who the hell she was, or why she was here.

A friend of Bob's, maybe.

This was a real mess.

He paced the room once, then twice. The apartment stank of stale takeout and nerves. Bob was still breathing—shallow, ragged, but steady enough.

The sedative would keep him down for a few more minutes, maybe.

He'd have to dose him again soon.

But the woman... her breathing had already changed.

Shit again. He needed to move—fast—before she woke.

He crouched and pawed through her purse. Wallet. Phone. Notebook.

Becky Fletcher.

His gut twisted.

The goddamn reporter.

The one writing the story about Paul Max.

The one clawing at Marcus's grave.

She'd been in Boise yesterday. Back already.

Right in his hands now.

Jack's jaw tightened until it hurt. This wasn't just bad luck—it was a grenade with the pin pulled.

He looked at Becky sprawled on the floor, hair fanned across the carpet. For a second, he almost admired the irony.

He'd been hunting her—and she'd walked straight into him.

Maybe someone had whispered Bob Malone's name, maybe just instinct. Either way, her reporter's nose had led her here. She was good. Too good for her own sake.

Now he had a problem.

A beautiful, fragile problem.

And Jack only knew one way to solve problems.

Eliminate them.

Becky was no exception.

But first, Bob. He was supposed to move him, drag him to a quieter place, break him apart for answers, then report back—and only then finish him.

That plan was already gone.

He pushed to his feet, his one good eye sweeping the apartment, calculating.

Ten minutes, maybe fifteen, before someone walked by or got curious.

If the neighbors had half a brain, he was already behind.

He'd have to make a call, see if a change of plans would stick.

But deep down he knew—there wasn't one.

Both of them would have to be dealt with here. No other option.

And first—Becky.

The order hadn't changed. Yesterday it was her. Today it was still her. She'd be the first to go.

That's when she moved.

A twitch. A groan. Then suddenly she was up—stumbling, half-dazed, but moving.

Becky bolted toward the door.

"Goddammit!" Jack hissed, lunging.

He caught her before she reached the hallway, slamming her into the side wall with a dull thud.

She let out a cry but kept fighting, kicking wildly.

She reached for something—a lamp? No.

A small metal statue from a side table. She turned and swung it fast.

Crack.

Pain shot through his jaw. The world tilted. He staggered, stumbled back two steps. Saw red.

She ran again.

Jack recovered just enough to dive. His hand latched onto her ankle just as she flung the door open.

With a grunt, he yanked her backward, sending her crashing to the floor.

He kicked the door shut with his heel and shoved her across the room, toward Bob's limp body. She sprawled out, gasping.

Enough of this, thought Jack.

No more hesitation. No more screw-ups.

Jack stepped toward her, raising the statue she'd smashed against him. He turned it in his hand, weighing it. Cold metal. Heavy. Perfect. He'd end it now. Kill her.

Worry about the cleanup later.

Becky's eyes locked on his. No begging. Just raw defiance.

Jack couldn't help but admire her strength. Was she truly unafraid—or was something else at play?

But then—her gaze shifted. Just for a second. He couldn't react in time.

Jack saw Becky raising the pepper spray, aimed straight at his one good eye, and fired.

Jack roared, vision exploding in fire.

Still, he clung to the statue, slashing blindly through the air.

Becky staggered back, but he drove her toward the wall, closing the gap.

He knew he had to finish it—end this fast.

Neutralize her before she struck again.

Before anyone else showed up.

Pain seared through his eye—white, pulsing—but he fought it, desperate to see.

And then—something. Through the blur, Jack caught Becky's gaze shift over his shoulder. Her eyes widened, sharp with shock.

A voice on his back ripped through the room.

"Police! Drop it!"

Jack spun, half-blind, the world smeared in shapes and shadows. A figure filled the doorway, gun raised and steady.

He didn't drop the statue. Couldn't. No more uniforms in sight.

His only chance was to strike first. Jack lunged, statue raised high.

He moved—fast.

Straight for the shadow in the doorway.

Chapter 45

Grace Fletcher didn't mind silence.

Not Charlie's. Not Mona's. Not anyone else's. But Becky's? Becky's silence she couldn't stand.

She'd called three times that morning. No response. Texted. Nothing.

A few hours ago, she'd called Jim Bamford—Becky's editor at *The Hollywood Star*—again.

"Grace? Hi. We're talking a lot these days," he said, his voice tight with concern.

"Hi, Jim. I don't want to bother you, but I need to know where Becky is. I heard she just got back from Idaho, and I have reason to believe she might be in danger."

"Shit, I did not know," he said. "She called from the airport, asked me to get an address—someone named Bob Malone. Said he's the last surviving Red Stage cofounder. We found it and texted it to her maybe an hour ago. She's probably on her way there now."

"Send me that address. Now."

"I'm sorry—I thought you knew. She seemed calm. I don't think she believes she's in any trouble."

Of course she didn't.

Classic Becky—charging into the unknown with a notebook in her bag and danger in her blind spot.

The irony was that she was smart.

Sharp enough to smell news from a mile away.

Sharp enough to recognize risk when it was staring her down.

But for some reason, she acted like she was invincible. Or maybe she just believed nothing would ever happen to her. And that's why she moved in reckless ways.

Grace didn't waste another second. She grabbed her keys, her sidearm, and flew out the door.

No more phone calls. No more waiting. It was time to act.

She was going to find her sister.

On the drive to Bob Malone's apartment, Grace called Charlie.

Her knuckles were white on the steering wheel, jaw tight.

"Hi," Charlie answered.

"Charlie, I just spoke with Jim Bamford—Becky's editor. He says she's on her way to see Bob Malone."

"What? That's dangerous!"

"I know. Do you have his address?"

"Yes. We got it today."

"Good. Stop whatever you're doing and meet me there. And bring backup." The city blurred past her windows.

"On my way. See you in a few."

Night dropped hard over L.A., city lights flaring to life like sparks on a fuse.

Grace blew through red lights, engine snarling, tires spitting over cracked asphalt. She cut through alleys without slowing.

Every turn hammered her pulse faster. Every block felt like borrowed time.

Becky was in trouble. Again.

And this time, Grace had a bad feeling it wouldn't just be close.

It would be *too* close.

Grace parked half a block away, engine ticking as it cooled. She slid out of the car, shutting the door softly, quietly, like the night itself.

The street was dim, a patchwork of shadows and sodium glow.

Old stucco buildings, peeling paint, and iron balconies that hadn't been safe in twenty years. Somewhere down the block, a dog barked and then went silent.

She walked fast, her shoes tapping against the cracked pavement, eyes scanning the building numbers.

Her pulse picked up with every step.

No sign of Charlie. Not yet.

So, she was on her own.

Because she had to move now.

The apartment complex where Bob Malone lived was old, low-rent.

Quiet—but not the kind of quiet that felt peaceful. Cracked sidewalks. Peeling railings. Windows patched with foil.

A place where people disappeared without anyone asking why.

Becky's car sat beneath a wide oak tree. Shaded. Still.

Too still.

Then she saw her—Becky—walking toward one of the units. Alone. Focused.

Reckless.

Grace picked up her pace, her hand near her holster.

Becky knocked. Waited. Knocked again.

Then—typical Becky—she tried the doorknob.

It opened.

She stepped inside.

Grace's stomach dropped. She screamed Becky's name, but there was no answer. Not from this distance.

She drew her Glock.

And ran.

Straight for 5B.

When she reached the door, it was shut tight—but noise bled through. Thuds. A crash. A muffled shout. A fight.

Grace didn't hesitate. She slipped inside, low and fast, gun raised.

The smell hit her first—sweat, stale bourbon, a sharp tang of metal.

And then—she saw it.

Becky was pressed against the far wall, terrified.

A man loomed over her—tall, dressed in black, a statue raised mid-swing.

Behind him, another figure lay on the floor, half-wrapped in plastic, barely conscious.

Becky's eyes locked on Grace's, wide with recognition.

Grace didn't think.

"Police! Drop it!" she barked.

The man turned. One eye hidden under a patch. Vision compromised.

But he didn't drop the statue.

He lunged at her, swinging hard.

Grace fired. Once.

Then again.

The statue slipped from his grip, clattering to the floor.

His body twisted, then collapsed face-first into the carpet—right at Grace's feet.

A beat of silence.

Then, from outside, the rising wail of sirens—police cars closing in.

The first thing Grace did was run to her sister and pull her into a hug.

Becky was crying silently against her shoulder.

Grace wanted to scream at her—shake her for being so reckless—but instead she just held on. Held on tight. Held on long.

When Charlie arrived seconds later, they were still locked together. He went straight to Bob Malone, cutting away the plastic as the man groggily stirred from sedation.

Another uniform knelt beside the man in black, trying to stanch the blood pouring from him.

The ambulance pulled up outside, blue and red lights flooding the street.

Chapter 46

Becky looked pale, but steady. A faint bruise bloomed along her cheekbone.

She sipped orange juice from a paper cup, seated stiffly in a vinyl chair in the hospital's hallway.

Grace stood beside her. Arms crossed. Jaw clenched.

Becky glanced up, then away. "I'm sorry," she said, voice small. "I didn't think something like this would happen."

Of course not, Grace thought. *You never do.*

"You could've died," Grace said, voice low, steady. "You were fighting for your life. He was about to kill you."

Becky winced but stayed silent.

The pause stretched. Fluorescent lights hummed overhead. Somewhere down the hall, a monitor beeped. A nurse passed by, shoes squeaking, clipboard in hand.

"How did you know I was there?" Becky asked at last.

"I called your editor," Grace said. Her eyes didn't waver. "At least *he* answers my calls."

Becky looked away. "Well... you got there just in time."

Grace nodded. "Yeah. Just in time."

Another silence. Tighter this time.

Grace took a slow breath. "Becky, I'm going to say this once, and calmly—but you cannot ignore my calls. You need to tell me where you're going. You need to stop—" She paused. "—acting so irresponsibly."

Becky's shoulders stiffened. "I'm not a child."

"Then stop acting like one."

Becky opened her mouth, closed it. Looked down at her juice.

"I'm sorry," she whispered. "I'll change. I promise."

Grace didn't answer. She'd heard that one before.

Instead, she exhaled and shifted the conversation.

"Becky, what matters is that you're OK—*miraculously*. Let's change the subject. So... Idaho. How was it?"

Becky's expression softened. "It was good. Intense. I met Marcus O'Brien's daughter. Lisa. And her boyfriend, Mark—he's a detective with Boise PD. They think Marcus was murdered."

"Why?" she asked, keeping her tone steady, her expression calm. She'd wait—just a little longer—before revealing what she knew: Marcus was innocent.

What she wanted now was to see if the Boise detective had anything solid. Anything that could prove Marcus hadn't just died—he'd been murdered.

"They did an unofficial autopsy. Found signs of injected medical-grade ethanol. Nothing conclusive without toxicology, but enough to raise questions. No one's taking it seriously. But Lisa and Mark are convinced."

Grace let that sink in. "Interesting. If we assume Marcus was killed... that makes two murders and one so-called accident. Paul, Marcus. And Rebecca."

"Right."

Grace looked at her sister. "Tell me everything else you know."

Becky hesitated. Then nodded.

"I think they're all connected through Red Stage," she said. "Marcus went to prison for embezzlement. But Lisa swears the documents were faked. Their accountant—Tom Harper—disappeared after the trial. So, Lisa doesn't have proof."

Grace's eyes narrowed. "We found proof the embezzlement case was fabricated."

Becky sat up straighter. "What?"

"Yes. Someone, known only as CC, came up with the plan—so Paul could get out of the Red Stage contract that forced him to pay up to fifty percent of his income for five years if he wanted to leave," Grace said.

"Tom Harper sent the evidence to Marcus. Marcus passed it to Rebecca. And before she died, Rebecca forwarded it to her mother, who never opened it. We just did. Pages of documents. Letters. Copies. All of it."

Becky's eyes widened, her voice sharp. "You're serious?"

"Yes. And here's the working theory." Grace's voice dropped, quieter. "Marcus confronted Paul. Maybe threatened to go public. Paul killed him—to silence him. But not before Marcus mailed the evidence to Rebecca. Which means she knew—five years ago."

Becky's brow furrowed. "Then what?"

"This part's twisted. Rebecca probably knew about Marcus's death—maybe even suspected it was murder. But instead of going to the police, she used the information as leverage," Grace said. "She might've believed Paul still liked her, that he wouldn't touch her. We don't know.

What we do know is she got a role in *Silent Sun*—blackmail, essentially. But eventually they had a serious falling-out. That's in the court transcripts from Paul's trial."

"So, he killed her?"

"We think so. But we don't have concrete proof. Except for a note."

"A note?" Becky asked.

"Right. The one Rebecca left for her mother. She wrote that Paul killed Marcus. She was afraid. And then she died."

Becky leaned back in her chair, staring at the floor. "So, Paul was a murderer..."

"He fooled everyone. You included."

"I believed him when he said he didn't kill Rebecca."

Grace shrugged. "He was an actor—better than we gave him credit for. His whole life was just a role. None of it was real."

Becky didn't respond. To her, Paul hadn't seemed like he was acting—not at all. And if he was, then it wasn't performance. It was psychosis.

Grace added, "Charlie ran a check on the guy I shot today. Jack Taylor. Professional. A hitman. Military background, clean history, but with whispers in dark corners. He's still in intensive care, but the doctors say he'll make it."

"We'll talk to him?"

"As soon as he's stable in 2 or 3 days, according to the doctor. He may have answers."

Grace crossed her arms again, shifting her weight.

"We also found something else. Payments from Paul to Peppy La Font. Spread across several months, starting during the trial."

"Payments?"

"Alimony. But not from the original settlement. It came later—an amendment the Court granted during the trial. Our guess? He paid her to lie. To give him an alibi for the shooting."

Becky looked sick. "Jesus. So, he manipulated the trial too?"

"That's what it looks like. And it gets worse."

Becky didn't say anything.

"Otto Fisher's dead. Suicide—at first glance. They found incriminating web searches, stuff linking him to the death of a child. But we talked to the detectives on that case—doesn't add up. So, we're treating it as a homicide until proven otherwise. If it was a hit, it ties back either to Paul's murder... or to whoever's working to keep the truth buried."

Becky stared ahead. "So, Paul faked the embezzlement to get out of Red Stage and start his solo career. Then killed him to protect his image. Then killed Rebecca to protect his secret."

Grace nodded.

"But now Paul's dead."

"Right."

"Do we know who killed him?"

Grace shook her head. "No. Not yet."

The silence returned.

Becky whispered, "But if Paul's the one who started this... maybe someone's just trying to finish it."

Grace didn't answer.

"What about Bob Malone? How is he?" Becky asked.

"He's fine. I'll talk to him tomorrow, first thing in the morning."

"Bob may confirm the working theory."

"Yes, I think he will."

Chapter 47

Grace Fletcher hated hospitals. The quiet, the bleach-scrubbed walls, the way time slowed down. She preferred crime scenes—at least there, the silence had a reason.

She walked alongside Charlie Bonelli down a bright corridor. Early morning sunlight spilled through the windows, too cheerful for what they were about to discuss.

Becky had already been discharged and was resting at home.

But Bob Malone was still here, recovering from the attack.

They reached his room. Grace knocked once and pushed the door open.

"Good morning, Bob," she said.

He looked up from the hospital bed. Pale, bruised, but alive.

"It's bad," he said, trying to sit up straighter. "Sore all over. Still waiting on x-rays and a few scans, but the doctor said I'll be fine."

Charlie offered a nod. Grace stepped closer. "Glad to hear that."

Bob's voice softened. "Detective Fletcher... I just wanted to say thank you. You saved my life yesterday."

"You're welcome," Grace replied. "I was just doing my job. But yeah—it's good you're still with us."

A moment of silence passed.

"Now," Grace continued, shifting gears, "we have some questions. If you're up for it."

"Go ahead," Bob said, voice cautious.

"Did you know the embezzlement charge against Marcus O'Brien was fake?"

Bob blinked. "What? No. I remember Paul making the accusation. But the accountant—Tom Harper—presented documentation. It seemed legit."

"Marcus always said he was innocent," Charlie added.

Bob shrugged, wincing at the movement. "They all say that. I didn't think much of it. We all just... moved on."

"Did you keep in touch with your Red Stage colleagues after that?"

"Some of them, here and there. But the truth is, we hated Paul. Not because he was successful. We could've lived with that. It was the way he left us behind. He never looked back. Marcus took it the hardest, of course. In the last few years, I stopped talking to any of them. It just got depressing. The same conversations, the same old bitterness."

"Did Marcus or Rebecca ever tell you they were blackmailing Paul?"

"Only what you told me. No, they didn't say any-thing about that. I had no idea."

Grace crossed her arms. "Did you know Marcus had a daughter?"

"Barely. He mentioned her once. Lisa, I think. Never met her."

Charlie made a note. Grace leaned forward slightly.

"What was Red Stage really about, Bob?"

Bob exhaled slowly. "It started with a good idea. We were all struggling actors. We decided to pool our money into a shared account. To fund plays, short films, maybe even a feature. The idea was freedom—no bosses, no producers. Just us."

"And it worked?"

"For a while. We scraped together a few things. A small theater run. One terrible indie film. But then Paul started booking commercials. Bigger roles. And sud-denly the contract didn't feel so fair."

Grace nodded. "You had a clause, right?"

Bob nodded. "Five-year lock-in. Anyone who left early owed 50% of their income to the rest of the group. For five years. Harsh, maybe—but we all signed it. We all helped write it."

"Paul's first real success came one year after he left," Grace said. "It was the first production he signed with Peter Woodford's company. You think he left to avoid paying?"

"It wouldn't surprise me," Bob muttered. "He com-plained about the contract constantly. But legally, he was stuck. The only out was proving wrongdoing by another co-founder. That's when he pointed fingers at Marcus."

"And if the embezzlement was fabricated..." Charlie said.

"Now it makes sense. Then Paul used it to weasel out of the contract," Bob finished grimly. "And saved himself millions. We calculated once—as a joke—he probably owed us tens of millions based on his career earnings."

"So, Paul had motive," Grace said quietly. "To silence anyone who could expose him."

Bob looked away. "Yeah. I guess he did."

"But if that's true, Bob—who killed Paul?" Grace asked.

He shook his head. "I don't know. Maybe someone who found out what he did. Maybe revenge."

"Or," Grace said, "someone from Red Stage. Some-one who discovered the truth later—and wanted it all."

Bob turned sharply. "You're not suggesting me?"

Grace stayed calm. "You're the last one left. You were almost killed yesterday. Maybe it was self-de-fense. Maybe you knew too much."

Bob scoffed. "That's insane. First of all, I didn't know any of this until recently. And second—I'm not a killer."

Grace didn't reply. Just watched him.

"Look," Bob said, more forcefully. "If I wanted revenge, I wouldn't have waited this long. I hated Paul, sure. But not enough to kill him. I'd moved on."

Grace leaned against the wall, arms crossed. "Then who did this?"

Bob met her stare. "You tell me."

Charlie's eyes narrowed. "If someone had access to the evidence about the fake embezzlement—and wanted to use it for leverage—they'd need the competition out of the way."

"Meaning?" Bob asked.

"Meaning," Charlie said, "maybe they killed Marcus and Rebecca. Then went after Paul."

"To take it all," Grace murmured.

Bob shrugged. "It's a theory. One that doesn't involve me."

"Except," Charlie added, "you're the only one who nearly ended up dead and lived to talk about it."

Bob leaned forward, his voice edged with frustration. "It doesn't work like that. Sure—logically—it might make sense to kill Marcus and Rebecca, then use the Red Stage contract and the accountant's proof to sue Paul. That way, yeah, you could chase the money without sharing it."

He paused, looking from one detective to the other.

"But why kill Paul? Killing him now just complicates everything. His estate gets tied up in probate. Lawyers. Delays. If this was about money, it was a terrible move."

"Unless you were afraid he'd kill you first," Charlie said.

Bob scoffed. "If I'd killed Marcus and Rebecca, what would I be afraid of? That Paul would come after me for something he didn't know I had? Makes no sense."

He took a breath. "Now, if Paul killed Rebecca? Fine. That's a theory. But then, who killed Marcus? Me? For the evidence I didn't even know existed until yesterday?"

Charlie tilted his head. "What if Paul killed both Marcus and Rebecca to stop the blackmail. Then he came for you. Something happened. You fought back. Killed him. Wrote 'murderer' on his chest."

Bob blinked. "So let me get this straight. I didn't have the evidence. Didn't know about it. But I killed him in advance? Before he could maybe kill me? That's the theory?"

He let the silence linger. "I would've gone to the police. He'd already been on trial for killing Rebecca. I had leverage—don't you see?"

Grace watched him carefully. He was sweating, but not panicked. Not dodging.

His eyes stayed locked on hers—clear, steady.

And deep down, she knew it.

He didn't have the proof.

He didn't have the leverage.

Which meant—he didn't have a reason to kill anyone.

Not for the money, anyway.

Chapter 48

"Did you kill Otto?" Peter Woodford asked flatly.

Silence.

He stood by the window of his office, watching the city blur beneath the morning haze. He hadn't slept.

Police questions had swallowed the night before—first his statement about finding the body, then an endless barrage about Otto, Paul, and everyone orbiting them.

By the time they were finished, he was drained. Hollow. Exhausted.

Then CC's voice, sharp as glass. "I'm getting tired of your calls. And your stupid questions."

Peter didn't blink. "It's not stupid if it's true."

"For the record," she snapped, "I don't owe you a damn thing. But no—I did not kill Otto."

Peter exhaled slowly, though nothing in him relaxed.

His hand clenched the windowsill.

He knew something had happened years ago—something critical—when Otto first started working for Paul.

He never learned what it was, but it mattered.

Paul had been rattled then, spiraling into panic attacks.

CC had stepped in, coordinated something with Otto, and days later... calm.

The storm vanished. Life went on.

But Peter knew better. Something had happened—something Otto carried.

Now Otto was dead. Shot in his own bed. A supposed suicide. But Peter didn't believe that. Not for a second. It was too clean. Too timely.

And only one person stood to gain from Otto's disappearance. Someone who couldn't risk him talking. Someone who didn't trust his silence. Someone who needed a loose end cut—permanently.

"You were close to him," Peter said, voice quieter now. "He trusted you."

"That's rich," CC replied. "Everyone trusted Otto. And yet somehow you ended up with the money."

"That transfer was arranged through him. I wanted to make sure everything was handled legally."

"No," she hissed. "You just wanted to make sure you got paid. That's all you care about—money."

She let the words hang, then added, colder: "Look, Peter, I don't like you—you know that. But I'm a professional. The transfer's predated, every digital trace wiped. You're clean. And I've already taken my cut. So, stop bothering me with this."

Peter didn't argue. It was true enough.

The money had come in, and within minutes, he'd cleared the debts that had been strangling him.

For the moment, he was fine.

The numbers kept climbing, and the movie was shaping up to be a success.

Without Paul Max, the future would look different—he knew that.

But at least now, he had time to think about it.

But even money wasn't worth what this was turning into.

Fine—assume the transfer wouldn't raise alarms.

Otto was still dead. Should he go to the police? Or keep his mouth shut?

Truth was, he didn't know much. Something had gone down, sure, but he couldn't say what—or even if it was illegal.

Maybe not.

What he did know was that whenever CC had her hands on a problem, the "solution" was, at best, crooked.

Still, he had nothing concrete.

Which meant the smartest move was to forget it.

Leave Otto in the ground, and keep clear of CC.

But something else gnawed at him.

"The police know about Red Stage," he said.

"I know," she said, her voice cool again. Too cool. "I have contacts. I'm aware."

"What do we do?"

"We?" Her voice dripped with disdain. "There is no we, Peter. You sit tight and pretend you know nothing. Because you don't. That's your specialty."

"CC, the police will dig into Red Stage. They'll find out. We'll be implicated."

"There are only two people who know what happened—you and me. So, keep your mouth shut."

"Fine. But what if they track down Tom Harper?"

"I'm taking care of that."

And then—nothing more. Silence. Classic CC.

Tom was the only other person who could explain what he'd done with Paul and CC. But he'd vanished ten years ago—no trace, no word.

Best case, he was already dead.

Worst case, the police found him. And if they did, they were both finished.

Peter rubbed his forehead, a headache creeping behind his eyes.

He hated this—being in the dark.

Dependent on someone like CC to steer the storm.

And she was the storm, whether she admitted it or not.

Peter knew the police would uncover his link to the Red Stage embezzlement.

Paul, CC, and Tom—the accountant—had handled it directly.

He hadn't taken part. Not exactly. But he knew.

And if things spiraled, knowledge alone could make him an accomplice.

He'd spoken to Peppy La Font earlier.

She was already bringing in her lawyers. Said she wasn't willing to risk it.

The detectives had grilled her hard, dragging everything back to Paul's trial and the accident with Rebecca Fontaine.

They were pointing fingers in every direction.

No way to know what they'd ask next—or why.

She didn't want to be misinterpreted, didn't want her words twisted.

Peter realized he needed to start thinking the same way. Up until now, he'd been far too candid with the police.

That had to change. He needed to be smarter.

"They caught the guy who went after Bob Malone," Peter said. "And the reporter—Becky Fletcher—was there. She's been asking too many questions, and she almost paid for it. The police shot him."

"And?" CC pressed.

"He's alive. The hitman. Intensive care. Stable, they say. He'll wake up soon, CC—in a day or two."

A beat of silence.

Peter pushed. "Who is he, CC?"

"I have no idea."

Chapter 49

Matt McGregor showed up twenty minutes early. After months of trying, he wasn't about to blow this.

Grace Fletcher had finally said yes. Dinner. A real date.

Mario's Cantina wasn't exactly central—it was tucked away in Brentwood—but Matt loved it. The food, the low hum of conversation, the little patio strung with lights, candles glowing under the trees.

He couldn't think of a better place for a first date.

He still remembered the first time he'd seen her—almost ten months back, in the courthouse halls. He'd just been torn apart by a prosecutor, blindsided by his own client, and all he wanted was a stiff drink and a hole to crawl into.

He stormed out of the courtroom and collided head-on with her.

They both went down.

"What the hell—watch where you're going!" she snapped from the ground.

He lifted his head, ready to bark back. Then he saw her. Blonde hair cropped short, part of it falling across vivid green eyes. Tall, athletic, black leather jacket, jeans. Beautifully angry.

His tongue refused to work. "Bbb...mm..."

"What? Spit it out."

He finally managed, "I'm...sorry. Let me—" He helped her up. "You okay?"

"I'm fine," she shot back, brushing herself off. Then she disappeared into a courtroom.

Twenty minutes later, he was waiting at the door. When she came out, he held out peace offerings: a coffee and a donut.

She arched a brow. "Really? A donut? To a cop?"

"Cliché, I know," he grinned.

Her lips quirked.

"My dad was a cop. Breakfast was always black coffee and donuts," he said.

She took them both.

"Tough childhood."

"You have no idea. Sometimes they forced me to eat dessert."

She smiled then—an honest, disarming smile—and they walked outside together. Talked. Names exchanged. She told him about her sister. Old movies. *Casablanca*, *Witness for the Prosecution*.

Then her phone rang mid-sentence. Work. Always work. She walked off with a quick thanks and a laugh about the donut.

After that, chance meetings. A few texts. Good conversations. But never a date. Always her family. Or her job. Always something.

Until tonight.

Now here she was, walking into the restaurant in a blue dress that knocked the air out of him. She saw him, smiled, crossed the room. They kissed hello. Sat.

"This is a great place," she said.

"The lasagna's phenomenal," he replied.

The waiter came. They ordered. She followed his lead and chose the lasagna, like him. He suggested a Chianti— "House rule," he joked. "You order lasagna, you drink Chianti. We're practically in Italy."

She smiled, agreeing.

They talked easily. Life in general. Friends. Grace mentioned that Mona loved the spiritual world. He asked if she shared the same interest. "No," she admitted, "but I let her have it."

He told her about his small law office with a partner. Not glamorous, but steady.

They laughed about how she probably arrested some of his clients. The wine flowed. The food was good. The company even better.

Matt thought Grace was exactly who he'd imagined—unpretentious, funny, sharp, grounded.

When the tiramisu came, with a small glass of *limoncello*, he asked: "So, are you working on anything big? A famous case?"

"You could say that," Grace said. "Paul Max's murder."

"Wow." He leaned in. "That's as high profile as it gets. How's it going? Do you know who did it?"

Matt was genuinely impressed—and curious. Crime was his business, too, just from a different side.

Grace hesitated. "We've been working crazy hours. It's strange—we're nowhere near finding who killed him, but we did uncover... another side of him."

"Another side?"

"He had secrets. Old ones. Buried ones. He wasn't who he appeared to be on camera—or in life."

Matt grinned. "Now that's a hook. You can't just drop a line like that and expect me to sleep tonight."

Grace smiled. "Maybe it sounds more intriguing than it really is. Let's just say, we found links to old cases. Maybe two. Still confirming."

"Did he kill that actress—Rebecca Fontaine?"

"The jury's still out," Grace said quietly. "But I think he did. He had motive. She might've been blackmailing him."

"And someone killed him to even the score."

"Could be. We're still fitting the pieces."

"I heard about his assistant. Suicide?"

"Too many deaths around him for it to be that simple. Between you and me, I think it was murder. We've requested a full autopsy. My guess? Someone took him out because he knew something. Something big. And maybe he was ready to talk."

"Who's killing all these people?"

"We've got a key witness in the hospital. He should be ready to talk tomorrow. He may have the answers we need. So, park those questions for now. We might not have to wait long."

"In my experience, people with money don't kill directly. They hire someone to handle the dirty work. There's always a hand pulling the trigger—but someone else is always behind it."

Grace turned it over in her mind. Yes. That could explain why the act hadn't been linked to the main suspects. Someone else had been the fixer.

Her phone buzzed. Charlie.

"I'm sorry," she said, lifting it. "I have to take this."

Matt watched her face as she listened, reading the tension in her eyes. His gut told him the night was about to end.

"Okay. I'm on my way. Twenty minutes." She hung up, then turned back to him with the most apologetic smile he'd ever seen.

"Matt, I was having a great time. Really. But I have to go. It's a special operation."

"It's okay. Go. We were finishing anyway. I had a great time too."

She glanced at her glass. "Didn't even finish my limoncello. I'll call you, okay?"

And just like that, she was gone.

Leaving Matt more interested than ever.

Chapter 50

A car parked three blocks from Westwood General Hospital, headlights off, engine ticking as it cooled. Inside, a shadow waited. At last, a door opened, then shut softly.

The night was heavy, air pressed low. The streets were nearly deserted—just the occasional car whispering past, nothing more. Perfect.

The shadow started walking. Pale blue scrub top. Matching pants. White shoes. An ID badge clipped neatly to the chest—lifted from a real nurse two days ago.

A wig tucked under a disposable surgical cap.

Clipboard in hand, not clutched too tightly. Natural. Practiced.

The breeze carried the faint tang of asphalt and exhaust, but the walk itself was calm, almost pleasant.

No need to rush. Time was on the shadow's side. Each step measured, deliberate.

As the hospital grew nearer, light spilled from the ambulance bay—harsh fluorescents cutting through the dark.

A few paramedics milled about, one wheeling in a patient.

The waiting room, visible through the sliding glass doors, looked nearly empty.

At precisely 3:07 AM, the shadow crossed the threshold, slipping into the hospital through the ambulance entrance. Unseen. Unnoticed.

Hospitals at night are places of subdued motion.

Not the chaos of daytime, except in the ER.

The night shift was thinning. Hallways grew quiet, lights dimmed to spare energy—and nerves. Machines beeped in steady rhythms, comforting the sick, sedating the dying.

Just nurses gliding from room to room, checking charts, adjusting drips, offering a hand when needed.

For the most part, though, it was silence.

The shadow walked with purpose, but not haste.

Smiled if someone passed. Nurses are ghosts in hospitals—always there, rarely noticed.

The shadow had spent the last day buried in schematics, memorizing hallways, shifts, names. Watching the guards.

Tracking the nurses. Every move rehearsed, every risk weighed.

The plan was airtight. And yet time was slipping away.

One night—that was all. No chance to bring in help. No second window. This was it.

The one way to keep the risk at its lowest. The job had to be done now.

The shadow glided through the corridors of Westwood General Hospital like a practiced whisper. Past Pediatrics. Left at Recovery. Down a sterile hallway that smelled of bleach and plastic tubing. Room 412B.

Jack Taylor.

The name was there.

On the chart clipped neatly outside the door.

Same as in the hospital's visitor system—already checked, double-checked, three hours earlier through a terminal in the ER. No mistakes.

This was the room. This was the patient.

And this patient wasn't like the others. This one mattered. This one was important.

A uniformed officer stood posted outside, leaning against the wall, posture sagging with fatigue. The graveyard shift was always the same—long, dull, sleep pressing heavy against the eyes.

The shadow approached with practiced calm.

The disguise carried authority and the quiet confidence of someone who belonged.

The voice, when it came, was low, even, almost kind.

"Evening, officer. We just finished brewing some coffee in the kitchen. I can bring you a cup—just need to administer a pain reliever to the patient first."

The cop's face softened with relief. Human reflex. Gratitude. He straightened slightly, tried to look alert. His smile was small, tired, genuine.

"That'd be great. Thanks."

The shadow tilted the clipboard against the chest, head inclined just enough to appear casual.

"Don't mention it. Two minutes."

The officer nodded, already imagining the coffee.

The man inside, Jack Taylor, was in intensive care.

Bullet wounds. Sedated. Under observation.

But if he woke up—if he spoke—it would all come apart.

The shadow had come too far to let it fall apart now.

Jack knew too much—names, jobs, the past. All of it.

A single word from him could rip the whole operation wide open. Too much risk. Unacceptable.

Jack had to die.

Tonight.

One hand on the door handle.

A slow inhale.

A quiet twist.

The room was dark. Quiet. Machines beeped beside the bed.

The figure on the mattress was still, bandaged, face turned to the side, pale under the glow of the monitors.

The shadow stepped in, closed the door without a sound.

The shadow slipped a hand into the side pocket, fingers brushing cool metal.

A capped syringe. Inside, a thick amber solution. Succinylcholine.

One push and the lungs would lock; the heart would follow. No struggle. No sound. No second chance. Just silence.

The dose was measured—enough to finish the job and still leave time to walk away unnoticed.

Gloved fingers pulled the cap from the needle. It moved closer to the bed, careful not to cast a shadow on the face. The IV line was already in. All it had to do was insert the syringe and press.

The shadow leaned down.

But the moment the hand touched the line—

The lights snapped on.

Bright. Blinding.

The figure in the bed sat up like a puppet on a string, eyes flashing open—not glassy with sedation, but alert. Smiling.

Not Jack Taylor.

A cop.

"Gottcha," he said.

The shadow whirled—too late.

The room filled with sound and movement. Four plainclothes officers surged in through the side door.

Another two stepped in behind from the hallway. Guns raised. Calm, but ready.

One of them tackled the shadow before it could reach for the small blade taped to the thigh.

The shadow hit the ground hard. The syringe rolled under the bed.

Hands wrenched arms behind. The wig came loose. The cap fell.

The silence shattered as the door opened again—and she stepped in.

Detective Grace Fletcher. Cool. Controlled. Wearing her badge on a lanyard and a gun on her hip.

Grace crouched beside the woman now pinned to the floor. Her voice was steady.

"Hi there," she said. "You would be Connie Carson."

She smiled coldly.

"Or as most people know you... *CC*."

Chapter 51

Five days had passed since the takedown at the hospital.

For the first time in weeks, Grace Fletcher felt like breathing came easier.

She wasn't sure if the case was close to being wrapped—but the center of the storm was beginning to show. And for now, that was enough.

The sky outside was the color of chilled steel, with the faint scent of impending rain, but Grace was in a good mood. A rare, almond-croissant kind of mood.

She pushed open the door to Becky's apartment, balancing a pastry box in one hand and two steaming skim lattes in the other.

"Truce offering," she said, nudging the door closed with her boot.

Becky looked up from the couch. Papers were scattered across the cushions; her laptop open in front of her.

Her hair was pulled into a loose bun, pencil behind her ear, and that familiar frenzied look in her eyes.

She smiled the moment she saw the croissants.

"God, I love you."

"I know," Grace said, dropping the box and the coffee onto the table. "But say it again. Louder."

"Let me eat first," Becky said, already reaching for the pastry. "You only bring almond when something big happens. Did you solve it?"

"Not yet," Grace said, settling in beside her. "But we're closer than ever. So yeah, it qualifies."

Becky took a bite; eyes closed in pure reverence. "This is actual heaven. So? What's the news?"

"Connie Carson, better known as CC."

Becky paused mid-chew.

"Who is she?"

Grace nodded. "We picked her up at the hospital. Dressed as a nurse. Syringe in hand. She was going to kill Jack Taylor."

Becky blinked. "Jesus."

"Yeah," Grace said. "But we were ready. We had moved Jack to a different room earlier that night and replaced him with an undercover. She walked right into the trap."

Becky put the croissant down slowly. "How'd you know she'd show up?"

Grace leaned back, sipped her coffee. "Peter Woodford called the day before. He wanted to talk about Otto—said he believed the suicide wasn't real. He mentioned being scared of CC or Connie Carson, a very expensive freelancer. He told us that she worked for Paul as some type of security provider."

"Scared of CC?"

"We didn't know much about her until Peter called. Just the initials referenced in the documents Marcus sent to Rebecca. The thing is, Peter believed she had a hand in Otto's death. He wasn't sure how—but the timing was too neat. And he was scared shitless.

Our best guess? She wasn't just tied to Otto. She could've been behind the attempt on Bob Malone too. And others. Which meant Jack was a liability. He knew too much, and she might decide to cut him loose. So, we set the trap.

We moved him to another wing under a fake name and built the sting around that. If I was right—and CC was tied to Jack—she'd try to eliminate the one person who could incriminate her. And she did."

Becky nodded slowly. "And how is Jack?"

Grace glanced toward the window. "He's alive. Banged up, but alive.

"So, she was behind Jack Taylor?"

Grace nodded again. "Looks like it. We're still digging, but here's what we found—CC used to be FBI. She was kicked out years ago. Something about a case involving a former President's inner circle. He wasn't happy about an investigation she led, one that linked him to a group of radical neo-Nazis responsible for a deadly riot. It was a mess.

According to the files, she tampered with evidence and twisted witness statements. The Bureau fired her in disgrace. She dropped off the radar after that. But around the time Red Stage fell apart—she reappeared."

"And Paul started paying her."

"Exactly. Quiet transfers. Not huge—but significant and steady. Coming from a shell company tied to one of his old accounts. Same trail we'd already been following for the payments linked to Peppy's alibi.

When you layer it all together, the pattern's clear—Paul was paying her for services. And based on Peter's statement, we believe those services were less about security... and more about cleaning up messes. A fixer."

Becky frowned. "But why would she keep working after Paul died?"

"I asked myself that same question," Grace said. "But here's the thing—she's a fixer, Becky. The kind who does things that could land her in prison. Maybe she was the one behind the deaths of Marcus, Rebecca, and Paul. Maybe she was trying to clean house—eliminate any loose ends that could trace back to her. I can see her hand in Marcus and Rebecca. Paul had reasons to get rid of them.

But Paul himself? That's the part I don't get. Maybe it was a misunderstanding. Maybe something went sideways. I'll find out."

Becky shook her head, still chewing it over. "And Peter?"

"He's nervous, but I don't think he's guilty," Grace said. "He's just afraid of getting dragged down with the rest. But he knew about how Paul and CC orchestrated the embezzlement case against Marcus O'Brien.

That was Paul's way out of Red Stage so he could launch his solo career with Peter. We pressed him. Told him we were closing in on CC. That got him talking. He didn't know much about Jack, but he'd seen the signs. He believes CC was using him. Feeding him targets, one by one."

"So, Jack kills Marcus and Otto. Tries to kill Bob. But it was CC pulling the strings, trying to clean up the mess before anyone talked."

"Exactly," Grace said. "But now they're both in custody. Which means, if we can get them to talk, we might finally get the full story."

Becky leaned back on the couch, hands resting on her notebook. "We're close."

Grace nodded, finishing her latte. "After breakfast, I'm heading to the penitentiary hospital. I'll sit down with Jack. Try to crack him."

"And if he doesn't talk?"

"He will," Grace said.

"Eventually. They always do."

Chapter 52

Grace Fletcher stood outside the interrogation room, arms folded, expression flat. She glanced at Charlie, who gave her a small nod.

It was time.

They'd spent the last five days digging deep—with forensic accountants, digital experts, and jurisdictional clearances. The evidence was solid. Now they needed leverage.

She opened the door.

Jack Taylor sat under the buzzing light like he owned the place. Calm. Crisp button-down. Hair combed back like a banker. His wounds were healing—two gunshots, clean exits—but he still looked like someone on vacation, not a professional hitman caught mid-job.

"That's what made him dangerous—he could hide in plain sight," Charlie had said.

Grace stepped inside and shut the door.

"Morning, Jack," she said, pulling out the chair opposite him.

Jack didn't flinch. "Detective Fletcher."

"No tricks today, Jack. I'll lay it out straight. You're smart. Methodical. A professional. We don't need to play games with you."

She dropped a thick folder on the table.

"You were caught in the act. Two attempted murders—Bob Malone and Becky Fletcher. And you're lucky you're here and not in the morgue."

She opened the folder slowly.

"We also have evidence linking you to the murder of Marcus O'Brien in Boise. Five years ago. You used a chemical compound designed to mimic alcohol, leaving only faint traces. But the full autopsy confirmed it wasn't intoxication that killed him.

Almost perfect. Except we found a surveillance clip. Blurry, yes—but enough. Witnesses place you in the area. And the payment trail? It leads to a crypto wallet tied to an offshore account... which brings us straight to Connie Carson, CC."

She watched for a twitch. Caught the slightest flick of an eyebrow.

"She hired you—just like she did with Otto Fischer. You staged it as a suicide, but we know you killed him. This time, we found traces of chloroform. And we know you planted that crap about the murdered child."

Still nothing. A poker face carved in stone.

Grace flipped another page in the folder. "We even pulled one of your burners from the scene. Calls to CC. We hit your hotel too. You weren't planning to get caught, but you left plenty behind. Do you want me to read you the list?"

Grace leaned forward. "You're not walking out of this, Jack. But you get to choose how deep you sink. You want to rot in a maximum security cell for the rest of your life? Or do you want a way out?"

She paused. Charlie stepped in, placed a new folder in front of Jack.

"This is real," she said. "Signed by the prosecutor. Already run past the judge. If you help us—fully—you'll get a reduced sentence. Five years max. Maybe out in three."

Jack finally moved. He reached for the paper. His fingers were steady.

"You're offering a deal?" he said, voice low. "Just like that?"

Grace nodded. "We're offering a way out. And yes, just like that."

Jack's eyes flicked through the pages. His gaze sharpened.

"We need your help tying loose ends. You've got knowledge we don't. Payment methods. Contacts. Timelines. But more than that, we need you to help us prove what we already suspect."

She paused again. Let it sink in.

"You and I both know Connie Carson is behind this. But we think there's someone else pulling the strings. Someone above her. Paul Max."

That got him. A subtle shift. His shoulder stiffened. The name still carried weight, even now.

"We also believe you were behind Paul's death—and maybe even Rebecca Fontaine's so-called 'accident.' But we don't have enough to prove it yet," Grace continued. "That's where you come in. We need you to connect the dots.

"I know you're not the mastermind here, Jack," Grace said, softer now. "You're a tool. A weapon. They pointed you at the problem and you pulled the trigger. That's not justice. That's exploitation. And you—if you help us—you can walk away with something."

Jack tapped the table once, then looked up.

"How do I know this isn't bullshit?"

"You have a lawyer?" Grace asked. "Call them. Let them verify it. We'll wait. We're not playing games."

Charlie slid a phone across the table.

Jack stared at it.

Grace leaned back, arms crossed.

"I don't think you're a good man, Jack. But I don't think you're the worst, either. You've done terrible things. No denying that. But this—" she nodded toward him, her voice low, steady "—this is your chance to stop being someone else's weapon.

I'm betting you've got money stashed away. Enough to disappear if you wanted. But here's the truth: this is your only shot at something better. A chance to help us take down the people who really pulled the strings.

A chance to stop. To maybe spend what's left of your life in peace.

You want redemption? Then give us what we need. That's the price.

And one more thing, Jack. Why protect a dead man—and a woman who wouldn't lose a minute of sleep selling you out? Deep down, you know I'm right. The second she gets the chance, she'll pin everything on you. You'll be the monster, the killer, the scapegoat she needs to walk away clean. That's how she plays the game.

But it doesn't have to end like that for you. Look at that document. That's not a trap—it's a door. Your door. A way out of the mess they dragged you into. Take it, Jack, or you'll be the one left holding the bag. And that's not the life you want. They're the ones responsible—not you. You were just the weapon. Don't let them win."

He looked down at the paper again. Silence stretched thin. He was weighing every option, calculating the angles. Grace knew Jack was smart—cold, efficient. He'd reach the logical conclusion.

And then:

"Alright," Jack said and reached for the phone.

"I need to call my lawyer."

<h1 style="text-align:center">Chapter 53</h1>

Grace and Charlie had spent two full days piecing together the final leg of the case. Long hours, walls of documents, statements, timelines. Jack Taylor had been surprisingly cooperative. Methodical, even. A killer's mind, now repurposed for justice.

But today was different.

Today, Grace was facing the person who had orchestrated it all.

Connie Carson.

The former FBI agent sat quietly in the penitentiary's interrogation room, smaller than Grace remembered. No makeup. Her gray hair tied back roughly. Her eyes—once sharp and unshakable—looked tired, dulled by days in isolation.

Grace entered with a paper bag and set it on the table.

"Good morning, CC," she said, placing coffee and a croissant in front of her. "Figured you might want something decent."

CC eyed the bag with mild suspicion, then took it. Slowly.

"You were FBI. You know how this works," Grace continued. "No games. We can give you a reduced sentence if you cooperate."

She dropped a thick folder on the table with a thud.

"Here's everything we have on you. Summary form. We know you orchestrated the embezzlement scheme that sent Marcus O'Brien to prison. We also know you hired Jack Taylor to kill Marcus—after he got his hands on proof from Tom Harper. And we know you paid Jack again to eliminate Otto Fischer. And Bob Malone."

She paused. Watched for the twitch. There it was—just a flicker in CC's jaw.

"All of it backed up by financials, crypto trails, surveillance data. And most importantly—Peter and Jack's sworn statement."

Grace opened the folder. CC didn't even look but she felt the punch. She'd been betrayed, and that was painful.

"Jack gave us details," Grace said. "Names. Payment logs. Patterns. He knew things only someone on the inside would. We verified them. Cross-checked them."

Still nothing.

Charlie leaned forward. "We know the truth, CC."

CC inhaled slowly. Her chest rose and fell like someone sinking under water. She said nothing. Not yet.

"Look," Grace continued, shifting her tone, "I get it. You were good at what you did. Maybe too good. Maybe you believed too much in the job. Maybe that's how it all started. The whole mess with the Bureau—tampering evidence during that case with the riot and the president. Pushing too hard. Trying to force the truth into the light."

CC's expression cracked for the first time.

"You don't know a damn thing!" she snapped, her voice low and sharp. "I didn't tamper with evidence. That was the story they gave the press—but it wasn't mine. I uncovered connections they didn't want exposed—links between a neo-Nazi cell and the president's inner circle.

I brought it forward. And they buried me for it. You're clinging to a version of the truth *they* built. That's what they do. They fabricate reality. They create illusions all around us... and you believe them!"

Grace kept her tone even. "So, you were the scapegoat."

"Damn right I was." CC's eyes burned now. "My boss fed me to the wolves. It was political. I was silenced. Stripped. Blacklisted."

Silence.

It hadn't started the way Grace expected—but it was something. At least she was talking.

"And then," Grace said, "you reemerged. Right around the Red Stage days."

CC went quiet again.

"Paul needed someone to clean up his past. You became that person. And when Marcus threatened to go public with the truth—"

"He paid me to handle it. And I did. The problem was, I never found the proof Tom provided—or Tom himself. Paul also told me not to meddle with Rebecca. I never knew why. Recently, I tried again with Rebecca's mother. No luck." CC's voice stayed flat, emotionless.

Charlie spoke next. "And Otto? Bob?"

"Otto was a loose end. I knew he'd talk. He knew about Marcus. He had to be eliminated. I never thought Peter would betray me, at least not so soon—but he did. In this business, there are no friends. No family. Only assets and liabilities."

"And what about Rebecca?" Grace asked.

"No," CC said. "That wasn't me."

"She was threatening Paul too. She had leverage. Paul needed to eliminate her," Charlie added.

"But it was not me. Because killing her the way she died would've risked Paul's reputation," CC said. "A set accident? During a production tied to him? That's sloppy. That's not how I work. If I wanted her gone, she'd disappear—quietly, cleanly. No mess, no noise. That wasn't me. I didn't even know she was blackmailing Paul.

I asked him straight out—*did you do it?* He swore to me he didn't. And Paul didn't lie to me. Not about things like that. He truly believed it was an accident. Pure and simple. But when the proof started to stack up against him... he panicked. Paid Peppy to protect him. Not because he was guilty—but because he knew the system might decide he was."

Grace studied her. "And what about Paul? Did you kill him?"

CC rolled her eyes. "Are you kidding? I didn't kill him. He was my client for over a decade. Paid well. Trusted me."

"You were the only one who knew where all the skeletons were buried."

CC held her stare. "I didn't kill him. If I wanted leverage over Paul, I had a thousand ways to get it. I didn't need him dead."

Grace nodded slowly. "Alright. You didn't kill Rebecca. You didn't kill Paul. But you admit to everything else?"

"Yes. Because I was paid to do it."

"And you're willing to sign a formal confession?"

"I will. But I want the deal you promised—reduced time, protection, full cooperation."

"We'll make it happen," Grace said. "But then, who do you think killed Paul?"

"I only had two leads, one was Bob. Jack was supposed to do whatever was needed to get the truth out of him. But you got him first. If he's not the one, then the only option is Tom Harper. I'd been tracking him for years. He vanished. My working theory? Witness protection. Or dead."

But then CC lowered her voice, "however, just last week, I found a guy who forged new papers for him years ago. Fake ID, new identity. He didn't know where Harper went after that. So, I was starting to backtrace the alias when you arrested Jack."

Grace leaned in. "Do you have the name?"

CC reached into her memory, squinted, like she was dragging the name from the bottom of a well.

"Yes," she said finally. "Daniel Reed."

"Thank you, CC," Grace said. "We'll keep our end of the deal. But you're not done yet. We'll need every-thing."

Grace exchanged a quick look with Charlie. A new lead.

A new ghost to chase.

Chapter 54

The restaurant was tucked into a corner of Melrose, all soft light and warm brick. Tables draped in crisp white linen. Brass chandeliers casting gold halos over half-eaten plates of pappardelle.

A Sinatra tune murmured in the background. The kind of place you only picked when you needed comfort—or closure.

Grace Fletcher sat across from her sister Becky, a glass of red wine balanced between her fingers. Barolo, this time. Charlie Bonelli nursed an Old Fashioned, cube ice clinking softly as he swirled the amber liquid.

"Tough day?" Becky asked, already halfway through her second glass. "I need something stronger than pasta."

Charlie gave her a crooked smile. "You and me both."

Grace raised her glass. "To surviving."

They clinked. Quietly. No toasts, no speeches—just the weight of everything unsaid.

"By the way, a little birdie told me someone had a date," Becky said, grinning at her sister. Grace's cheeks warmed instantly.

"What? Mrs. *'All I do is work'* finally took time to meet a fellow mortal?" Charlie teased.

Mona, Grace thought. Of course she told her.

"Okay, okay. Yes—I had a date. And it was good. End of story. Let's leave it there."

"Fine," Becky said. "More details when you're ready. For now—let's drink. To dates!"

"To dates!" they echoed, Grace joining in reluctantly but with a smile. Their glasses clinked again.

Silence followed—long enough to bring the elephant in the room lumbering back between them.

"So," Becky leaned in. "Where are you two on the case? I'm almost done with the story, but I've got no ending in sight. No clean villain. No ribbon to tie it all together."

Charlie sighed. "I confirmed with Peppy what CC told us. She admitted she received the payments from Paul—he really did pay her for that alibi.

At first, she didn't want to cooperate, but we convinced her lawyers we weren't after her for wrongdoing.

We just needed to know whether Paul killed Rebecca on purpose... or if it was truly an accident."

"And," Grace added, "according to Peppy, Paul told her he was innocent. Swore it."

Becky's brow furrowed. "Not just her. Remember—he did the same with me. And I still don't think he lied... but if that's true, then who the hell killed Rebecca?"

"The only motive we know of is blackmail," Grace said. "Rebecca had the proof. She pressed Paul. But he gave her roles in his films—maybe that's all she wanted. And Paul... he liked her, once. He went along with it... But if Paul didn't kill her..."

"Then who did?" Becky insisted. "And why?"

"That's the million-dollar question," Charlie muttered. "Everything still points to a freak accident."

A silence fell over the table, broken only by the scrape of cutlery. The pasta was excellent—handmade pappardelle with mushroom truffle cream—but none of them were really tasting it.

"Maybe we need to go back to the start," Grace said finally. "Back to Red Stage."

"Marcus was innocent," Becky said. "That's confirmed. And Paul's the one who accused him."

"With forged evidence," Charlie added. "Tom Harper helped him pull it off."

Grace nodded. "Which means Tom could face obstruction, perjury, conspiracy—maybe even accessory to murder, depending on the timeline. He had motive to keep Paul quiet."

"Still," Becky countered, "that's not enough to kill him. He'd kept his mouth shut for years. Paul wasn't about to go public—he'd be incriminating himself. And we know he was willing to kill to protect what he did to Marcus and the other Red Stage founders. So why kill him? Why now?"

Charlie leaned back, his glass halfway to his lips. "Unless something else happened recently. Something that pushed someone over the edge."

"Secrets don't just rot," Grace said. "They evolve. New events reframe old ones."

"Or die with the person keeping them," Becky murmured, thinking of Paul.

There was a long pause. A waiter approached to refill the water glasses and vanished just as quickly.

"Did you track Tom Harper using his new identity?" Becky asked, breaking the quiet.

Grace sighed. "We traced him as far as Atlanta, Georgia. Then... nothing. Dead end."

"You think he changed his identity again?"

"We don't know," Grace admitted. "We're working every angle. Financials. DMV records. Old colleagues. But it's like he disappeared... again."

"Maybe he's dead," Charlie said. "Maybe someone already got to him."

"If that's the case, we don't have a body," Grace replied. "No proof. Until we find Harper—or his body—we're stuck circling."

They picked at their plates again. Becky twirled a strand of pasta covered in Parmesan; let it fall. She sipped her drink, eyes distant.

"This case is a goddamn puzzle," she said. "Too many pieces, and half of them don't fit. And the worst part? We're digging into the past. The people who matter most are either dead or vanished."

"If we don't find Tom," Charley said, "we may never know the truth."

"It's like *Murder on the Orient Express*," Grace said suddenly.

Charlie blinked. "The hell does that mean?"

"You know—everyone had a reason. Everyone was part of it. Multiple killers. Shared guilt."

Grace tapped her fingers against the base of her glass. "So, you're saying Paul didn't kill Rebecca. CC didn't kill Paul. Maybe each death has its own killer."

"Exactly," Becky said. "Maybe we're looking for one monster when there are three."

Charlie rubbed his temple. "Great. Just what we need—a gang of killers."

"But if we're right," Grace said quietly, "there are still one, maybe two players out there."

Becky nodded. "Tom Harper's still in the mix."

Grace stared at the candle flickering between them. "Find him... and maybe this all starts making sense."

Charlie raised his glass again. "To ghosts. And to finding the last one."

They drank. The wine burned warm down Grace's throat.

Outside, the night thickened.

Inside, the story was snapping into focus—*for Becky*.

Her intuition whispered of something the others had missed.

Something that could complete the puzzle.

Chapter 55

The lobby of *The Hollywood Star* buzzed with artifi-
cial calm. Too much glass. Too much polished
chrome. The air smelled of stale coffee, overused
printer toner, and faint ambition.

Becky stepped through the revolving door with her
usual messy bun, notepad sticking from her oversized
leather tote, and a restless mind that hadn't shut off in
days.

Ideas drifted like smoke. She had something—but
not the whole thing. Not yet.

Paul Max was still with her. Not in body, obviously.
But in memory. In contradiction. In mystery.

He'd lived two lives.

The public one—charming, talented, magnetic. A
box-office darling. Golden smile. Golden touch. America and the world adored him.

But behind that polished image, something cracked.

A shadow that didn't match the light in his eyes.

He hadn't just hidden secrets.

He was made of them.

Dark ghosts that may have tormented his second life—hidden, insecure, ruthless. A man who either committed or ordered others to commit terrible crimes.

Like the roles he played, Paul had built an illusion. A carefully rehearsed version of himself. But was it an act... or was it the real man?

Maybe people are like that. Maybe we all carry secrets. Some we whisper to ourselves. Others we bury so deep, we forget they're there. We want to escape the darkness, build clean lives, forget the parts that don't fit the story.

But Paul?

Paul was different.

He didn't just hide the darkness.

He used it.

And maybe that's the difference. The Pauls of the world go one step further. They lie, they scheme, they kill—literally kill—to get what they want. Or to keep the truth buried.

Now, looking back, Becky saw it clearly. The secrets were real. But not all the answers were.

The problem was—some of those secrets seemed to have died with him. With Marcus O'Brien. With Otto Fisher.

And with Rebecca Fontaine.

Her death still didn't sit right. Becky had followed the trial closely. She was there in person. Depositions, statements, reconstructions. At the end everyone said the same: it was an accident. A tragic, freak accident on set.

But if that was true... why didn't it feel like it?

There was a thread. Thin. Faint. But real. Something linking Rebecca's death to Paul's. Becky couldn't name it yet, but she felt the pull.

Paul had sworn he didn't kill her. Was that the truth—or just another lie?

There were too many pieces that didn't fit.

On one hand, it made no sense to use that method to kill someone—unless it was the shooter. A shooter who could later deny it. But if that was the plan, wouldn't you at least try to shift the blame? Create a scapegoat?

Paul didn't do that. He stuck with the accident story, even though it sank him with the jury. He only dodged disaster thanks to a last-minute gambit—Peppy's deposition. That wasn't strategy. That was desperation. His last card to stay out of jail.

And no one else had access to the gun. Only Paul. He alone had the key. It was never proven, but that was the fact. Except the assistant—he'd called in sick that day. He had the other key.

So, if not Paul—then who? And why?

Becky believed Paul's defense had crumbled because they couldn't point to anyone else with a motive to kill Rebecca. If no one else had a reason, then it came down to two possibilities: either Paul did it—especially with the new blackmail angle—or it was an accident. And in the end, Peppy's deposition tipped the balance his way.

The elevator pinged. Becky rode it up to the third floor. A whiteboard by the newsroom entrance read "BREAKING: CRIME, CELEBS, SCANDALS." Under it, someone had added in Sharpie: *And Becky Fletcher's absences.*

She smiled. Sort of.

She made her way to her desk—cluttered with past drafts, trial notes, lipstick-stained coffee cups—and dropped her bag. But before she could sit, she was summoned.

Jim Bamford. Her editor. The man who once called her "the only real reporter left in this dump."

She knocked gently on his office door.

"Just come in, Becky. You don't need to knock," Jim barked.

"Hi, Jim."

He leaned back in his chair with that half-annoyed, half-affectionate smirk. "Hi, Jim? That's what you lead with?"

"It's customary," she offered with a dry smile.

He wasn't having it.

"Let's cut the crap. You know why you're here. Let me boil it down for you: You spent a month interviewing Paul Max. Then he turns up dead. Perfect setup. I asked you for a quick piece. You said, 'No, Jim. Something bigger's coming.' Fine. I played along. But Becky—where the hell is my article?"

She blinked. "It is not ready... but..."

"Exactly! Meanwhile, the *LA Times* has three op-eds. *BuzzMag* posted a goddamn podcast. And us? Crickets. Do you want to hand our ad revenue to competitors gift-wrapped?"

He was loud now. This wasn't casual Jim. This was final warning Jim.

"I know," she said, quietly. "I really do. I almost have it. One more lead. One more trip. Give me three days. You'll have your story."

Jim narrowed his eyes. "Becky... I'm not bluffing. I need that article. Or you'll be reassigned to cover celebrity divorces and daytime soaps. Clear?"

She didn't answer. Because just then—someone knocked.

A young assistant poked his head in. "Miss Fletcher? You asked me to alert you immediately... The production company is on line three. They have something you requested."

Becky's pulse quickened.

That was the missing piece.

She rushed to the phone.

Chapter 56

Grace could be a pain in the neck.

Becky loved her sister—sure, most days—but Grace had a knack for hovering like a helicopter mom who happened to carry a badge.

Becky'd promised to keep Grace informed. And she had. Every detail, every update, every theory. But did she really need to tag along for this?

Becky didn't think so. She wasn't a little girl. But here she was, back in Boise, Idaho, Grace planted beside her like a stubborn oak, both of them waiting for Mark and Lisa to come back from the kitchen with coffee.

"Are you okay?" Grace asked. She could see Becky wasn't. Not on the flight. Not now.

"Yes, Mom."

Grace gave her a look, the kind she reserved for suspects and irritating family members.

Becky knew she didn't like it. Which made it even more tempting.

"Becky, we made a pact," Grace said, voice low. "I'm here to help you. To support you. Nothing else. I am not going to write your article, for God's sake."

Becky let the silence stretch.

Then: "Okay. Okay."

She paused, then added, "Mom," and stuck her tongue out.

Right then, Lisa walked in, balancing a tray of cookies. Mark followed with a carafe and four mismatched mugs.

"We have a couple of good Joes," Mark said with a smile. "I know in L.A. you prefer something more... sophisticated."

Grace smiled. "This is perfect. Thank you."

Lisa didn't smile back. She looked worried.

Becky took a mug, inhaling the bitter steam. "I told you I had to speak to you in person," she said to Lisa. "About your father's case. Something important."

They knew the broad strokes—Paul sending a hitman after Marcus, the cover-up, the years of lies. But this was more than a refresher. This was the piece Becky hadn't dared to put in an email or over the phone.

Her mistake had been telling Grace she was going back to Boise. That had sparked a very serious "conversation," and now here they were. Grace glaring over her mug, Becky ignoring her, Mark and Lisa settling into the couch.

They drank coffee, complimented the cookies, made polite talk about the weather. It was maddening. The air was thick with the thing they weren't saying.

Finally, Lisa leaned forward. "Becky, you can't keep me waiting."

"Okay, okay." Becky set her cup down. "Let me go for it."

She took a breath. "This case was an enigma from the start. Paul turns up dead, shot, a note written in his own blood: Murderer. Someone knew he was a killer. But who?"

Lisa's eyes narrowed.

"Later," Becky continued, "we learned he'd killed Rebecca. But was it really an accident? At first it made sense—she'd been blackmailing him. He had motive. But the way it happened... risky. Messy.

Why stage it like that when he had CC on speed dial to make people vanish cleanly? If Paul did it this way, he created a trial that nearly put him in prison. Not exactly a smart plan."

Mark shifted. "Maybe because he was seriously threatened."

"Maybe," Becky said. "Or maybe he didn't want to kill her at all."

Silence.

"I've talked to people who swore Paul wasn't responsible for her death. He told me that himself—crying. He was a good actor, sure, but *that* good? So, let's assume, just for a moment, he was telling the truth. If Paul didn't kill Rebecca... then who did?"

Mark shook his head. "The court decided it was an accident. A real bullet left by mistake in the gun. No one tampered after the prop check. It was the only explanation."

"No one really believed it," Becky said, "but it stuck because no one had anything better. But what if it was a mistake of a different kind? What if someone wanted to kill another person—not Rebecca—and screwed it up?"

Lisa leaned in. "What are you saying?"

Everyone's eyes snapped to Becky, confusion written across their faces.

"That bullet wasn't meant for Rebecca," Becky said. "That was the trial's crucial mistake. *The bullet was meant for Paul.*"

Lisa blinked. Mark scoffed. "What? How?"

"It's just a theory," Becky admitted. "But think about it. Paul ends up dead a year later. Could it be the same person who tried the first time... finished the job the next year?"

"That's crazy," Mark said. "The first was Paul killing a blackmailer, even if the court called it an accident. He paid Peppy La Font for her alibi, didn't he?"

"That's true," Becky said. "But Peppy swore the alibi was only because the jury was leaning toward guilty—not because Paul really was. So please, just indulge me. Let's keep pretending he was innocent, even if he bought that innocence."

"That's still crazy," Mark muttered. "Lisa, we shouldn't—"

"Please," Becky cut in, eyes on Lisa. "Indulge me for a couple more minutes."

Lisa glanced at Mark. "Sit."

He did, reluctantly. It was clear Mark would never go against Lisa. Even the smallest gesture from her was a command he obeyed.

"Okay," Becky said. "Let's assume Paul didn't kill Rebecca on purpose but was the intended target. How do we prove it?" She let the question hang, watching their faces. "I spent hours turning it over. Thinking about it. Then I knew.

There's one reason—*one obvious reason*—for the killer to make that kind of mistake."

Chapter 57

Two days earlier, something happened that shifted the case.

Grace felt a jolt of adrenaline when the call came in—a small police department in Blue Ridge, Georgia had uncovered a lead. Maybe, just maybe, it could finally crack the long-cold trail of Tom Harper. Or Daniel Reed, as he went by now.

According to the officer, someone in Blue Ridge had recognized Tom's new look.

Not the clean-cut Red Stage accountant from the old photos, but a man with graying hair, a softer jawline, and eyes that never seemed to land on you for more than a second.

The tip came from Penny Lee, a local waitress.

Grace and Charlie flew down and met her in the back booth of a roadside diner—the kind with cracked red vinyl seats and coffee that tasted like it had been burning since the Carter administration.

Penny didn't bother with pretense. She was blunt about the nature of her "relationship" with Tom.

"'Dating' is a generous word for what we had," she said, stirring sugar into her mug. "We hooked up for a while. Friends with benefits, I guess. Mostly just... benefits." She smirked, but her eyes softened. "He was lonely. Sad. Never talked much about his past...or anything."

But there was one thing she remembered—the dreams.

"He'd thrash in his sleep, mumble nonsense," Penny said. "Mostly gibberish. But every so often, a word cut through. Twice—maybe three times—I swear I heard him scream 'kill'... and 'Paul Max.'

Scared the hell out of me."

The first time she brought it up, he froze. Went pale. Then brushed it off like she'd imagined it. A few weeks later, he ghosted her. She never saw him again.

Before they left, Penny handed over a small spiral notebook. "Found it under the bed after he took off," she said. "Most of it's crap—stuff about birds, random news clippings, places he visited. But you're cops. Maybe it means something to you."

Most of it was junk. But in the middle of a page about Appalachian songbirds was a note that made Grace stop reading:

Blue Ridge Buddhist Monastery – nearby – quiet, isolated.

Two days later, Grace and Charlie were behind the wheel of a rental car, winding through the North Georgia mountains. The road narrowed to a ribbon, thick pines closing in on either side.

The monastery appeared suddenly, as if it had grown out of the forest. Nothing grand—just a cluster of low wooden buildings, their roofs dark with weather. A small garden bloomed near the entrance, rows of neat vegetables bordered by stones.

Ten monks lived there, the deputy had told her. They accepted donations from a few Buddhist charities and devoted themselves to meditation, vegetable cultivation, and silence.

A young monk in a saffron robe met them at the gate. His head was shaved, his eyes calm. Without a word, he led them down a narrow path to the main hall. Inside, the air was cool and smelled faintly of incense and wood polish.

An older monk, the apparent leader, waited for them. He smiled gently. "Welcome. What can I do for you?"

Grace glanced at Charlie, then stepped forward. "We're detectives from Los Angeles. We're investigating a series of murders. We believe someone connected to our case may have stayed here." She slid a driver's license photo across the low table. "Do you recognize this man?"

The monk studied the picture for a long moment. "I do not think so. My memory..." He trailed off, handing it to another monk who had silently appeared at the doorway. "Show it to the others."

While they waited, he poured them green tea.

"Why do you believe he was here?" the monk asked.

"He lived in Blue Ridge about eight years ago," Grace explained. "We found notes in his handwriting mentioning this monastery."

"It is possible. Many come to visit. But the picture... it is old."

Grace gave a small shrug. "We know it's a long shot."

The second monk returned with another robed figure—a man with deep lines around his eyes and a voice like gravel. They exchanged a few words before the leader turned back to her.

"Yes," he said. "He was here. Daniel. I did not recognize him because when he arrived, he shaved his head, and he looked different. He stayed for some time."

"Stayed?" Grace leaned forward. "As in—lived here?"

"Yes. He was one of us." The monk's gaze softened. "He became a monk and practiced Buddhism with us."

"Tom Harper, a monk? That was unexpected... You said he *lived* here. When did he leave? Do you know where he went?"

The monk rose, motioning for them to follow. "Please—come with me."

They left the hall, winding down a narrow trail at the back of the compound. Birds called in the trees overhead. The scent of pine and damp earth filled the air.

The path ended in a small clearing, sunlight spilling across rows of simple stone markers. A cemetery. Each grave was marked only with a name and a date, carved into the rock.

The monk stopped before one of them. He placed his hands together, bowed his head, and stepped aside.

Grace read the inscription. The name was the one from the driver's license, Daniel Reed.

"He died two years ago," the monk said quietly. "Cancer. We buried him here."

Grace stood still, staring at the stone. The wind moved softly through the trees, carrying the scent of incense from the hall. CC had chased Tom Harper across years and states. She'd followed whispers, dead ends, and shadows. And now here he was—six feet under in a quiet corner of Georgia.

Grace thought it made sense—guilt had driven him to confess to Marcus. He couldn't undo what he'd done, but at least he confessed to the one he'd hurt most.

Charlie shifted beside her. "So that's it," he muttered.

In his head, the words followed: This is *literally* a dead end...

Chapter 58

Becky waited. All eyes were on her.

"I had a suspicion," she began, voice steady. "So, I reached out to the production company from the film where Rebecca was shot. It had been more than a year, so I didn't have high hopes. It was a long shot. But maybe—just maybe—someone would remember."

And I got lucky—someone did."

She leaned forward, the energy in the room tightening.

"I talked to a screenwriter who'd worked on the film—he remembered it clearly. Three days before Paul accidentally shot Rebecca, the writers, director, and production team pushed through major script changes. Not a tweak here or there. Big changes. Multiple scenes, different beats in the story. And one of them was... *who would be shooting who.*"

Grace felt the pull of Becky's words but kept quiet. This was Becky's theory—her moment to lay it out. Across from her, Lisa and Mark sat frozen, staring at Becky.

"The production company sent me the scripts they'd used during filming," Becky continued. "There were four in total.

In the third version the wife, driven by jealousy, confronted her husband with a gun and shot him. But he survived. The rest of the story followed his recovery, his penance, and eventually, their reconciliation.

But in the rewrite—the fourth and final version—everything flipped. Now it was the husband, driven by rage, holding the gun. A confrontation of jealousy and fury.

In the chaos, he shoots her. On the page, she survives, and he rushes her to the hospital, ashamed and wracked with guilt."

Becky let the information hang in the air before remarking, "That change happened three days before the shooting on set."

Grace reinforced the point. "In the third version Rebecca was not supposed to be in the line of fire. Paul was."

Mark stared at her. Lisa's face had gone pale—eyes wide, terrified.

"Exactly," Becky said. "But then the script changed—and suddenly Rebecca was the one in the line of fire. The killer or killers didn't know that.

"And here's the thing—it wasn't Paul who asked for the change. He wasn't even part of those discussions. This wasn't about him. The director is the one who pushed it. He had a reputation for being a perfectionist—hands-on, willing to take risks mid-production. Nothing unusual there. The crew didn't think twice. They'd seen him do it before, even earlier on the same film.

And if you're curious, I checked the director," Becky went on. "He didn't even know Rebecca before this movie. No connection. No motive. And think about this—Rebecca spent her whole life in low-budget films, modeling gigs, and off-Broadway plays. This was her first time on a serious, big Hollywood production.

She was new to almost everyone on set. The only person who knew her was Paul. He's the one who brought her in. Which means..."

And she made a pause looking at them.

"Which means," Becky continued, "if Paul killing Rebecca was unlikely, and no one on the crew had a reason to target her, then the killer had to be someone outside the production.

And here's the key—my theory is that the real target was always Paul, who wound up dead a year later. We checked thoroughly. Aside from Paul, no one had a motive to kill Rebecca. She lived a quiet life—caring for her mother, working long hours just to pay the bills. No enemies, no scandals, no personal life to speak of.

The trial proved the same thing. Paul's own defense team tried to find someone else with a reason to kill her. They came up empty. Whoever swapped the blank for a live round was working off the old script—the third version. They wouldn't have known about the rewrite.

And if they didn't know, that tells us something: they weren't permanent crew. Maybe they had temporary access. Maybe they leaned on a contact to slip in. But they weren't around long enough to realize the roles had been flipped."

"So, someone wanted to kill Paul. But because of the last-minute script change, Rebecca was the one holding the wrong end of the gun," Grace said slowly.

Becky nodded. "Exactly. A fatal mistake. They got the wrong victim. But the motive was there. And a year later... the same person finished the job.

The problem with Rebecca's death was that it never made sense in the context of Paul. He had cleaner ways to kill. He had a fixer. He wasn't the type to risk everything on a reckless stunt. But the script change—that changed everything.

Suddenly, Rebecca's death started to make sense. Someone outside the crew, working off the old script, had swapped a blank for a live round. The target wasn't Rebecca. It was Paul. Risky, yes—but this person didn't care.

If it failed, they could always try again. Someone with some skill, but not the precision of a professional like CC."

Becky's voice softened, but her words carried weight. "It had to be someone who wanted Paul dead.

Someone who knew he was a murderer, or at least believed he was.

Someone who could see through the charm to the narcissist underneath. And it had to be personal. Deeply personal. Not just business. Someone who'd been living with anger and injustice for years."

She let her gaze travel around the room before it landed on Lisa O'Brien.

"Someone," Becky said, her voice barely above a whisper, *"like you, Lisa."*

Chapter 59

"What? Are you saying I killed Paul?!" Lisa shot to her feet, eyes shining with tears that were about to spill. "This is crazy!" She turned to Mark. "Mark!"

He was already moving, wrapping his arms around her protectively while glaring over her shoulder at Becky. "Are you out of your mind?"

Becky didn't flinch. "You had the motive, Lisa. The reason. Who else—"

"But I didn't do it!" Lisa's voice cracked. "I'm not a criminal! Yes, I hated Paul—with all my guts. I'm not afraid to say it. But I wanted him to pay in court, in prison—not like this!" Her words broke apart, collapsing into sobs.

Becky pressed forward. "Who else was so invested in bringing him down? Bob Malone had checked out years ago. Your father and Rebecca were dead. Tom Harper was in a Buddhist monastery. You were the only one still carrying that grudge."

Mark's voice cut low but sharp. "That's your proof? Really? Other people are dead—monks or whoever—and that's enough? This is insane! You come into our house as a guest and accuse Lisa without a shred of proof? Unbelievable. 'My assumption is that Paul Max didn't kill Rebecca'—are you out of your mind?"

Mark was furious, but he kept his arms locked around Lisa. She was his priority.

Her shoulders began to tremble, soft sobs breaking free.

"No," Becky said. "But I'm sure we could prove it—with flight records, hotels, the works—"

Then Lisa turned her head toward Becky. Her eyes sharpened, suddenly alert—the look of someone who had just remembered something important.

"Wait. Wait a minute." Lisa's tone shifted—still sobbing, but steadier now. "I remember when I heard about Rebecca's death. I was in class with my students. Another teacher came in and handed me the paper. I was there all week. You can't prove I was in L.A., because I wasn't. I was here."

She smiled faintly and turned to Mark. The tension eased from her face, replaced by relief.

The room fell silent.

It was a solid alibi. A good one. Becky felt the air drain out of her confidence. She had been so sure Lisa was the killer—everything pointed to her. Who else could it be?

"Detective," Mark said, still holding Lisa, "this is getting out of control. We all need to calm down." He stroked her hair gently as she wept, quieter now. "Is this what you came here for? To accuse her of murder?

It's absurd. I do not know what you want from us, but you need to leave."

No one spoke. No one moved. Becky looked confused.

Then, softly, Lisa mumbled, "I didn't do it. I was here. Remember, Mark? You called me that night—we talked for hours. We couldn't believe Paul had the audacity to kill her. We even talked about celebrating... not Rebecca's death, but the way he was hitting rock bottom. The way America's hero was finally showing his true face."

Mark's voice was steady. "Yes, honey. I know. I know. They don't know what they're talking about."

The moment felt heavy, awkward. Grace and Becky stood there, unsure how to move forward.

And Becky felt defeated. She'd been so sure.

Slowly, she crossed to the chair, grabbed her bag, and headed for the door. Nothing left to do here. She was wrong. And now she didn't even have the article she'd promised Jim. A total disaster.

Grace felt bad for Becky and moved to follow. She picked up her bag and turned toward the door.

And then Becky's expression shifted—that familiar look she got when something clicked.

She stopped, turned back, and fixed her eyes on Lisa.

She straightened. "Wait," Becky said slowly. "You two talked that night... *on the phone?*"

"Yes," Lisa said. "I remember that day clearly. I'm almost certain the school logs and my phone records will confirm it."

Becky turned to Mark. "From where did you call?"

"Why?" Lisa asked, still sniffling.

Becky's gaze stayed locked on Mark. "Just answer."

"We talked," Lisa said, "why does it matter?"

Mark said nothing.

"Mark?" Lisa's tone sharpened turning towards him. "You were in L.A., remember? For that police event?" She searched his face. "Remember?"

Mark's silence stretched.

"Mark?" Her voice trembled.

He lowered his head, sinking onto the couch.

Lisa's breath hitched. "Mark? What's going on?"

Neither Grace nor Becky spoke. They stopped near the door, facing back toward Mark and Lisa.

Lisa stepped toward him. "Mark, you told me you were in L.A.... Did you go somewhere else? What did you do? Where did you go?"

Mark finally looked at Lisa, and the tenderness in his eyes—soft, endless—made the hair on Grace's neck stand on end.

This man loved Lisa more than his own life. Grace had never witnessed such intensity of feeling before.

Tears welled in his eyes, sliding down his face as he kept staring at her. Lisa looked back, confused, unsettled.

Lisa's fear broke through. "Mark? What's happening? Tell me—what did you do?" Her voice shook. She looked suddenly small, defenseless. Confused. She couldn't understand what was unfolding.

Mark turned his face away. Ashamed. Tormented by the gaze of the woman he loved.

Lisa spun toward Grace and Becky, her voice breaking into a scream. "What is going on?! What are you saying?"

Becky hesitated only a moment before stepping forward. Her voice was calm, almost gentle. "Lisa... Mark went to L.A., but not for that event."

Lisa's eyes darted between them. "What?"

Becky's voice didn't waver.

"Lisa, *Mark killed Paul.*"

Chapter 60

L isa was in total shock.

She looked hollow, as if something vital had been drained from her in an instant. Her eyes—still wet, still focused a moment ago—seemed to have shut down.

She stood there for a long beat, staring into a void only she could see.

What was running through her mind? Grace couldn't say. Was it betrayal? Loneliness? The unbearable weight of realizing the person she loved—trusted—was a stranger? A killer? How do you reconcile the warmth of a heartbeat ago with the cold blade of that truth?

Slowly, Lisa sat. In slow motion. It was almost dreamlike, as though she were moving in another reality.

She stayed there, hands slack in her lap, not crying now—something worse. Something inside her had broken.

Mark walked deliberately to the small bar in the corner. His movements were slow but steady. He poured a bourbon, then turned to the room. "Anyone else?"

Silence.

No one answered.

Tears still streaked his face.

His hands trembled around the glass.

Grace's hand rested near her holster. She watched every movement. She didn't know if Mark was pouring a drink or reaching for an exit.

But he didn't try anything. He took a seat in a chair near them, glass in hand.

Grace thought of the final scene in *Dial M for Murder*—Ray Milland, his plot exposed, calmly pouring drinks.

This wasn't the same, but the acceptance was there.

Mark wasn't going to fight. He knew it was over.

Maybe he even knew proof of his actions wouldn't be hard to find.

He understood the end had come.

He kept his gaze down as he spoke. "I love Lisa more than anything in my life. More than I've ever loved anyone. More than I ever will again."

He wasn't talking to Lisa—he was talking about her.

"I've watched her suffer for years," he went on, voice steady. "Crying. Living with the injustice of this world. I tried to find the man who killed her father, but I had limits.

And the hate... it just grew. I'm not asking for forgiveness. I'm not justifying myself. I'm telling you what's been inside me for a long time."

He drank.

"Lisa was—is—my whole life. Watching her carry that weight, facing pity—or worse, ridicule—it killed me. Paul was responsible for Marcus's death. We didn't have proof, and Marcus never told us what he had.

Maybe he was going to... until the hitman got to him. A rich man like Paul wouldn't do it himself. He'd hide behind layers, hire someone to hire someone. Keep his image intact. Keep the illusion alive.

And I decided it had to end.

I wanted to wipe that smile off his face. I wanted justice. I wanted Lisa to have peace."

Lisa's tears returned, silent this time. She sat stiff, rigid—present, but distant.

Mark didn't look at her. Maybe he couldn't. He didn't look at Becky or Grace either.

His gaze fixed on a corner of the room, but it wasn't seeing anything.

His eyes were blank—empty, as if the images had all drained away.

"I got hold of a copy of the script," he said. "I thought I was looking at the script—not some outdated draft. I didn't know about the changes. That was my fatal mistake. I figured I could swap a blank for a live round and make it look like an accident. The production would take the blame.

I targeted a crew member—the assistant with one of the keys to the gun locker—who happened to be sick. I made sure he stayed that way by slipping something into his food. Nothing serious, just enough to keep him out for a day.

I convinced him to let me cover for him. No one knew I had the key—not even the assistant I'd taken it from. Everyone believed Paul's was the only one on set that day.

I used mine when no one was watching, swapped the round, and slipped away. Just another face in the crowd, moving paperwork."

He stared at the bourbon in his hand. Half a glass left, the amber liquid clinging to the sides. Waiting. Watching him.

"When Rebecca died, I didn't understand at first. The only explanation was that someone had changed the scene. I couldn't believe how naïve I'd been. And then... another innocent gone because of Paul.

My anger only deepened. I waited. Followed the trial, certain the police would come knocking at my door. But they never did. They missed the script change. The case twisted off in another direction. Everyone stayed focused on Paul and his actions. Even that—I hated."

Mark leaned back, eyes dull.

"So, I decided to end it. I blackmailed Paul. Threatened to kill Lola—his girlfriend—unless he met me alone. I knew he loved her. I told him to drop his security and come to an abandoned gas station. He did. I shot him. I didn't take the money.

I didn't want anything from him. I wrote murderer on him for the world to see. Even if no one believed it, the illusion was broken.

At least to me."

Grace took out her phone and called it in.

Mark added one last thing, still not looking at Lisa. His eyes were fixed somewhere far away.

"I love you," he said quietly.

"And I always will."

Chapter 61

Becky stepped out of the sunlight and into the glass-and-marble lobby of *The Hollywood Star*. A perfect L.A. day—clear sky, warm breeze, palm fronds swaying like they were on payroll.

The receptionist looked up, her smile wide. "Congratulations on your latest piece, Becky."

"Thank you," Becky said, smiling back.

It had been a week since her exposé had dropped. The response was staggering—front pages, trending hashtags, endless cable news debates. It wasn't just Hollywood gossip anymore.

It had gone national.

Global!

She had brought the hidden truth to the public.

That morning she'd even gotten a call from *Le Monde*. Unreal.

She walked straight into Jim's office without knocking. He was finishing a call but waved her in, pointing toward one of the leather chairs.

Since the article was published, Jim had been nothing but sweet—almost too sweet.

Becky glanced around. Corner office. Wall-to-wall windows framing the sprawl of Los Angeles, the mountains hazy in the distance. She picked up one of the magazines on the coffee table.

Paul Max stared back at her from the cover.

The headline read: *Paul Max, the Master of Illusion.*

The subhead: A Great Actor. A Web of Deception. And the Revenge That Ended It All.

"Becky!" Jim said as he hung up. "I just got a call from *60 Minutes*! They want you for a full episode on Paul. CNN is calling too. You did it again! The country—hell, the world—is crazy about your exposé!"

Becky smiled. "It's been... insane. Reporters from everywhere have been contacting me nonstop. I've agreed to a few interviews, but now it's the story of the story. NBC wants to profile me and *The Hollywood Star.* Looks like we're in for a hectic couple of weeks."

Jim was practically bouncing in his chair. "Exactly. We need to ride this wave. This will put us on the national radar for weeks. That means more sales, more ad revenue. I've got a board meeting next week, and they'll want to know every detail."

"Well," Becky said, "you took a risk on me by holding the piece until it was ready. It paid off. Thank you, Jim."

"I knew you could do it, kid." He leaned back, still grinning. "By the way—I heard they're considering exhuming Tom Harper's body for a full autopsy. There's talk he might have been murdered too."

"It's possible," Becky said. "CC knew who he was, and if she knew, she might've known where he was. She could have had him killed. But neither she nor Jack ever said a word about it. We know CC handled some jobs personally, so it could've been her—and Jack wouldn't necessarily know. Or she might've hired someone else.

Then again, if he really had cancer, maybe she didn't see him as a threat. He was living in a remote area. She might've thought nature would take its course."

Jim shook his head. "Still... what a character CC turned out to be."

"She was Paul's weapon," Becky said. "Kept in the shadows to protect his illusion, his life, everything he'd built."

"But in the end..." Jim began.

"In the end," Becky said, "he never had a chance. Lies and deception always surface—one way or another. In his case, they came back to not just haunt him but to do him in."

Jim tapped his desk. "I also heard Bob Malone's writing a book about his role in all this."

"Yeah," Becky said. "He's cashing in on his fifteen minutes. Speaking of books—I convinced Lisa O'Brien to write one from her perspective. I'm going to help her."

Jim's eyes lit up. "That's a great idea. Got a publisher?"

"Not yet."

"Well, we can talk. You know we've got that small imprint for celebrity memoirs and Hollywood histories. This could be perfect."

Becky smiled. She'd already thought the same thing.

"How's Lisa?" Jim asked. "I heard she visited Mark in jail."

"She did," Becky said. "I think she's still conflicted. She's furious at him, but part of her still connects with the Mark who did it because he loved her. And she loved him. That's a lot to untangle."

They were both quiet for a moment.

"But was it proven she was in Boise during the murders?" Jim asked.

Becky smiled faintly. "The records say she was in class when Rebecca was killed. Investigators are talking to witnesses to confirm—or see if those records were tampered with. As for Paul's death, she was supposedly on summer vacation."

"Do you think she was involved?"

Becky thought about it. "I don't know. She was convincing when we confronted her. She seemed genuinely shocked. But... that could be another illusion. Maybe she and Mark were in it together. Maybe he's covering for her. We might never know."

"Or we'll find out during the trial," Jim said, his tone more business than journalistic. "Or in the book."

"Maybe," Becky said. "Time will tell."

"For now," Jim said, pushing back his chair, "let's celebrate. My assistant got us a table at the best restaurant in town. Grace and your grandmother already confirmed?"

"Yes, both of them."

"Perfect. We'll have the best dinner—and the best wine Napa or Sonoma ever bottled. Or France, why not? Tonight, there are no limits."

Becky stood, her smile easy and genuine. She'd done it. The truth—at least as much of it as she could get—was out there. The story had reached further than she imagined.

And tonight, for the first time in a long time, they could all just... breathe.

About the Author

Allegra Pope is a master of deception and suspense, whose fiction is defined by intricately layered plots and unforgettable twists. A lifelong enthusiast of puzzles and enigmas, Allegra began her literary journey by crafting short detective stories in the margins of her notebooks.

Drawing inspiration from classic whodunits and modern psychological thrillers, Allegra's work often centers on illusion and deception. Her protagonists -flayed yet brilliant- navigate a web of lies and sinister motives that keep readers guessing until the very last page.

When not writing, Allegra can be found exploring hidden corners of cities and reading crime fiction. She believes the best mysteries aren't just solved - they're unraveled piece by piece.

www.ingramcontent.com/pod-product-compliance
Lightning Source LLC
Chambersburg PA
CBHW071344300726
48976CB00006B/1761